THE DANCER *and the* THIEF

THE

DANCER

and the

THIEF

a novel

Antonio Skármeta

TRANSLATED FROM THE SPANISH BY KATHERINE SILVER

 W. W. NORTON & COMPANY   NEW YORK • LONDON

For information about special discounts for bulk purchases, please contact
W. W. Norton Special Sales at specialsales@wwnorton.com or 800-233-4830

Manufacturing by RRDonnelley, Harrisonburg
Book design by Chris Welch Design
Production manager: Andrew Marasia

Library of Congress Cataloging-in-Publication Data

Skármeta, Antonio.
[Baile de la victoria, English]
The dancer and the thief : a novel / Antonio Skármeta : translated from the Spanish
by Katherine Silver
p. cm.
ISBN 978-0-393-06494-0 (hardcover)
I. Silver, Katherine. II. Title.
PQ8098.29.K3B3513 2008
863'.64—dc22
2007033340

W. W. Norton & Company, Inc.
500 Fifth Avenue, New York, N.Y. 10110
www.wwnorton.com

W. W. Norton & Company Ltd.,
Castle House, 75/76 Wells Street, London W1T 3QT

1 2 3 4 5 6 7 8 9 0

To Jorge Manrique, Nicanor Parra, and Erasmus of Rotterdam

My trio of aces

The deeper the blue becomes, the more strongly it calls men toward the infinite, awakening the desire for the pure and, finally, for the supernatural.
—*Wassily Kandinsky*

THE DANCER *and the* THIEF

ON SAINT ANTHONY'S DAY, the thirteenth of June, the president declared an amnesty for certain common criminals.

The warden of one prison ordered one prisoner brought to his office before being released. Ángel Santiago arrived with an air of contempt, the raw beauty of his mere twenty years, his haughty nose, and a lock of hair falling over his left cheek. He stood in front of the warden and stared defiantly into the eyes of authority. Hail pounded against the windowpanes through the bars, wearing away at the thick layer of dust.

The warden looked Ángel up and down without blinking, then lowered his eyes to the game of chess on the table in front of him and slowly rubbed his chin, contemplating his next move.

"It seems you're leaving us, young man," he said with a touch of melancholy, never taking his eyes off the board. He then picked up his king and absentmindedly placed the tiny cross on its crown into the space between his front teeth. The warden was wearing an overcoat and a brown alpaca muffler; a heavy sprinkling of dandruff decorated his brow.

"So it seems, Warden. I've had to put up with two years in this place."

"I guess you wouldn't say that the time flew."

"It didn't fly, Mr. Santoro."

"But something positive must have come out of the experience."

"I'm leaving with a few interesting plans."

"Legal?"

The boy gently patted the backpack where he carried his few belongings. He edged a piece of sleep out of the corner of his eye and gave the warden an ironic smile, as if to negate the veracity of his own words.

"A hundred percent legal. Why did you call me here, sir?"

"Two little things," said the warden, tapping himself on the nose with the king. "I am white and it's my turn. What should my next move be?"

The young man looked contemptuously at the board and scratched the tip of his nose. "And what would the second *little thing* be?"

The man put the king down on the chessboard and smiled with such overwhelming sadness that his lips quivered and swelled as if he were about to cry.

"You know."

"No, I don't."

The warden smiled. "Your plan is to kill me."

"You aren't important enough to say that my plan, my only plan, is to kill you."

"Let's just say it is *one* of your plans."

"You didn't have to throw me naked into that cell full of brutes that first night. It hurt, Warden."

"So, you *are* going to kill me."

Ángel Santiago's senses sharpened significantly at the sudden, horrifying thought that someone might be listening to this conversation and that a reckless answer might endanger his imminent release. He spoke cautiously. "No, Mr. Santoro. I'm not going to kill you."

The man grabbed the lamp hanging over the table and turned it so the bare bulb shone in the boy's face like a spotlight. He left it there for a long time without saying a word, then dropped it and let it swing back and forth.

The warden swallowed hard and spoke with a hoarse voice. "As far as I see it, my participation in the events of that night was an act of love. You can go crazy with loneliness in this place."

"Shut up, Warden."

The warden began to pace around the room, his eyes glued on the concrete floor as if searching there for the right words. Finally, he stopped in front of the young man and with melodramatic slowness began to remove the muffler from around his own neck. In a sudden burst of humility he held it out to Ángel without looking at him.

"It's old, but it'll keep you warm," he said, then shivered and lifted his eyes to the young man's.

The phrase "act of love" had made the boy's face so red it looked as if he had swallowed gasoline. A scarlet patch spread over his ears.

"May I go now, Mr. Santoro?"

Santoro moved toward him, but Ángel's icy stare stopped him in his tracks. The warden shrugged his shoulders and spread out his arms in a gesture of resignation, as if begging for mercy.

"Take the muffler, young man."

"It would disgust me to wear something of yours."

"Come on, take it."

The young man decided that anything was preferable to further delaying his departure. He took the muffler and walked toward the door, dragging it behind him. When he got there he stopped, wet his lips, and said, "Play queen's pawn. Black will take pawn, then move white bishop to black queen. Checkmate."

THE MOMENT ÁNGEL left, the warden turned on the intercom and told the guard to bring him another prisoner, Rigoberto Marín. While he waited, he lit a cigarette, took a puff, and exhaled the smoke through his nostrils. Then he went and placed the kettle on the burner.

He opened a jar and placed one spoonful of instant coffee and a couple of spoonfuls of sugar in two cups; when the water boiled he filled the cups, stirring both with the one spoon that still remained from the government-issued cutlery set.

The guard brought in the prisoner; the warden pointed to the chair and to the coffee. Marín's hair was greasy and disheveled, his eyes dark and darting, as if his scrawny body had been subjected to a strong electric current. He took his first sip of coffee with a secretive air.

"What's up, Marín? How's it going?"

"Same as always, Warden."

"Too bad you weren't included in the amnesty."

"I'm not your run-of-the-mill thief, sir. I'm in for murder."

"It must have been serious. You got life. And even that was an act of mercy. How many murders have you got on your rap sheet?"

"More than one, Warden."

"So there isn't much chance you'll get out on good behavior in a few years."

"More like no chance at all. They agreed not to execute me only on the strict condition that my sentence never get reduced for any reason whatsoever."

"Wouldn't you have preferred the firing squad? After all, this isn't much of a life, is it?"

"Not much of one, but life is life, after all. Not even a worm likes to be squished."

The warden handed him a cigarette and lit another for himself. Marín sucked in his first drag with hungry ferocity, like a winded athlete inhaling a deep breath of fresh air.

"For instance, take this cigarette, Warden. A few puffs like this make my day. God always provides."

Santoro studied the man in front of him: he had all the classic characteristics of a scoundrel. He decided to come right out and say what was on his mind.

" 'God always provides.' That's a good saying, Marín, and just to show you how true it is, I'm going to make you a little offer."

"What's it about, Warden?"

"Obviously I couldn't include you in the amnesty, but there's nothing that says I can't let you out of here for a few weeks so you can do me a little favor. I'll just say you're in solitary, that way nobody will suspect you. As you know, not even the pope is allowed in there."

"I don't even gotta ask you what it's about. . . . Who is it?"

Santoro took comfort in another sip of coffee and indicated to Marín that he should do likewise. "Ángel Santiago."

Marín blinked long and hard, then glued his eyes on the cup as if he were trying to make out a hieroglyphic. "The Cherub?" he whispered.

"The very one."

"Such a handsome kid. He's like a fly on the wall, hasn't hurt nobody."

"But he's going to kill me."

"Did he threaten you?"

"He's going to kill me, Marín. And I have a wife and two kids and a lousy salary, but that's all we've got to live on."

"I understand. My problem is that I don't got nothing against the kid. Maybe a little envy, is all. Who wouldn't want to be so young and good-looking?"

"Make it look like a drunken brawl, whatever you can come up with. The important thing is to make sure he's really dead."

"It's just that every other time I had a good reason. But this . . ."

"You'll think of something. After ten years in jail, a whore a day for a month, let's say, would give a little meaning to your life, now, wouldn't it? And 'life is life,' as you said."

"I don't go to whores. I've got enough gals who'll do it for love."

"But they know you, Marín. I'm sorry for them, they'll miss out on the fuck of the century, but you are still officially in jail. One careless move on your part could turn your life sentence into a death sentence. What do you say?"

"It's a little complicated."

"Just think: a month on the streets, Marín, for the last time in your life."

Marín was silent. Without waiting for an answer, the warden walked over to the bathroom door, opened it, then directed Marín's attention to the shaving cream and razor.

"Shave."

IN A SEPARATE section of the same prison complex, Vergara Gray was told that he had been granted amnesty right after he asked the guard to buy him some more pomade for his hair. He took his tailored suit off the hanger and tried it on, pleased to find that he could fasten the top button by sucking his belly in just a little bit. The last five years of sedentary life had wrought only minimal damage to his physique, thanks in part to the yoga he had learned in the distant past when he was a seaman in Thailand.

His glistening gray locks found their final flourish in two salt-and-pepper sideburns; a thick mustache of the same color emanated a sense of authority and serenity. Standing in front of the mirror held for him by a guard, he drew a comb through his hair, confident that in spite of his years in prison his deep-set eyes could still make a woman dizzy. He cast aside this momentary indulgence in male coquetry with a sad sigh: he loved only his wife, Teresa Capriatti, and he suspected she would be less than overjoyed that her husband had been set free; she had not visited him once in five years, not even at Christmas.

Their son had not been the most affectionate nor the most frequent visitor, either. The boy would show up on his father's birthday in the last week of December, recite his full and unvaried schedule for the coming year, and after a few simple exchanges about their favorite soccer teams and how his high school studies were coming, he'd hold out his hand to avert the good-bye kiss Vergara Gray always tried to plant on his cheek.

This amnesty, which had cut his sentence in half, was a gift from Above, a chance to recover his lost love. He made a solemn vow to God, the press, and the prison authorities that he would never again break the law, and with the money his partner owed him for having kept his mouth shut throughout the trial, he would be able to lead a modest and honorable life without fleecing anyone or groveling for a few pesos.

He was on good terms with some influential newspaper editors who specialized in crime reporting, and he would beg them, as old friends, to stop publishing special editions on the anniversaries of his more spectacular heists. They would surely understand that now, with his newfound freedom, he would wish to maintain a low profile, that it was the only way he could hope to regain his family and, finally, his dignity.

He thanked the guard for holding up the mirror and flashed himself a final smile before turning away. This was the man he wanted to be. The warm smile, fraternal and virile; the secret light in the depths of his eyes; the deep lines etched by pain and solitude; and above all, the hunger, the desire to live, which in other prisoners had melted away into indifference, as if their own destinies had become as alien to them as somebody else's.

He took one last look around the walls of his cell and saw two remaining personal items: the calendar of the Virgin Mary with the days until June thirteenth marked off with a red X, and the poster of Marilyn Monroe, she and her luscious breasts stretched out across a red velvet cloth. He placed the calendar in his suitcase along with his clothes, then took an old fountain pen out of his bag and wrote across the length of Marilyn's body: "To my successor. Nicolás Vergara Gray."

On his way to the office of *his* warden, Huerta, he was joined by a number of prisoners who wanted to wish him good luck; some had tears running down their cheeks as they hugged him good-bye. The man humbly accepted this outpouring of love and admiration, always careful to maintain his upright bearing and impeccable grooming: the silk handkerchief discreetly peeking out of the breast pocket of his tweed jacket, his tie perfectly knotted, and his hair groomed like an elderly movie star's.

Huerta made sure Vergara Gray's arrival coincided with the boisterous uncorking of a bottle of champagne, and after another official poured out the bubbly for the guards and a select group of prisoners, glasses were raised and shouts of *Salud* rang out. The warden cleared his throat, paused histrionically, then pressed his hand to his chest before beginning to read a statement that had been carefully handwritten on official government stationery.

"Esteemed Professor Vergara Gray, dear Nico: It is with strong and conflicting emotions that we watch you leave today. We are overjoyed that you are free, that such a refined and gracious gentleman is emerging, reborn, into the civilian world. We are, however, also saddened at the loss of your delightful company, the pleasure of your stories, the depth of your reflections, and the stoic wisdom of your counsel, which has brought comfort to prisoners and guards alike.

"There is no denying that you strayed from the path of the law, and it was reasonable for the judge to sentence you to ten years for your spectacular robberies. In none of your deeds, however, did you use violence, you left nobody wounded or dead along your path, and I doubt if you have ever so much as carried a weapon. You are a far cry indeed from those unscrupulous miscreants who fill our jails and teem through our streets.

"Your crimes have been unanimously acclaimed as true works of art, and through them you have achieved renown that extends far beyond the courthouse. I am certain that more than one of Chile's great authors will write about you, thereby spreading your fame beyond our national borders. Today, however, I do not speak to the artist, but rather to the man of flesh and blood who is now taking his leave of this, our small corner of the world, a man bursting with life and integrity, and purified by many blessings of friendship. I offer you the two words that express all our hopes for you: Good luck."

He walked up to the prisoner, threw his arms around him, gave him a great bear hug, and with a sigh of resignation made room for other effusive expressions of congratulations. After everybody had had a chance to slap him on the back, shed their tears, and shower him with affection, they gathered around to listen to the words of the honored guest.

"My esteemed Warden Huerta, dear guards, fellow prisoners: Carried away by our long and tedious nights in prison, I was sometimes long-winded and told exaggerated accounts of my criminal deeds. But now, at this pivotal moment, I feel I am the most taciturn of men. Today, I am at a loss for words, as if a great stone were lodged in my throat. I leave here with an abundance of faith in myself, knowing I will forge my way back into life on the outside. I fear nothing but loneliness, and God willing, I will win back my family. May all of you also regain your freedom sooner than you expect, for only God can decide in the long run who is guilty and who is innocent. May He bless you all."

Out in front, in the small plaza, Vergara Gray felt June's cold breath on his neck and momentarily regretted giving away his trusty scarf and wool coat. The warden accompanied him to the taxi, solicitously carrying his suitcase. As he opened the door, he turned to Vergara Gray and said, "The taxi is paid for. We took up a collection."

The ex-prisoner passed his hand over his graying temple and smiled melancholically. "The money isn't really the problem, Huerta. Something else is."

"What?"

"What address should I give the driver?"

ONCE THE DRIVER had loaded the suitcase in the trunk, he sank into his seat and looked through the rearview mirror. Then he solemnly posed the momentous question, "Where to, Mr. Vergara Gray?"

"Do you know of a store that sells leather goods?"

"There's a good one on the Alameda. Stuff from Argentina. And with the crisis there, the prices are rock bottom."

"Take me there."

Vergara Gray had expected to hungrily devour the sights, smells, sounds, and people he encountered these first moments of freedom, but now, on the contrary, he felt he was immersed in a process of introspection that left him oblivious to the urban sphere surrounding him. He stroked his temple and realized that he was too old to embark on such a precarious life. He was a compass whose only north was his family: it was for them that he had worked, broken the law, and, of course, kept his mouth shut. "The Tomb," his partner had dubbed him, and it was supposed to be meant as a compliment. Nor could he complain about his luck: the president's amnesty—sharply criticized by the news media, which simultaneously condemned the overcrowding of prisons as inhumane and denounced the number of criminals wandering with impunity through the streets and alleyways of the nation—had been an act of divine justice. If he had squealed instead of remaining silent, he would have been spared the exact same five years the amnesty had erased with the stroke of a pen. "I'm a lucky fellow, after all," he mumbled under his breath.

After asking the cabdriver to wait, he trusted his instincts to lead him to the finest bags. With delight he touched the kid leather of a sturdy briefcase with two gold-plated clasps, which required a special code to open, then let out a deep, self-satisfied sigh when he discovered that it was by far the most expensive item: his choice had been the right one. The salesman asked Vergara Gray for a number so he could set the combinations—a different one for each lock—and without hesitating, he told him his own and his son's birthdays.

"Are you paying with cash, check, or credit card?" the salesman asked as he wrapped it up.

Lifting his brow, Vergara Gray wondered if he looked honest enough to be offered such choices.

"Cash," he said as he laid the bills out on the counter.

"Today is Saint Anthony's Day," the salesman suddenly said. "A miraculous saint. Single women stand his statues on their heads so he'll help them find a husband."

"I'm sure they do," Vergara Gray said as he took the change and the plastic bag containing his purchase. The man looked at him strangely, and the ex-convict risked a smile and a question. "Does my face look familiar to you?"

The salesman scratched his head. "Are you on TV?"

"Oh . . . no!"

"Nope, I can't place you. Sorry, sir."

"On the contrary, I am grateful for your tact. How old are you?"

"Twenty-five."

"History has passed me by. Five years ago, a shopkeeper like you would have asked for my autograph or called the police."

T HAT'S JUST HOW Ángel Santiago had imagined *his* Santiago: buses careening down the streets, pedestrians plunging into subway stations, scooters backfiring, office workers dressed in suits and ties and carrying briefcases, waves of women wearing brightly colored sweaters cut off right above their freezing-cold belly buttons, kiosks overflowing with newspapers announcing prison sentences for government ministers, and glitzy magazines plastered with pictures of naked women.

"My city!" he shouted. "My Santiago!"

He strode through the streets of downtown, feeling more energized every time he brushed against or tripped over somebody. He inhaled and exhaled with the prowess of an athlete until a deep and ferocious hunger overtook him: he knew he could devour at least two, maybe three, of those *completos* "with everything" from one of the restaurants in the Portal Fernández Concha, where hot dogs, nestled in fluted rolls, were piled high with a leaning tower of mashed avocado, chopped tomatoes, a long, thin line of El Copihue hot sauce, a pile of pickled cabbage—German-style—and crowned with a feverish delight of mayonnaise and mustard. These sandwiches begged to be downed in two bites that left the front of your shirt covered with the unstable ingredients and your face smeared all the way up to your eyebrows with a voluptuous carnival of flavors.

His hunger, however, was infinitely more ample than his funds. The two coins jingling against each other in his pocket would be barely enough for a couple of rolls: two pathetic *marraquetas*, naked and defenseless. He considered that poverty was a second prison, then dispelled this defeatist idea by punching his fist into the air: better to die eating smog in the streets than languishing in his cell. If his hunger got worse, he would steal. An apple from the produce stand, a package of crackers from the grocery store. The judge couldn't convict him. His pal, Fernández, a lawyer and prison colleague, had taught him a magic trick to avoid being sent back to jail. If they nabbed him, he would simply claim that the crime had been "motivated by dire hunger," that he had stolen food "to avoid dying of starvation."

"It's the only law in Chile that actually favors the poor; all the others pulverize them," Fernández had stated, with the air of a misunderstood aristocrat waxing eloquent behind bars.

Cold and hunger added alacrity to his steps, as did his backpack banging against his back and the joy of feeling healthy, in one piece, and above all, in no need of the warden's filthy muffler to ward off the cold. His blood grew warmer as he walked, turning him into his own portable heater, his own unique solution to the freezing temperatures that assaulted the necks of the other pedestrians, who tried to bury their noses into their belly buttons.

He would never bury his nose, no way, not that mighty spur that sucked in Santiago's smog as if it were the purest mountain air. And with that same grace and power that made him feel alive, intact, and virile, he would one day slice the warden's throat. Not now, not while the villain expected him to attack, but in a few weeks, a month, once he had grown accustomed to his fear and finally decided, What the hell, I'll go out with my buddies and have a glass of wine.

Then (at this point, he started walking faster) Ángel would find him in a drunken stupor. The white tablecloth would be decorated with flowery red wine stains, and the chairs would be held together with duct tape. Ángel would wait until the warden was alone, maybe when the bartender had gone to the bathroom, then come up behind him and grab his chin with his white-gloved hand, and press his knife into his jugular. Everybody else walking down that street might lack a purpose in life, flitting from one state of anonymity to another with nothing to ennoble their existence.

Not he. Not Ángel Santiago.

Of course (now he was leaning against the pole of the streetlight), the lifers who had carried out that repulsive rite against him had done so with more perversion than desire, their aim being to humiliate him more than anything else. They were uneducated men driven by a code of resentment. To do that to him, who had been educated in a good school, who was able to recite by heart several poems and figure out a percentage to offer a guard a bribe without using a calculator, was a way of telling him that his beauty and education weren't worth a rat's ass. The following morning in the infirmary he didn't know if more blood or more tears were flowing out of his body, nor which caused him more pain. His determination had been forged out of those bodily fluids, but he never suspected that an amnesty would hasten its fulfillment.

Before turning onto the central pedestrian walkway lined with hair salons, movie theaters, shoe-repair shops, and pawnshops, he looked affectionately at the watch Fernández had placed in his pocket before he left jail: "You are returning to a world where you can invest each moment with meaning. Here, in prison, time measures only the passing of nothingness."

He felt a wrenching in his gut at the thought of parting with this token of affection, but he had nothing else he could offer up for sale. His generous and well-worn leather jacket? Not a chance. Not only did it protect him from the cold but it lent him a certain air of toughness that was well worth cultivating in a city like Santiago. In addition, girls were drawn to the rugged air of old leather garments. It reminded them of movie stars and gave them the illusion that a guy wrapped in leather and stinking of black tobacco could offer them exotic adventures, when the only action they'd probably see would be a bit of pumping and thrusting in the bed of a seedy hotel room.

Right in front of the pawnshop was a stairway that led to an underground movie theater, and just above the ticket window, which was still closed, a poster proclaimed the virtues of the movie of the week: "A Japanese woman betrayed by her husband gets her revenge by sleeping with everybody she meets." The title was *Tokyo Emmanuelle*. Ángel was intrigued as he approached the window, not by the pleasures promised therein but by a tall, thin girl squishing her nose up against the glass. She seemed to barely be able to stand up under the weight of the backpack slung over her oversized coat. Standing there next to this young woman, feeling the warmth and tenderness emanating from her body, he got dizzy. Before his ill-fated run-in with the law, only two minor incidents separated him from his virginity, and the adventures he dreamed about in his cell were infinitely more exciting than those quickies he'd enjoyed under the stars.

He placed his cheek very close to the girl's face and read the names of the Japanese cast as if they were well-known stars like Brad Pitt or Leonardo DiCaprio. "Kumi Taguchi, Mitsuyaso Mainu, Katsunori Hirose."

The girl turned to look at him and, moving her backpack from her right to her left shoulder, smiled. That minimal expression of kindness, completely absent from his life for so many years, inspired the young man to take a pack of cigarettes out of his jacket and offer her one. The girl firmly refused; he placed the cigarette in his mouth and a moment later had it lit and burning. "Are you going in?"

"It looks kind of boring. You?"

The young man turned his head to blow the smoke away from her dark brown eyes and, without reading the poster, he declared, "A film with Kumi Taguchi, Mitsuyaso Mainu, and Katsunori Hirose can't be all bad."

The girl's cheeks shone with surprise. "How did you learn those names?"

"I am a useless marvel," he answered. "I read something once and never forget it."

"I wish I had that talent. I'm flunking out of school because I have such a terrible memory."

"What school do you go to?"

"*Went.* I got expelled."

"What are you doing now?"

"Waiting for them to open the movie theater. There's nowhere else to go in this cold. What about you?" The girl pointed at his bulging backpack.

"I've been on the road. I just arrived from the south."

"Where do you live?"

"Nowhere yet."

He pulled on the imitation-gold chain and took Fernández's watch out of his pocket to show her its face. On one half was a sun with a winking eye and on the other an owl sitting on a waning moon. The girl laughed.

"The sun is shining!" she exclaimed.

"At eleven at night, the stars around the moon begin to shimmer."

"It looks like a watch from *A Thousand and One Nights.*"

"How much do you think they'll give me for it?"

She held it in her hand as if she had lots of experience in such matters.

"It's very unique; at least, I've never seen anything like it. Maybe they'll give you a small fortune."

"I don't think so. It's Japanese junk. Like the movie."

He invited her to come with him to the pawnshop, where he placed the watch on the glass countertop. The pawnbroker sized up the couple with a quick glance, then picked up the object and held it in his hand as if it were the tail of a filthy rat.

"We don't buy stolen goods."

The young man winced at the pawnbroker's tone, and his hand instinctively moved into his pocket and clutched his knife. A moment later, however, he loosened his grip and pawed the floor with his tennis shoe to calm himself down.

"My father gave it to me for my eighteenth birthday."

The man tossed the watch onto the glass and faked a yawn. "That's what everybody says. That their gold medals and watches have great sentimental value but that they're forced to sell them because of some emergency. Is that what you were going to tell me?"

"Sir, you stole the words right out of my mouth."

The pawnbroker smiled at the girl and patted Ángel on the shoulder. "Now we understand each other."

"How much will you give me?"

"Thirty thousand pesos."

"But this watch shows day from night. It tells you if it is ten in the morning or ten at night. This watch is one of a kind."

"It's a useless feature."

"It might be useless, but it's cool and no other watch has it. This watch is poetic. The stars shine at night."

"Here, kid, take thirty-five, and be grateful I'm not asking you for the original receipt."

Ángel Santiago stuffed the bills into his pocket and deeply inhaled the cold air that swirled through the arcade's archways. He took the girl's arm and led her to the Plaza de Armas.

"In the Portal Fernández Concha, there's a cafeteria that serves hot dogs loaded with so many toppings you can barely get your mouth around them. I've been dreaming about biting into one of those for two years."

"I'll come with you."

"What about the movie?"

"It's always playing. I can go anytime."

"Do you go a lot?"

"Sometimes, that is, it depends. . . ."

He stretched his arm across her shoulders and together they crossed San Antonio Street.

"What does it depend on?"

"A lot of things."

"Like whether or not you've been expelled from school?"

The girl perked up, and answered cheerfully. "Exactly."

The restaurant was called Ex Bahamondes, and the boy asked one of the twelve hardworking waiters—who showered the customers with heavenly steaks, beers, broiled chicken, and hot dogs—if the "ex" in the name might suggest that the *completos* weren't as complete as they used to be.

"Better than ever, sir," the waiter responded. "I guarantee that when you bite into one the juice will drip all the way down to your belly button. Would you like two?"

"Not for me," the girl said.

"Aren't you hungry?"

"No."

"You don't mind if I eat?"

"On the contrary."

Rubbing his hands together, his smile stretching wider with each topping he mentioned, the young man sang out his order.

"Bring me a *supercompleto*. Cradle the extra-long hot dog in the bread, heat it up in the microwave; then smother it in a layer of sauerkraut, two slabs of avocado, a blanket of chopped tomatoes, and top it off with a dollop of mayonnaise decorated with a line of red hot sauce and another of mustard."

With Santiago's first bite, the waiter's prophecy came true, and a torrent of mayonnaise and tomato streamed over his leather jacket. The girl stuffed a dozen napkins under the collar, then encouraged him to keep eating. Every once in a while, Ángel Santiago would lift a finger, as if to signal that he was about to say something, only to decide instead to devote himself to another bite. Still chewing heartily, he seemed to continue to formulate the words he would utter once he had finished savoring every exquisite flavor.

Crowds of office workers on their lunch breaks poured in, steaming up the windows and making the restaurant hot and stifling.

"I need some fresh air," the girl said.

On their way out, Ángel bought two cartons of milk. They crossed over to the Plaza de Armas and sat down on a wooden bench, placing their feet on their respective bags: he, on his backpack full of everything he had brought with him from jail; she, on her bag with her schoolbooks and supplies.

She undid the top buttons on her coat, exposing the indecipherable insignia on the sweater of her school uniform.

"How long have you been playing hooky?"

"A month. They kicked me out of school and I still haven't dared tell my mother."

"So what do you do?"

"I get up in the morning, pretend I'm getting ready for school, then walk around until the movie theaters open. After a while, I go back home."

The boy knitted his brow, looked up, and considered the possibility of a sudden downpour. The clouds overhead were dark: some were compact and puffy, others stringy and fast-moving.

She followed his gaze, then ran her fingers through her hair. As they both looked down, their eyes locked for a brief, intimate moment. She smiled at him; he thought it would be attractive and virile to do nothing, so he held her stare and brushed his hair off his forehead.

At the precise moment they lifted their milk cartons to their mouths, and just as they were about to take a sip, lightning flashed through the clouds and a ferocious peal of thunder boomed across the sky. They both looked back up at the ominous sky, glanced at each other, then swallowed their milk as if they were enjoying a picnic in the countryside on a spring day. She wiped the white foam mustache off her lips with the sleeve of her coat and, seeing that the boy's upper lip was also thus adorned, wiped his off with her finger.

Under the lash of the downpour, the girl hunched up her shoulders, drawing herself into her large coat. Ángel seemed oblivious to the deluge around them.

"This is what I am," he told the girl. "I am absolutely and totally *this* moment. I have no home, no friends, no past, nothing I want to remember, and no money. I am a stomach stuffed with a delicious *supercompleto* and this is my city of ice and mud. What's your name?"

"Victoria."

"And they call you Vicky?"

"Yes, but I prefer to be called Victoria, or *La* Victoria, like Victory; it sounds more hopeful."

She brushed away the water seeping underneath the collar of her coat, then noticed a brown alpaca muffler poking out of the boy's bag. She pulled it out and placed it over her head.

"Take that off," the boy ordered sharply.

"Why?"

"Because it's contaminated."

"With what?"

Before answering he pulled it away from her and stuffed it back into his pack. The rain seemed to wash away her smile.

"That muffler belongs to somebody I despise. I'd rather be carried away in a flood than owe that person anything."

"So why not just throw it away?"

"It may come in handy someday."

She made a tent by covering both their heads with her overcoat. Inside that cozy darkness, they finished drinking their milk. Having him there so close and so serious made her laugh, and she remembered the games she played as a child with her cousins when they'd pretend the sheet was a teepee and they were Eskimos, rubbing their noses together. Santiago began to feel the warm vapors of her laughter melt the icy armor that had helped him survive the last few years, and something viscous and musty seemed to evaporate from his soul in a feverish swirl.

He touched Victoria's cheek, then brought his fingertip to his lips and rubbed them together solemnly. Watching the concentrated gravity of his gesture, she stopped laughing and became serious and alert.

"What's your name?" she asked in a whisper.

"Santiago. Ángel Santiago," answered Ángel Santiago with a wink.

H E TURNED BEFORE reaching Las Cantinas Street, wanting to see for himself how the neighborhood had changed during his absence. Sauna studios, massage parlors, and bars—where cocktails came garnished with the promise of girls wrapped in leather and a joint or a line of coke on the side—now reached all the way to the Costanera Highway. He regretted that he was carrying that old, beat-up suitcase and looking like a tourist who had been given the wrong directions. His picture still appeared in the papers whenever a journalist decided to once again extol the consummate artistry of his crimes. He'd even considered shaving off his ostentatious mustache to avoid calling attention to himself, but such a desecration would have been like amputating his manhood. At the first corner, his goal of keeping a low profile was thwarted by Nemesio Santelices, a purveyor of stolen goods and valet-for-hire, who every once in a while got a few coins tossed his way for parking someone's car and watching it so it didn't get stolen.

"What a pleasure to see you a free man, Nico!" he exclaimed as he fell into step alongside the maestro, not daring to offer his hand or give him a hug. Nico was encouraged that the lowliest scum in this world of scum still knew how to show proper deference to his status.

"I doubt if everyone feels the same way."

"Why shouldn't they? Everyone knows you didn't squeal."

"Vergara Gray, the Tomb, eh?"

"The Tomb of Gold. Business has been thriving while you were inside. Santiago is now a great metropolis."

"Sounds like my partner's bank account should be doing quite well."

"Hey, Nico, if you're planning something, you know you can count on me."

"You better look elsewhere, Santelices. I'm retired."

During this brief stroll, and without even turning to look, he had felt many eyes on him. Then with a quick touch of his finger to his forehead, Vergara Gray took leave of his companion. When he reached Monasterio's place, he placed his suitcase down, loosened his belt, tucked in his shirt, pulled his pants up over his belly, took a deep breath, and retightened his belt. It had just gotten dark, but his partner's cantina was almost full, and even though the girls stared at him as he entered, not one of this new generation of hookers wrapped in fashionable garb seemed to recognize him.

He made his way to the far end of the bar and studied the room's every detail until he caught sight of Monasterio giving instructions to the cashier. With the power of his gaze alone, he forced his partner to look over at him. Recognition was instantaneous, as was a dark cloud that spread over the man's face. By the time Monasterio reached him, however, he had skillfully wiped away the shadows, and proceeded to shower his partner with affectionate hugs and the requisite backslapping. The ex-convict received his partner's enthusiasm with a cautious smile.

Monasterio complimented him on his elegant suit, his perfect haircut, and the youthful shimmer that lent an ironic sparkle to his eyes. Feeling suddenly quite modest, Vergara Gray said, "Ah, but styles change in five years."

"What are you talking about? You are as elegant as ever."

"The suitcase doesn't shut. I had to close it with tape."

Monasterio awarded it a gentle, affectionate kick. "The suitcase of so many great feats, Nico. When you have your own museum, this will be one of the most valuable exhibits. Don't laugh. In London there's a crime museum, with a wax statue of Jack the Ripper. Champagne?"

The guest waited confidently for his partner to utter one additional word, then smiled when he did.

"French, of course. You are, after all, the one and only Nicolás Vergara Gray!"

He told the waiter to bring the bottle, the bucket, and the glasses to a private booth in the back; once they were seated, Monasterio patted Vergara Gray's cheek with paternal affection.

"Free at last, old man."

"Outside, time flies; inside, it crawls."

"I want to ask you to forgive me, Nico, for not visiting you this whole time."

"I hadn't noticed."

"It's not that I didn't want to, it's just that my visit would have given the police a lead. In other words, my *not* going fit right in."

"With what?"

"Your silence."

"That silence, Monasterio, is now my only capital."

"We really must talk about that. But not now. Now is the time to celebrate your return. Now is the time for champagne."

His partner raised his glass, but Vergara Gray left his untouched. Instead, he placed the suitcase on his knees, pulled back the tape, and took out a large envelope. "I brought you a present."

"For me?"

"For you, partner." He emptied the contents of the envelope onto the table. Out tumbled five calendar pads with each of the days of the five years circled in red ink.

"Nico, I sent your family a money order every month."

The ex-convict picked up one of the many pages that had come loose from the pad and placed it in front of his host's eyes.

" 'The year is 2001 and it's the hottest summer I ever remember in Santiago. The cockroaches stagger past the rusty bars.' "

"I'll show you your room."

"Where?"

"I've got a little hotel across the street."

"A family hotel?"

"We're in an economic crisis," he said, attempting to appease his partner.

"You mean it's a hotel for couples."

"And miscellaneous."

"And miscellaneous."

"Just for a few nights, until I find you something more appropriate."

"That won't be necessary. I'm going to live with Teresa Capriatti."

"Let me carry your suitcase."

Without waiting for Vergara Gray's consent, Monasterio picked up the suitcase and started walking toward the door. The night had grown colder and darker. The wet sidewalk reflected the pathetic flashing of the neon lights.

As they crossed the street, Vergara Gray, at least four inches taller than his companion, had to lean over so he could hear him over the roar of traffic.

"Take good care of those calendars, partner. You can put them on exhibit in the Vergara Gray Museum, too."

The room had a small, modern closet where Vergara Gray hung

up his jacket. He pulled a speckled gray sweater out of his suitcase and put it on, sat down on the bed, and picked out a pair of thick wool socks to warm up his cold, aching feet. Then he lay down on the bed without even bothering to pull back the covers and began to study the stains on the ceiling.

He feared nothing, he told himself, nothing but loneliness.

He heard a knock on the door and propped himself up on his elbow. "Come in."

Someone pushed the door open with a knee, and at first all he saw was a metal tray carrying a bucket, the bottle of champagne, and two fluted glasses. The intruder was a woman about twenty years old, dressed in a tight outfit that showed off more than just her belly button and with a mass of black hair framing a pair of fuchsia-colored lips.

"Monasterio says you forgot this."

"You needn't have bothered."

"He said it would be a shame for it to get warm. It's French champagne, after all."

"You can just leave it on the table."

The woman followed his instructions, then filled the two glasses and held one out to him. She sat on the edge of the bed. "Why does Monasterio take such good care of you?"

"He's an old friend."

"He's got lots of old friends, but only you get a double treat."

"What's that?"

"The champagne, and me."

"Ah, I understand. Since we're occupying the same bed, maybe you should tell me your name?"

"Raquel."

"Look, Raquel—"

"Of course, my name isn't really Raquel."

"Of course. Look, Raquel, you are a beautiful young woman and any man would feel privileged to have the opportunity to be with you. But there is only one woman in my dreams, and I am saving myself for her, as if I were a teenage virgin. It's nothing personal."

"What do you mean, nothing personal? It is me, *personally*, you are rejecting. I'm a skilled professional. I promise I won't hurt you."

"I trust you implicitly; it's myself I don't trust."

"Afraid you won't be up to it?"

"I'm sixty years old."

"So, you don't trust me."

Vergara Gray took a sip of champagne and indicated that the woman should do likewise.

"I can't stand champagne. It gives me a headache."

"What do you like?"

"Mint frappé."

The man handed her a ten-thousand-peso bill. "Here, go buy yourself a bottle."

"I never refuse a good tip. But what should I tell Monasterio?"

"Tell him I appreciate the thought, but that I never accept gifts. Tell him I'm waiting for him to bring me the fifty percent he owes me."

"He's going to yell at me."

"I don't think so."

He drained his cup and wiped his mustache with the back of his hand. She patted the back of his other hand and stood up.

"What's the lucky woman's name?"

"Teresa Capriatti."

The woman took a cube of ice out of the silver bucket and placed it in her mouth. She switched it back and forth from one cheek to the other with a thoughtful expression on her face, as if she were trying to interpret a hieroglyphic. "You're an odd duck," she concluded.

VICTORIA LED ÁNGEL SANTIAGO down the staircase of the dance academy and from there to the rehearsal studio, where the heater was on full blast. The young man leaned against the wall while the girl spoke to her teacher. A half dozen teenage girls were at the bar doing stretches and practicing pirouettes on tiptoe. The teacher's gray hair was pulled tightly back from her temples. A thin layer of mascara lent a certain weight to her lashes, which seemed to leap off her pale face. Victoria returned carrying a stool. "She says you can stay."

"I don't know what to do here."

"Just watch."

She ran off to the other end of the studio and stripped down to her tights and leotard. The teacher placed a ring of keys on top of the piano, called the girls to attention, then began playing a tune with a strong beat.

At first the young man was interested in the dancers and even found it entertaining when four of the girls linked arms and performed a short routine. About half an hour later, while they all stood at the bar and the teacher corrected them by tapping them lightly with a pointer, he grew bored. Absentmindedly, he reached for the girl's backpack and started rummaging around inside.

Only about half the exercises in the math workbook had been completed, and these had been corrected by the teacher with painful results. The assessments at the bottom of each page ranged from "bad," to "very bad," to "terrible."

Her language arts binder contained a poem by Gabriela Mistral with two lines highlighted in bright yellow: "*From the frozen niche where men have put you, / I will lower you to the humble, sun-drenched earth.*"

As Ángel turned the pages full of grammar drills and lists of synonyms and antonyms, he noticed that those same two lines appeared again and again, written like a slogan and highlighted each time in a different color, on every fourth or fifth page.

On another sheet, at the end of the poem "Tarde en el hospital" by Pezoa Véliz, Victoria had written, "so many people everywhere dying." In her music binder he found lyrics by Elvis Costello and a few lines from Beethoven's "Ode to Joy."

His clothes were beginning to dry, and he moved on to his own bag to verify the extent of his worldly possessions. He emptied the contents onto the floor and poked through them with his foot: the warden's muffler, two shirts, two pairs of boxers, a turtleneck sweater, and his faded leather jacket with the broken metal zipper. There were also two books: *Heart*, by Edmundo de Amicis, and *Where I'm Calling From*, by Raymond Carver. A special gift for a certain special person, he thought with a smile.

Soon night would come and he would have to find himself a place to sleep. There were several mattresses in this very studio, and if the heat stayed on until morning, the problem would be solved.

The other possibility was to go to a hotel with Victoria, a doubly crazy idea because they had yet to exchange so much as a kiss and because they didn't have the money to pay for their room in advance, always required in the cheaper places. They could possibly go to a more respectable establishment and find some way to disappear in the morning. No, that was also a bad idea: they'd ask him for ID when he arrived and then he'd have the whole police force after him.

There were always parks, plazas, and pneumonia. It would be a sorry blessing indeed to exchange the prison cell for a cot at the public hospital next to a bunch of indigents in their final death throes.

Victoria approached with her teacher and introduced him as her brother from Talca. The teacher, introducing herself as Ruth Ulloa, asked him what he did. In a moment of inspiration, he said that he owned a small plot of land and was studying agronomy. After all, he knew that the Piduco River ran near that city and that there were meadows and cows and lots of grapes on the vines. The teacher responded that there must be a future in agriculture because of all the new exports to Asia, and he, in turn, noted that dance was an even more promising profession because all you had to do was watch television to see that this generation was crazy about dancing and everyone who wasn't already on television hoped to be there one day. The teacher explained that the kind of dance she taught at this academy never ended up on television but rather in prestigious venues, such as the Municipal Theater of Santiago and the Colón Theater of Buenos Aires, when and if, of course, there was talent. Ángel Santiago considered it appropriate to ask what exactly it meant for a dancer to have talent, and she answered that talent was a dancer's ability to express with physical precision the fantasies that obsessed them.

"For example, I am now helping your sister choreograph a dance based on a poem."

"By Mistral!" the boy exclaimed.

Victoria looked at him perplexed, and Ángel Santiago licked his smiling lips, feeling certain that his luck was improving by the moment. His guardian angel had found her way back to him and was watching over every step he took, offering him one inspiration after another.

"Yes, Mistral," the teacher confirmed with gravity. "She wants to dance nothing less than *The Sonnets of Death.*

" 'I will lower you to the humble, sun-drenched earth,' " the young man was quick to recite.

"I see you are interested in poetry," the teacher commented, already seduced.

"No, only that poem. After all, it has a lot in common with agronomy, don't you think?"

The teacher acknowledged the exchange with a smile and, putting on her coat, gave them each a kiss good-bye and a couple of blankets. Victoria went over to the hot plate and put on water to make some instant coffee. She filled two ceramic cups and sat down cross-legged on the floor. The boy burned his tongue with the first sip while she blew cautiously into her cup.

"Who goes first?" she said after a brief pause.

"With what?"

"The truth."

The boy wrapped his hands around the warm mug of coffee and silently praised his good fortune as he stared into the profound intensity of her brown eyes. He didn't want to make one false move. He didn't want to lose her. Not that night, not ever. "Shoot."

"Your name. I mean, your real name."

"Ángel Santiago."

"It sounds like the name of a trumpet player in a salsa band."

"That's the name they gave me."

"Your parents?"

"Or the local priest. I was too young to remember."

"What do you do?"

"Here and there."

"What do you do here and there?"

"Nothing. I don't do anything here and there."

"And what's this about agronomy? Do you really own land in Talca?"

"The only land I own is the dirt on the soles of my shoes."

"How do you live?"

"I've got a few plans."

"What kind of plans?"

"A few ideas for making money. Lots of money."

"Tell me all about them."

"It's a secret. If I tell you, it'll ruin the whole thing."

They finished drinking their coffee in silence, then Ángel took off his shoes and placed them next to the heater. She pulled the rubber band out of her hair and, with one shake of her head, let it fall in charming disarray down her back.

"My turn," said the boy.

"Go ahead."

"I don't want to ask you any questions, but I do have three wishes."

"What's the first?"

"That you let me know when you are going to dance at the Municipal Theater."

"Why?"

"I saw a movie on television once about a guy who sends his ballet-dancer girlfriend a bouquet of roses. I would love to send you a bouquet of roses at the Municipal Theater."

"That will never happen. The girls from this academy never get to dance at the Municipal."

"Well, anyway, if by some chance you do one day dance there, I want to know."

"Agreed."

"My second wish is that you go to school tomorrow and ask them to let you back in."

"There's more chance that I'll dance at the Municipal than that they'll let me back in school. I was expelled, Ángel."

"Everybody gets kicked out of school at some point, but then they let you back in."

"That already happened to me. They suspended me twice; the third time, they expelled me."

"Why?"

"Partly because both times they made appointments to meet with my mother, and she didn't show up."

"Didn't she want to go?"

"I don't want to talk about my mother."

"Okay, okay, calm down."

"I am calm."

"You are calm. Good. Now relax."

Victoria began to pull on the rubber band she'd taken out of her hair, then turned to watch the rain falling against the basement windows. "They threw me out of school because I can't concentrate. When I'm in class I'm always on the moon. I mean, I'm always thinking about the same thing."

"What's that?"

"My father."

"What happened to him?"

"When my mother was pregnant with me, the police arrested him in front of the school where he taught. Everybody saw it happen. They came with helicopters and cars without license plates. Two days later they found him in a ditch with his throat slit. I was born five months later."

"What had your father done?"

"He was against the dictatorship. He would have been able to identify some of the kidnappers who made people disappear. I think he was one of the last to be killed. Then democracy came."

"That doesn't mean you have to think about him all the time."

"If I don't, he'll disappear forever."

"But that's not good for you, not good for your head. That's why you can't concentrate on your schoolwork."

"I went to the same school he taught at. Everyone was really nice to me. They treated me like I was made of glass and was about to shatter. They even gave me a scholarship so I could study there."

"You can't just throw that away!"

"My mother wants me to study law. Can you imagine! Studying law in a country where my father was murdered with total impunity?"

"But she's your mother. You have to tell her the truth. She'll speak to the principal, and they'll take you back."

"My mother's depressed, totally indifferent to everything. After he was murdered, while everybody else was talking about my father being a hero, she just kept complaining about how she'd been abandoned. When I was born, I think she was more upset than happy because I reminded her of my father. Once she said to me, 'The Party might have lost a militant, but I lost my man.' "

Santiago tried to think of something he could say that would lighten the gloomy tone of their conversation, but he couldn't find the words. He also decided to stifle the caress destined for Victoria's cheek, afraid to show compassion that the girl might reject. Instead he walked over to the bars and did a few gymnastic exercises he had learned in school. Encouraged by his agility, he walked back to her and said, "Tomorrow I'll go to your school with you and talk to the principal."

Victoria laughed, but without derision. Suddenly she was in an irresistibly good mood. "You? In those rags?"

"I'm your brother from Talca. That should give me a certain amount of authority."

"They know I don't have any brothers. Every year, in every speech at the beginning of the term, the teachers mention my solitude and the tragedy Chile has overcome. The word 'overcome' makes me laugh. Nothing ever overcomes death."

"So I'll say that I'm your boyfriend and we're going to get married."

"But you don't even have enough money for bus fare. What would you support me with?"

"I told you, I've got plans."

"What plans?"

"Nothing you'd be interested in."

Victoria yawned and laid out a mattress against the wall. She took off her leotard, folded it up neatly, and placed it on a chair on top of her sweater. Her nakedness revealed to Santiago two firm, medium-sized breasts with an archipelago of freckles between them.

He carried over the other mattress, laid it down next to Victoria's, and spread a large wool blanket from the island of Chiloé over both of them. Its thick weave promised prolific warmth, and he grew dizzy at the proximity of the girl's body. When he moved his cold knee between her thighs, she murmured with closed eyes, "Remember, you are my brother from Talca."

But the boy's fingers had already grabbed hold of her underpants, and with one quick movement he had pushed them down around her knees. He brought himself up against her from behind and with more luck than skill found his way to her more humid regions. When he heard her first gentle moans of pleasure, he lost the last remnants of control and into her flowed all the frustration accumulated over so many nights of sadness and fantasy.

H E WAS WOKEN by a knocking on the door, hesitant at first, then more and more insistent. He got up and went to the bathroom to wash out his mouth, looking sadly at the almost-full bottle of champagne. Twenty years ago, two of those wouldn't have been enough to bring the night to life. As he was pulling his pants on slowly and deliberately, the knocking sounded more and more like a police raid.

"The louder you bang, the less I'm going to rush."

The racket stopped immediately, and he spent another few minutes combing his mustache and checking how quickly the white was winning out over the gray. Only then did he pull the door open suddenly and all the way, a trick gangsters use when they've got nothing to hide. He assumed this overzealous early bird could only be a cop.

Instead, the young man anxiously waiting in the hallway looked like somebody's assistant, an impertinent messenger boy poking his nose into other people's business. He carried two books in his left hand, and his hair clearly had not seen a comb in months. Behind his ear he carried a green highlighter pen, and he had the look of someone who had been up all night.

"What can I do for you?"

The young man brought his hands to his chest in a gesture of prayer and cleared his throat several times before he could get any words out.

"Vergara Gray?" he exclaimed finally. "I'm really face-to-face with the one and only Vergara Gray? I can't believe it!"

"Go light on the melodrama, young man. How may I help you?"

"May I come in?"

"I'd rather you didn't. This room is only very temporary. It's really not up to *our* standards."

"Oh, no, sir. It's perfectly fine by me."

Vergara Gray walked over to the window. He opened the curtain and felt comforted by the sight of the dim sun filtering through the inevitable June smog. Compared to the miserable day he'd been released, this Tuesday felt like a party. He lifted his eyebrows, trying to soften the stern expression he'd shown his visitor so far. "What can I do for you, young man?"

"I have here a letter of recommendation."

"From where?"

"Jail. They released me yesterday."

"They threw me out of prison, too. Same amnesty, eh?"

"Destiny has brought us together," the young man quickly added.

"Is it a letter from the warden?"

"Please, sir, who do you take me for? It's from a prisoner!"

"A prisoner?"

"From Lira the Dwarf."

"A letter of recommendation from a hoodlum like Lira? I advise you not to look for work in a bank."

"Open it and read it, please."

The man placed the envelope on the bed, took one dramatic

step back, then stood and stared at it with a furrowed brow. The boy picked it up and handed it back to him. Vergara Gray wiped his fingers off on his sweater, as if to erase his fingerprints, scratched open the envelope with his fingernails, and took out the thin piece of paper he then held in the air as if it were infested with lice.

"So, what do you say?" the boy asked impatiently, moving the books covered in graph paper from one hand to the other.

" 'I would like to introduce you to Ángel Santiago.' Signed, 'The Dwarf.' "

"That's it."

"That's the entire contents of this epistolary masterpiece? Lira the Dwarf's eloquence is as spare as his stature."

"It would have been too incriminating to say anything else. I'll tell you the rest."

"I'm happy to hear that, my boy, because this is about as informative as a brick wall."

"First of all, I'd like to give you these two books. They're used, but in good condition."

"Thank you. Let's see . . . *Heart* and *Where I'm Calling From.*"

"In *Heart*, I identified with Garron, the good boy in class."

"I take it, then, that your stay in jail was the result of a misunderstanding."

"Don't make fun of me, sir. In the other one there's a story about the death of Chekhov. Do you know who Chekhov was?"

"Sounds like the name of a chess player."

"He's a Russian writer."

"I've never been interested in politics."

"Chekhov was from before communism."

"You might have guessed that I'm not a big reader. Thank you anyway for the books. I will try to take a look at them."

Ángel waved his arms around wildly. "No, no. You don't have

to read them, Professor! What matters about these books are their covers."

Vergara Gray scratched his head, then rubbed his unshaven cheek. "Translation, please."

"In jail, it's impossible to find better book covers, so we used graph paper."

"I see."

"The graph paper is much uglier than the original covers, so we will remove them at once." Joining action to words, he took the paper off the books and spread them out on the bedspread.

"Mr. Vergara Gray, sir, Lira the Dwarf's genius is inversely proportionate to his size."

With one sweeping movement he turned over the book covers; the other sides were covered with intricate and complex hieroglyphics that looked something like a map. They were, in fact, miniature architectural drawings.

"What is this?"

"This here is the strategy for what I call *the big coup*, designed step-by-step by the Dwarf. It was going to be his next masterpiece, but he got arrested for some minor job that wasn't worth even a tenth of his talent. He sends it to you as a token of profound admiration and with very cordial regards."

"I'm sorry, but I'm retired."

"Please allow me to explain."

The man covered his ears. "Don't waste your breath. I don't want to hear anything."

"Okay, just one thing: we're talking about one-point-two billion pesos."

"What's that in dollars?"

"On the black market, with the dollar at seven hundred forty-five pesos, that would come to about one-point-six million dollars."

"Okay, now you listen to a different calculation: for every hundred thousand, that's one year away. In one million six hundred ten thousand dollars there's a hundred thousand, sixteen times, which adds up to sixteen years in the slammer. But in order to get your hands on that delightful sum, you can't just lift your arm and cut off a branch laden with bills, as if you were picking a bunch of grapes. You can bet that amount of money will be well protected by guards and guns. Let's say you have extraordinary good luck and you only kill one person. For homicide, add . . . Have you killed anyone yet?"

"No, not yet."

"Okay, let's see. For a first homicide, you'll get ten years, added to the sixteen you've already got, that's a total of twenty-six years in the shade. And if we figure that you're as good as your Garron in that book and they let you off five for good behavior, we've got twenty-one. How old are you now?"

"Twenty, sir."

"You'll get out at forty-one, probably with other pieces of paper like Lira's in your pocket."

"If I've come to you it's because I know you've never fired a shot. That's the beauty of your career."

"I am not infallible, young man. After all, they had me inside for five years. I've even got a few white hairs in my mustache."

"But they didn't catch you in the act. The judge gave you ten years because you wouldn't squeal."

"Either you know a lot or you presume a lot."

"You're all anybody talked about in jail, Professor Vergara Gray. Of course, Lira the Dwarf would like a commission."

"A 'small' commission, I hope."

"Lira has modest ambitions, and a really good sense of humor. He used to tell us jokes by Monterroso, a well-known writer of similarly short stature."

"Like what?"

"Like this one: 'Dwarfs have a kind of sixth sense that allows them to recognize each other at first sight.'"

The man smoothed down his mustache and walked over to the window to hide his smile. He preferred not to get the young ruffian's hopes up by showing him that he was amused; Vergara Gray also feared that if he allowed himself any weakness he would be more vulnerable to temptation. "Breakfast would be a good idea. Coffee or tea?"

"Coffee with milk, for me. Are you really going to treat me?"

"I'll ask them to bring it up from the bar. In the meantime, we'll have to get some fresh rolls from the bakery."

"I'll go."

"I would greatly appreciate that."

"What kind do you want?"

"An assortment. I eat a big breakfast and then skip lunch."

"Understood."

"Bring two *marraquetas*, two *colizas*, three *hallullas*, three *flautas*, four *tostadas*, three onion rolls, and three slices of kuchen with raisins and candied fruits."

"At your service, Professor. Oh, yes, and please forgive me, but could you give me some money? I left jail without a penny."

The man took a five-thousand-peso bill out of his wallet, rolled it up, and stuck it behind Ángel's ear. "Here you are."

"The bread is, of course, my treat. This loan is guaranteed by the loot."

"By the one-point-two billion?"

"By my share of the one-point-two billion."

The young man was about to shoot out the door when the older man stretched out his leg to stop him.

"What made Lira the Dwarf think that you and I could work together?"

"Lira said, 'The technical expertise of Vergara Gray combined with the energy of Ángel Santiago.' "

"That's pretty sad praise."

The young man pointed to the drawings on the bedspread. "What do you think, at first glance?"

"A lot of work has gone into this."

"Only three years. At first the little guy was worried about leaving any clues. He didn't want to write anything down, afraid they'd steal his treasure. So we'd sit in the yard, and he'd explain it to me over and over, drawing it out with a stick in the dirt. Whenever a guard approached, he'd erase it. We'd say we were playing tic-tac-toe. Until I had the idea of covering the books in graph paper. A simple but brilliant idea, don't you think?"

"So you're good at remembering things they tell you only once?"

"I don't like to brag, but that is my speciality. I'll just run out to the bakery and be back in a flash."

He walked out into the hallway, where the man's urgent voice reached him.

"Just out of curiosity, Mr. Santiago. What exactly are you going to buy?"

"Bread, of course."

"Which ones?"

The young man blinked for ten seconds, stuck his tongue out between his teeth, then recited while scratching his nose, "Two *marraquetas*, two *colizas*, three *hallullas*, three *flautas*, four *tostadas*, three onion rolls, and three slices of kuchen with raisins and candied fruits."

"May God be with you, my boy."

"Don't forget to do your part."

"My part?"

"Order me a coffee with milk."

VICTORIA CAUGHT THE first bus of the morning, the same one that carried the masons and carpenters from the outlying slums to the wealthy neighborhoods, and she crowded into a seat without feeling any relief from the cold. The men had wet hair, mufflers wrapped around their necks and up to their noses, and almost everyone carried a bag containing a sandwich and a thermos of coffee for lunch.

When she got off at the corner of the school, she almost passed out. Even though she was aware of the dangers of anorexia, she knew that even a few extra ounces could sabotage her *grand jeté* or a leap into the arms of her *partenaire*, and she preferred hunger to losing her ballet dancer's figure. After last night's precipitous explosion, Ángel Santiago spent hours caressing her skin with his unpracticed hands, and she felt more supple and flexible than ever. Those rough fingers seemed to be writing something on her skin, and she allowed him to do as he pleased, surrendering to his desire and his protective touch.

But this abrupt change in her life was also disorienting. A month had already passed since they had expelled her, and now, instead of heading in blind despair for a movie theater that opened early and showed movies continuously, she found herself in front of her school, trembling and not knowing exactly what to do when the bell rang. Santiago's arguments had been much more persuasive than her mother's silent reproaches; she was in her last year of school, just five or six months from graduating, and she simply couldn't allow her life to be ruined because of a simple case of poor academic performance.

"The teachers are there to teach you, and if they can't manage it, the failure is theirs, not yours," Ángel had whispered in her ear.

The girl explained to him, talking into the pillow without looking him in the eyes, that she was often incapable of expressing herself, and that for her, everything from the most insignificant to the most profound got transformed into movement. "I can dance sadness, but I can't cry it."

"But to get into the Escuela Superior de Arte you have to have your high school diploma. That should be our goal, *your* victory, or else you'll end up dancing in a chorus line or being a nursery-school teacher. You think your father would approve of that? I'm sure he would have wanted something better for you. He wanted freedom for the people!"

"Yeah, and instead he left my mother, a slave to me, a widow, pregnant," Victoria said, turning around, "indifferent to herself, to me, to life. What do you know about freedom?"

Ángel Santiago smiled at her words. "The fact that a small group of teachers threw you out of school, destroying your life and shitting on your father's dreams, is nothing more than an insignificant bleep in the entire history of the universe. If that's the way it is, then the people who killed him won. They defeated you, and him."

She had put the pillow over her head. She didn't want to hear a sermon, she said. She was sick of people who talked big.

Yet here she was, wearing her blue uniform stained with fruit juice and ink from her Bic pen, her backpack slung over her shoulders, and her eyes glued on the tiles in the hallway.

She was the first to arrive in the classroom. She sat down in her assigned seat and looked at the only name she had carved into the desk with the point of her compass—Julio Bocca, the dancer— surrounded by all the other honors generations of girls had paid to their idols and current boyfriends.

"Have they taken you back?" asked Ducci, the blond girl, as she sat down next to her.

The other girls also looked at her as they arrived.

"No."

"So what are you doing here?"

"I'm going to see what happens."

"They're going to throw you out. That's what's going to happen."

"They've got no right. This is a democracy and I want to study."

The class was art history, and according to what the girl could glean from peeking at her schoolmate's binder, they were studying trends in twentieth-century painting. The teacher had passed out photocopies with pictures of dozens of paintings, and the students were supposed to say which school each belonged to, then back up their answers with an explanatory sentence. At the bottom of the page, she saw the list of possible answers: expressionism, surrealism, pointillism, impressionism, cubism, abstract.

"Cézanne is a cubist," her friend whispered in her ear, "because he distorts figures into geometric shapes."

"Why did he do that?" asked Victoria.

"Because he felt like it, that's why. An artist who does something that hasn't been done before becomes the founder of a school."

"And Dalí?"

"He's a surrealist. For example, here you've got a clock melting in

49

the desert. It's not melting because of the heat, but because time is useless, sterile, like the desert. Understand?"

"Where did you learn all that?"

"I learn what interests me. For number three, write down 'Van Gogh.' That one first sees the colors, then the things. When he puts the things with the colors, it's as if he were seeing them for the first time."

"Like this sunflower?"

"This is just a stupid photocopy. If you saw this in Amsterdam, you'd faint."

"Have you been to Amsterdam?"

"Are you kidding? My family is dirt poor. Write there, 'Van Gogh.'"

"What are you going to do after you graduate?"

"I'm going to get a job as a bilingual secretary. Take the sheet to the teacher."

Ms. Sanhueza had kind green eyes surrounded by plump cheeks, and she often preferred to stay at her desk rather than move her ample body up and down the narrow aisles between the desks as the girls pretended to gasp in horror at the advent of her ample rear end. While the girls completed worksheets, she'd bury her head in a magazine of crossword puzzles about movie stars. She agreed with her students that Hugh Grant was divine, but she saw herself as having much more affinity with a more mature gentleman like Richard Gere.

She had once taken part in a television game show. Poised to win a hundred thousand pesos for answering questions about Jeremy Irons's life in a "double or nothing" round, she failed to remember the names of the entire female cast he had starred with in *The House of the Spirits*. To have missed such an easy question that was so relevant to Chile gave her rheumatism for two weeks, during which time she couldn't look anybody in the eye.

"You already finished?" she asked with surprise when she saw Victoria's paper.

"Yes, teacher."

She looked over the pictures and Victoria's comments and checked them off with a Faber fountain pen.

"Everything is correct."

When she opened her roll book to write an A-plus in the column next to Victoria's name, she found that it had been crossed out with a thick red line.

"My dear!" she exclaimed. "You don't exist. Look at this: 'Expelled for poor performance, May twentieth.'"

The girl smiled innocently.

"I left and now I'm back, teacher. As far as my performance, you can see for yourself that I've changed."

"An A-plus in art history is quite an event, my dear. I rarely give anybody such a high grade."

"I've grown up, teacher. Before I didn't know what to do with my life. Now the only thing I want to do is study. Get a scholarship. Go to the university."

Ms. Sanhueza nodded and placed the successful exercise on top of the roll book.

"And what would you like to study, young lady?"

"Art history education," she proclaimed.

She didn't know where those words had sprung from, and she couldn't believe they had just come out of her mouth. She somehow associated this strange lapse with a fleeting memory of Ángel. Could it be that just as Ducci had whispered in her ear the correct answers, her new friend had hypnotized her into articulating such madness?

Ms. Sanhueza had always been sweet, but the expression on her face now reached the heights of syrupy goo.

"Really, young lady?"

"Really, teacher."

"Never has any student I've ever had chosen my career. Don't you think it's because I haven't been a very good teacher?"

"No way, teacher. I would say that it is precisely your dedication that has inspired me."

"As a teacher you will never earn very much money and you'll go gray at a young age."

"I'm only seventeen years old! I'm way too young to worry about gray hairs. What matters to me is to follow my vocation."

She placed her hand on her chest as if she were swearing allegiance to the flag. Ms. Sanhueza removed with a sweep of her hand the tear that lingered in the corner of her eye.

THERE WAS A long recess at ten in the morning. The girls spent the time yawning in the hallways, sharing secrets, exchanging music they'd downloaded from their computers, smoking in the bathrooms, applying acne cream, trying to finish homework for the next class, and flirting with the French teacher, who was only five years older than they and had a certain George Clooney air about him that made them tremble.

In the meantime, Ms. Sanhueza, invoking a dispensation granted to teachers by the Ministry of Education to be used only in matters of the gravest consequence, called all the teachers to the principal's office to address the case of Victoria Ponce. The girl was placed in the middle of the room—whose walls were covered with oil paintings of illustrious citizens and rectors of the institution—precisely under a teardrop chandelier that had enough lightbulbs to dispel the gloom of winter.

The teacher laid out her argument with a vivacity and passion that brought a blush to her puffy white cheeks: the punishment this academic community had dealt out to Victoria Ponce had had the desired effect. The black sheep had returned to the fold, not only remorseful about her prior behavior but with a strong desire to study, an eagerness to excel, and a willingness to be obedient and polite to her teachers and friendly and congenial to her classmates.

And that wasn't all: Ms. Ponce had just completed an assignment in art history with such mastery she had given her the highest possible grade: an A-plus.

"What exactly are you trying to tell us, Ms. Sanhueza?"

"I believe we must rescind this girl's expulsion."

The principal turned to the teacher with a sardonic smile on her face. "Have you taken into account that Ms. Ponce was removed from this school after three suspensions? That her guardians did not even show up to discuss the deviant behavior of their rebellious and insolent child?"

Ms. Sanhueza rose from her seat with an accusatory finger. "You know very well that her father couldn't come because he was assassinated on the steps of this very school, where he was a great pedagogue. It seems that the events of that terrible day have silenced us all with fear."

The principal made a gesture of irritation and looked up at the chandelier, as if asking for patience from the heavens. "What fear are you talking about? That happened seventeen years ago and Chile has been a democracy for over a decade. When are we going to stop blaming everything on Pinochet? This girl never even knew her father."

The art teacher turned purple and broke out in a profuse sweat. "But she knew his absence!"

With the alertness of a predator about to leap on its prey, she looked from one to the other of her colleagues, awaiting their response. The other teachers docilely lowered their eyes; only the math teacher, Berríos, spoke while examining his well-groomed fingernails.

"I have great sympathy for your somewhat pathetic eloquence, Ms. Sanhueza. But in my class this student was performing well below grammar school level. I doubt she even knows her multiplication tables."

"Okay, my dear"—the art teacher turned to Victoria—"what's nine times nine?"

"Eighty-one, teacher."

The woman made a triumphal pause, like a defense lawyer who places his client at the mercy of the court.

"That was just a figure of speech," Berríos sighed. "She doesn't know anything about algebra."

"Did Picasso know algebra?"

"How should I know?"

"And Dalí?"

"I don't think so. He was crazier than a loon."

"So why should Ms. Ponce know algebra when her greatest aspiration is to be a humble art teacher?"

"But we have a basic curriculum, Ms. Sanhueza. It doesn't matter at all if an architect knows the difference between the liver and the kidney, but any civilized person must understand the circulatory system!"

"Blood knows better than you how to circulate. Air comes and goes through your lungs without you even realizing it. The birds and the bees don't need your sex education classes to breed."

Berríos covered his face with a handkerchief. "I'm ashamed to be in this room. Your arguments lower me, degrade me, Ms. Sanhueza."

"My esteemed colleague, anybody can learn algebra. But only Toulouse-Lautrec could have painted the *Moulin Rouge*."

The principal clapped her hands to put an end to the exchange. The clock told her that recess was over, and she hadn't even had her tea. The other teachers were also impatient.

"What do you say, dear colleagues? Shall we give Ms. Ponce another chance?"

The teachers, perhaps distracted by other concerns, simply shrugged their shoulders.

S EVERAL TIMES A day, every day for more than a week, Vergara Gray dialed Teresa Capriatti's phone number. Every time she answered, he recited her name reverently and she hung up. On three occasions she asked him never to call again, underscoring this more formal rejection by slamming down the phone.

Her scorn caused him so much distress that all he could do was sit in his room, shuffle a deck of cards, and dream about a sudden stroke of good fortune. In the evenings he went across the street, where Monasterio told the bartender to serve his partner vodka with orange juice and, on the pretext of having some urgent business to resolve, muttered something to Vergara Gray about how next week they would have a long chat about all their unresolved issues.

"There's only one I care about," Vergara Gray said, grabbing him by the lapel and lifting him off the ground. "Half-half. That was the agreement and I expect you to honor it."

"You don't have to remind me, Nico. We'll share whatever there is in a brotherly manner."

"Nothing brotherly about it, Monasterio. Fifty-fifty."

Then he'd take a stroll around the neighborhood and observe the changes of the last five years. Most of the girls on the street were very young, almost children, and they all wore what looked like a uniform: a skimpy top and blue jeans that came below the tops of their underwear. Between the two garments a shiny ring hung off their belly buttons, adorning their smooth, flat stomachs. Men's gazes could slide from their breasts to their bellies as if skating down a smooth sheet of ice.

Apparently, the heroines from his criminal past had abandoned the battlefield, mortally wounded by added pounds and a profusion of wrinkles. They had never learned how to use those portable compact disk players the young ones wore glued to their ears and strapped around their skinny waists, nor would they have been able to sing along to the latest hits in English. The more he observed his surroundings, the neighborhood, this world, the lonelier he felt. His expectations of freedom had been so different that he even began to feel nostalgic for jail.

On Saturday, after glancing at the sketch of an elevator in Lira the Dwarf's plans, he picked up the telephone and again dialed Teresa Capriatti's number, deeply resigned to the agony of another rejection. This time, however, his wife didn't hang up, but rather asked in a strictly disinterested tone of voice how he was.

"Good, my love. I'm very good."

"I'm glad, Nico. I didn't hang up this time because you and I have to talk."

"That's what I've been trying to tell you."

"It's about something important that affects you, me, and our son."

"My three aces." The man smiled.

"We should speak in person. I'd like us to meet tomorrow, once and for all."

"Lunch?"

"No. That takes too much time. Let's meet for tea. It's less complicated."

"Where?"

"There's a tea salon on Orrego Luco, just before you reach the Costanera. It's called Flaubert. I'll be there with Pablito tomorrow at five."

"He's really going to come?"

"He doesn't want to see you at all, but since it's something important . . ."

"He's my son. He shouldn't feel that way."

"You've caused him a lot of harm, Nico."

"I? Harm him? The person I love most in the world? I, cause harm?"

"Try to remain calm, or we won't be able to meet."

"You're right. It's better to talk about these things in person."

"Flaubert is a decent establishment. Keep that in mind."

"What do you mean?"

"Well, people notice what you're wearing."

"I understand."

"Styles have changed. Anyway, just so you know what to expect."

When he hung up, he rushed down the stairs, crossed the street to his partner's bar, and asked Elsa, the cashier, to give him some money. She told him there wasn't any money in the register this early in the morning. The money got locked up in the safe on Friday night, and on Monday the armored car came to take it to the bank.

Vergara Gray told her he needed a modest sum, about two hundred thousand pesos, to buy a more fashionable jacket, a silk tie, and a nice striped shirt, English-style. When the cashier pressed the electronic button that opened the drawer, he could see for himself that there wasn't even enough money in there to give change to an early bird buying cigarettes or a vodka sour.

Smoothing down his mustache, Vergara Gray asked her the location of the safe and the combination. Smiling, the woman informed him that she knew absolutely nothing about the numbers that gave access to the treasure within, but that the metal safe, weighing in at over four hundred pounds, was in the next room and was bolted to the floor and the wall.

"Let's go take a look," the thief said, winking at her.

"My pleasure, Nico. I just want to reassure you that it's impenetrable."

"I believe you. I'm just curious."

Vergara Gray stood in front of it and sighed deeply. How many times had he faced a similar contraption after sneaking through the labyrinthine hallways of banks and stores, then had to turn away, humiliated by defeat, unable to find the combination and open it. This particular model had a special kind of charm. Right in the middle was a wheel that had to be turned to open the first steel door, behind which there would be an electronic system, perhaps connected to an alarm, that would require either a load of dynamite or the fine manipulation of tiny screwdrivers.

He turned the wheel to the left and to the right, then turned it back to the middle; he brought his ear close to the lockbox and smiled when he realized that the music of that mechanism was not new to him. If he was remembering right, he was dealing with the same Schloss model he had encountered in the Petzold Jewelry Store that unsettled month of September 1973.

The owners had raised the Chilean flag to express their approval of the military coup that had overthrown Allende, then gone off to their mansion in the resort town of Zapallar to wait for the soldiers to finish killing off all the leftists still roaming the streets.

On the night of Wednesday, September 12, that very flag had inspired him to climb onto the roof of the jewelry store with a drill, for the first time unconcerned about the noise he would make—it would just blend in with the gunshots and explosions raging throughout the city—to open up a hole large enough to climb through and jump right onto the safe. It had been the quickest and most efficiently executed heist he'd ever pulled off. When the owners went to the police to complain about the disappearance of their most precious jewels, the captain accused them of being selfish shopkeepers, worried about some insignificant crime while his men were risking their lives in the battle against Allende's terrorists. He told them to get out of the police station immediately if they didn't want to be locked up in a cell where the blood of the torture victims flowed over the cement floors.

He figured that with his three jeweler's screwdrivers and his dental tweezers, he could disembowel Monasterio's safe in a few hours, as long as the cashier and the morning drinkers left him to work in peace.

"Elsita," he said to the cashier, "if I spent a few hours on this lady here, what would you do?"

"I'd have to tell Monasterio, Nico."

"Do you know your boss owes me money?"

"That's what everybody says."

"Oh, really? What *exactly* do they say?"

"That there's a lot of money involved."

"How much?"

"You kept quiet and the loot was never found. If it was sold on the international market, we must be talking about a whole lot of money."

"So why didn't they lock up Monasterio if everybody knows?"

"I'd rather not talk about that, Nico."

"It happened so many years ago. Tell me about it as if it were a legend, a movie somebody told you about."

"That's not so easy; I've been personally involved in this story. You see, ten years ago I weighed twenty pounds less and I kept off the wrinkles with makeup my niece brought me from the duty-free shop in the airport."

"So?"

"I'm trying to tell you that Monasterio noticed me."

"Were you his lover?"

"Oh, that word is so filthy!"

"You were his friend?"

"His friend."

"Intimate friend."

"You could say so. A few months after you got arrested, we had to get rid of the jewels. But it had to be done in a clever way."

The cashier seemed to suddenly realize that she had already said too much. She went to the refrigerator and pulled out two bottles of mineral water. She stuck a slice of lemon in each and offered the man a toast. Then she took a long sip and ran her tongue across her lips.

"If I'm telling you all this, it's for Monasterio. I want you to know so you'll still be friends. To him, you are more than a partner. He thinks of you as a brother."

"What happened to the jewels?"

"He got wind that the cops were going to come and question him, and he had the brilliant idea of beating them to it. He asked for a meeting with the first lady, and offered her half the jewels to give to the army to pay for the reconstruction of the country."

"Jesus Christ!"

"That's why he was allowed to keep the other half without anybody bothering him. I love Monasterio and I don't like to think that for a few pesos here or there a good friendship would be ruined."

"A few pesos here or there! I was sentenced to ten years in jail!"

"He did everything he could for you."

"Like come visit me in jail?"

"Every month he sent money indirectly to Teresa Capriatti."

"What do you mean, 'indirectly'?"

"*Directly* you'll see how he did it *indirectly.*"

The woman placed a checkbook on the counter and looked at the date on a calendar from a candle factory that had a picture of the Virgin Mary, the baby Jesus, and the motto: ILLUMINATING FROM END TO END.

"What are you going to do?"

"Write you a check to help you through these hard times."

"Elsita, I may be a thief, but I'm not a pimp. I just want Monasterio to give me what legitimately belongs to me."

The woman smiled as she scribbled on the newspaper to try to get the ink flowing through her Bic pen.

"What's so funny?"

"The word 'legitimately,' Nico. How much do you need?"

"I don't want charity, I told you."

"It's not charity, Professor. It's an advance."

Vergara Gray rubbed his chin, then his mustache, then one of his sideburns, and responded thoughtfully. "When you put it in those terms, it seems honorable enough."

"Will two hundred be enough?"

"Make it three."

"IN THE CRIMINAL world, the only things that work are violence and patience," proclaimed Lira the Dwarf. "The first will make you rich or lead you back to jail; the second will keep you poor but free."

Ángel Santiago was already losing patience with being poor.

He wanted to get to the ballet academy and invite his "sister" to a Chinese restaurant. If all had gone well with her return to school, he hoped he could count on a night of lovemaking, maybe even in a decent hotel in a real room with a real bed.

He wanted to make up to her for his overzealousness, for wildly shooting off his wad as if he couldn't care less about his lover's pleasure. He tried to comfort himself with a feeble explanation: that discharge was just a burst of energy accumulated over months and years of fantasy and frustration, when the only women he saw were in glossy magazine pictures that hung on the walls of his cell. But he still had not confessed to her that he had not traveled four hours by train from Talca to Santiago but rather three hours from two years in jail to the movie theater where they had met. The way things stood now, she might very well have gotten the impression that he was an uncouth, arrogant young man.

The problem was, he liked the girl. There was also, of course, her body, delectable wherever his hands happened to land. But most of all, he was drawn to her precariousness, a poor student expelled from school, frequenting raunchy movie houses just to keep warm, or so she said. He imagined her there, slouched down in her seat, less interested in the kung fu moves and erotic gymnastics than in her dreams about the routines she would practice that evening at the ballet studio.

When he pictured the girl dancing, she became even more enchanting and seductive. He imagined her surrounded by other dancers, also passionate about the precise execution of a *pas de deux* or a similarly exalted *tour en l'air*. But when the music stopped and the sand got swept out of the circus tent, as they say, all that awaited her was uncertainty: the streets, a depressed mother, poverty, and— he admitted to himself mercilessly—he, Ángel Santiago.

And who was *he?* A nobody she had met by chance. A starving interloper, an intruder, clueless as to his own destiny, but, when all was said and done, somebody she'd slept with. He had given her sermons, he realized, with the vehemence of a parish priest, not to harass her but out of pure, disinterested affection: a spontaneous impulse of his heart. Then he had shot her off to school like an arrow.

He needed money, even just enough to take the bus to the academy, and his hands were freezing as much from the cold as from the fear of being caught pickpocketing a sucker on the subway and being sent *express* back to jail, where the warden would not hide his glee, rejoicing in this welcome reprieve from the nightmare of his own murder.

His only path had to be prudence, but after two hours of hanging around the automatic teller machine at the exit of the Hippodrome of Chile, he began to get desperate and bored; that's also when his senses grew sharper.

A taxi stopped next to the curb, and a stuck-up woman rushed out of it and left the door open, shouting at the driver to wait. She ran into the cubicle, inserted her card, and impatiently banged out her password on the keyboard. Just as the money was coming out, Ángel Santiago approached her innocently and asked if the machine also gave out smaller bills. The woman looked at her wad, saw that it didn't, and, without saying good-bye, turned to run back to the taxi. Whatever had caused the woman's agitation, she had done exactly what Ángel had long been hoping for: she had walked away while the question, "Do you need anything else?" remained on the screen.

He pressed the *yes* key and tentatively asked for a hundred thousand pesos, which the machine gave him quickly and obediently. He then thought it prudent to let the machine remain in dialogue with itself, avoiding the temptation to commit other crimes he lacked the necessary experience to carry out successfully.

After crossing Vivaceta Avenue near the racetrack, he came across a groom leading a horse back from a training session. He patted it on its mane.

"Is he gentle?"

"Gentle? Like a lamb," the groom replied.

"How many races has he won?"

"Just one, when he was three. But he'll be able to again because he got downgraded."

"How does he do in the twelve hundred?"

"One-fifteen-two. If he goes down a fifth, he'll win."

"And how much is he worth?"

"Not cheap, about three hundred thousand. But he ain't mine."

"If I offer you a hundred thousand, will you sell him to me?"

"That's an insult, young man. There are six-year-olds who turn around. At that price it would be a steal."

"I'll buy him for a hundred thousand."

"Please don't insult me, sir. This horse has got a future."

"He won once when he was three. How old is he now?"

"Barely eight."

"Barely eight. He might win out in the desert, in Antofagasta, but forget about Santiago."

"How much did you say you'd give me?"

"Eighty thousand."

"Cash?"

"Cash. And since you're stealing him from his trainer, I'll give you seventy thousand and mum's the word."

"The trainer's crazy about him. He'll kill me."

"I'll give you sixty thousand cash and we'll forget all about it. How much did you say he ran the twelve hundred in?"

"One-sixteen. I can't lie to his new owner."

Ángel Santiago sought out the most deserted streets on his way to the dance academy. He had forgotten to ask the horse's name and in a way this made him happy: when you name something for the first time you make it yours. He and Victoria Ponce would baptize him at the fount of the church. He walked slowly up Einstein, following the signs toward the Virgin of San Cristóbal Hill. When he gave the horse his lead, the animal was obedient and attentive to his wishes.

He had not been free for even a week, and when he added things up, the balance couldn't have been better: he owned a horse, of sorts, that he could ride all over the city from end to end and corner to corner as he had done in the fields of Talca when he was a little boy. He had a girlfriend, of sorts, for although there was nothing

formal between them, the *starting gates had opened*. He could count the
ballet studio he had snuck into for the last few nights after having
secretly made a copy of the teacher's key as his own lodging, of
sorts. In addition, he had a fortune, of sorts, that permitted him to
take his slender friend out to eat with chopsticks at the Poor Chinaman Restaurant.

Not least among these few items in his private utopia was his
horse: a worn-out beast with matted hair, wide flanks, and more
than a few gray hairs; he was a creature, like Ángel himself, who
had dreamed in his youth of being a prince and in the end had only
been an also-ran. Society may have lowered its curtain on Ángel at
twenty, but both their lives were about to get turned around.

He evaluated his arsenal: a woman, a horse, Lira the Dwarf's
coup, and—sound the trumpets!—Don Nicolás Vergara Gray.

A FULL HOUR BEFORE the appointed time he snooped around the Flaubert Tea Salon, sniffing it out like a bloodhound. He leaned against the fence of a house across the street and spent a long time studying the customers and the cars they got in and out of, sensing that particular aura of an established, well-heeled clientele. He deduced that this was not a place for the kind of people he associated with but rather for those he stole from. By the same token, he was gratified by Teresa Capriatti's good taste, and he felt confident that his son's upbringing was in good hands.

Though he managed to maintain his upright posture and impeccable grooming, he feared he might be on the verge of passing out. By now, Pedro Pablo's gift had been carried around for so long that the red ribbon was unraveling and looked worn and secondhand. He wanted to avoid seeing them enter before him, so he snuck away toward the river and smoked two cigarettes, contemplating the turbid waters but unable to formulate even one clear thought.

For years now he had been preparing the conciliatory speech that would prove to them that he was a deserving man and that nothing remained in his attitudes or his plans that would lead him back to a life of crime. His decision to live a moral life and get a respectable job had been set in stone by nothing less than the decade-long sentence he'd been given. And if this hadn't been enough, he had recourse to the five long years he'd spent separated from his wife and Pedro Pablo, his teenage son, who, though he had made a few cursory visits to his father in jail, never even tried to hide his complete indifference.

At five minutes after five he entered Flaubert's and his instincts led him to the farthest, most remote corner of the dining room, a table in the back next to the oven where the aroma of baked delicacies was most concentrated. Though he had always thought Teresa Capriatti the most beautiful woman in the world, seeing her after so long—dressed in a close-fitting, tailored black suit with a pearl-colored scarf around her neck and the brooch she wore at her wedding on her lapel—gave him the anguished sensation that he did not, in fact, deserve her.

Time had done her little damage. On the contrary, any lines on her face were hidden under a layer of makeup, and the few extra ounces that filled out her cheeks only added the final touches of perfection to her beauty. On the heels of these observations came the unwelcome suspicion that she had a lover, a thought that cast a shadow over the ex-convict's face and distorted his well-rehearsed smile as he approached the table.

Somebody at the next table stared at him, perhaps sifting through his memory for where he might have met that man. Vergara Gray leaned over his wife's cheek and anointed it with a kiss: a mere peck for her; the entire world for him. Pedro Pablo rose, and his father stretched out his arms to give him a hug. The son, however, kept his distance and held out his hand. Vergara Gray sat down between them without uttering a word.

"We already ordered two mineral waters."

"Mineral water? But we must celebrate!"

"You can have whatever you like, but we're having mineral water."

"What would you like to eat?"

"We don't have much time, Nico. We'll leave the meal for another time."

"The pastries look wonderful. Aren't you just a little bit tempted?"

The waiter brought their order and turned to the man. "What would you like, sir?"

"Me? Tea, please."

"What kind?"

"Tea. Just tea."

"Sir, there are thirty kinds of tea on our menu."

The waiter held the menu out to him as if giving him a blow. As he read it he realized that all those exotic names of Oriental infusions meant nothing to him.

"Bring me the Flaubert mix, please."

"Yes, sir. Anything else?"

"I don't know."

He wanted to think of something that would stop time, slow down the clock, but nothing came to mind.

"Perhaps a pastry?"

"That's it, yes. A pastry."

"We have many kinds. Lucuma cake, black forest cake, mocha cake . . ."

"Just bring me a mineral water."

"Carbonated or plain?"

"What?" Vergara Gray asked, puzzled and suddenly distracted by the impatient little kicks his son was giving him under the table.

"Your mineral water, sir?"

"Carbonated, if you would be so kind."

The impertinent waiter's departure laid a tangled silence down among them.

"I love you," the man said abruptly. "I have come here to tell you that I love you, that the two of you mean everything in the world to me."

Teresa Capriatti brought the glass of water to her full lips, then dried them with the linen napkin. Her husband placed the gift on the table, offering it to his son.

"Thank you," the boy said.

"No need for that. Open it now, Pablito."

"Is that really necessary? Everybody's looking at us."

"Nobody will care if you open a present."

After trying several times to untie the knot with his fingernails, his son picked up a knife and cut the ribbon. He tore off the paper and nodded without uttering a word of appreciation.

"What do you think?"

"It's nice."

Vergara Gray lunged for his son's hand and placed it on the briefcase.

"Touch it, caress it. Can you feel the nobility of that leather?"

With both hands, he demonstrated the movement he was recommending. He then placed his hand over his son's and held it affectionately.

"It's nice. It's a good briefcase, thank you," the boy said, freeing himself from his father's touch.

"Now I'm going to show you the best part: how it locks. A lot of briefcases have two locks, but this one has a different combination for each one. You have to memorize them, then you, and only you, will be able to open it. The number on the right side is the day and month you were born, and the one on the left is the day and month I was born. A pact between father and son. Now open it."

"Here? Now?"

"I want to make sure it works. If there's a problem, I can still return it."

Pedro Pablo started to turn the lock; his father took part in the ceremony by whispering each number to the boy as he went.

"If you forget the numbers, you can always ask me."

"Where?" Teresa interrupted.

The man leaned back, dumbfounded. He spent half a minute scratching his mustache, then said in a very low whisper, "It's just that I thought that you and I . . . I mean, you and I and Pedro Pablo . . ." Then, correcting himself nervously, he said, "You're right. I'll write the combination down for you on a piece of paper."

He tore a page out of his small notebook and started to write. His son stopped him.

"You don't need to write it down. I've already memorized it. On the right—"

"Ssshh," his father said curtly, looking around. "This is a secret between you and me. Never say it out loud. If nobody knows the number, they'll never be able to steal your documents."

Pablo stopped, smiled, then suddenly started laughing out loud, even banging his chair against the wall.

"What are you laughing at?"

"The briefcase, man! Only a safecracker would think of buying such a secure briefcase."

A sudden tremor shook the man's hands, which he quickly moved under the table and held between his legs, trying to bring them under control. He felt like an idiot when he managed to say, "You don't like it?"

"No, I like it."

The waiter brought a cup, the mineral water, and a porcelain teapot. Pedro Pablo whisked away the briefcase, making room for the waiter to set the items down on the table. Teresa Capriatti took another sip of water and when Vergara Gray began to pour his into the glass, she spoke. "Nico, there are two issues."

"I should tell Monasterio to increase the amount he sends you every month. Everything in Chile has gotten so much more expensive."

"When will you be talking to him? I haven't gotten a check in six months."

"Today. And the other one?".

Teresa Capriatti looked at her son, who wiped his nose quickly with his finger, leaned conspiratorially on the table, and pulled a piece of paper in a plastic sleeve out of his jacket pocket.

"Nico, Mom and I have decided that I'm going to change my name."

"I don't understand."

"Vergara Gray. I don't want the name Vergara Gray."

"What name do you want?"

"Capriatti, Mom's name. It's totally legal."

"But you are my son, Pablito. Why do you want to change your name?"

"It has problems."

"What problems?"

"Well, every time they ask my name and I say Vergara Gray, they say, 'Vergara Gray, like the . . .'"

The boy twirled his fingers, making the universal gesture for a thief.

"So?"

"Well, it feels weird. And the other day I applied for a job at Citroën to learn to be a mechanic. I wrote down my name and underneath I had to put my father's profession—"

"Accountant. I am a certified public accountant!"

"It's better for me to change my name, Nico."

"There are hundreds of Vergaras and none of them would ever dream of changing their name."

"But there is only one Vergara Gray. Where did your family come up with such a pretentious idea of having two names?"

"We wanted to keep the name of the famous inventor."

"Who?"

"Gray, of course."

"What did he invent?"

Thoroughly distracted, Vergara Gray put sugar in his tea a second time, then drank it and made a face of disgust.

"What is this, son? An academic aptitude test?"

"I'm just asking!"

"It was one way to make up for a great injustice. Your great-grandfather, Elisha Gray, experimented with electrical and communication devices. On February fourteenth, 1876, he went to the U.S. Patent Office to register a patent for a new invention: the telephone."

"Gray?"

"Gray. But just a few hours earlier, Bell had registered the same invention in a different city. Your great-grandfather sued but lost, and the patent remained in Bell's name."

"A history of losers," the boy said with a smile.

"That's the way it was."

"You are so Chilean. Instead of commemorating victories, you celebrate defeats. Like our national hero, Arturo Prat: everybody remembers him with great affection because he lost the naval battle of Iquique against the Peruvians."

Teresa grabbed the document Pablo still held in his hand and placed it on the table. "The lawyer already filled out the papers. The only thing we need is your signature."

Vergara Gray leaned over the table; as he read his tongue got drier and drier. When he finished, he leaned back in his chair, wishing it were electric and the warden were on hand to lower the switch.

After clearing his throat, he said, "Do you realize, my boy, that since we came here you have not once called me *papa*?"

The boy shrugged his shoulders, and Teresa Capriatti handed Vergara Gray the gold pen he had given her for her fortieth birthday.

MONGOLIAN PORK, *seitan* chicken with almonds, glazed duck with noodles, conger eel with black bean sauce, deep-fried prawns, *reineta* fish in soy sauce, spring rolls, oyster cakes, Shanghai chicken in mushroom sauce, five-flavored duck, meat patties with pineapple, vegetable chop suey, Santa Rita Gold Star wine, Carmen Rhin, Undurraga cabernet: a small sampling of the dishes and wines on the menu at the Poor Chinaman Restaurant.

Victoria Ponce tended to go for lower-calorie dishes like stir-fry vegetables and Ángel Santiago for the furious fervor of the spicy Mongolian pork. She chose Cachantún mineral water; he, half a bottle of red wine. He had brought her from the ballet studio to the Plaza Brasil on his chestnut horse at a slow walk under the starry night sky, and Victoria had had to lift up the skirt of her school uniform to mount the horse, then cover herself from her waist to her knee socks with her large overcoat.

From their table next to the second-story window, lit up with dragons and red lights, they could see the horse, tied to a palm tree in the Plaza Brasil, patiently munching on the grass while some local kids stroked his mane. They had both expected that as soon as they saw each other they would breathlessly tell the other all the news of the last few days. But the process of mounting the horse instead of taking the bus and of going to a restaurant instead of grabbing a quick sandwich on the go had silenced them into smiles and circumspection. They were experiencing the onset of inhibitions so typical of those who begin to care deeply what the other person thinks of them. Once the dishes had been eaten and the absence of bread made it impossible to sop up the sauce and thus further postpone their communication, he asked her how things had gone at school.

"They took me back conditionally. They gave me ten days to pass an exam on everything that's been taught this year so far."

"Like what?"

"Natural science, world history, Chilean history, civics, algebra, physics, chemistry, French, English."

"I know a little English."

"Let's hear."

"*One dolar, mister, pleez.*"

"Where did you learn that?"

"*In Valparaíso harbor.*"

"On the docks? What were you doing there?"

"Getting by."

The waitress brought them jasmine tea and fortune cookies.

"How old were you?"

"Seven or eight."

"What did your father do?"

"He went out on the boats."

"And you?"

"I hung around."

"With your mother?"

"With several mothers. Listen, Victoria. I didn't learn the English I know at the Grange School; I learned it on the streets."

The girl stirred her tea without putting any sugar in it. "Now I feel sorry for you."

"You don't have to. Things have gone well for me. I had a knife to practice my penmanship before I had a pen, and I know how to peel an orange in one piece."

"Well, lots of people can do that. Even I can do that."

"Do you also know where to stab somebody most efficiently—in the liver, the lung, or the bladder?"

"In the heart, I guess."

"Well, that could be dangerous. If you're trying to hurt your victim rather than kill him, a stab in the heart could get you life."

"Why are you telling me all this?"

"So you know that I know a little about lots of things, like anatomy, languages, penal codes . . ."

"You should go to the university."

"I've got other plans. I asked my fairy godmother for four wishes because the standard three weren't enough."

"What are they?"

"There's one I can't tell you."

"It's something bad?"

"Yes, but not for me."

"You're going to hurt somebody?"

"Something like that. Though 'hurt' is a pretty gentle word to describe it."

"It's a euphemism."

"What's that?"

"It's a figure of speech. I learned it in language studies. A euphemism is a gentle way of saying something that isn't so gentle. For example, you might tell a really, really fat guy that he looks robust."

Ángel Santiago was momentarily distracted by a small statue of a smiling Buddha wrapped in colorful wreathes.

"That would be irony," he said after a moment, "not a euphemism."

"You can use a euphemism ironically. That's allowed. What are the other three wishes?"

"Well, I already have the horse."

"Where's he going to live?"

"Wherever I live."

"And where would that be?"

"I'll have to give that one some thought. In the meantime, I'll rent him out as a cart horse in the market."

Victoria took a sip from his glass of wine and swished the liquid around in her mouth. When she swallowed it, a rush of warmth rose to her cheekbones.

"You're a little screwed up in the head, Ángel. You have no sense of priorities. It's normal for some things to come before others."

"You're one to be giving me lessons about priorities. School should always come before the movies."

"Movies let you dream."

"But people who spend all their time dreaming get screwed up in the head, too. If you can't turn those dreams into reality, you'll end up in the loony bin. It's a good thing you're back in school."

"Thanks to you."

"I wouldn't want you to end up being bitter because you couldn't do what you wanted to."

"I have to pass that exam. I've got ten books in my backpack, and I've got to memorize all of them. I'll have to keep studying tonight."

"Not tonight."

"Why?"

"Now we're getting to the third wish."

Ángel donned his best smile as he leaned his elbows on the table and plopped his chin into his hands. The girl brushed her hair away from her temple again and again, as if with this gesture she could quiet all the storms in her soul. She wasn't certain about anything, but her dream was to dance ballet, of course, at the Municipal Theater in Santiago, the Colón in Buenos Aires, the Teatro de Madrid, the Metropolitan Opera House in New York. She didn't lack passion, and she'd be willing to burn every single one of her other bridges just to live out that dream. But for that she needed to graduate, she needed money, and she needed talent. Who could reassure her that she had talent? Her teacher at the academy, who doled out praise to all her disciples as if each of them were a Tamara Kasarvina, an Isadora Duncan, a Margot Fonteyn, a Pina Bausch, or an Anna Pavlova? No, her *maestra* had more delusions than objectivity, and her opinion wasn't worth a hill of beans.

Any girl with smooth skin, upturned buttocks, and a sassy belly could fancy herself a professional dancer because she had learned the simplest version of Shakira's newest dances, and she'd prance around hoping some television producer would discover her.

She also knew that there wasn't any chance that the kind of dance she studied would be profitable. She had seen so many people buy and sell themselves in order to live—first of all, herself—that she held ballet and modern dance in a sacred space, immune to all worldly corruption, beyond the reach of her depressed mother, her father's murder, the professors who looked down on her for her indifference, for her silence.

If she ever did dance professionally, even in the town hall of some tiny city in the provinces, she wouldn't ask to be paid. This would be the triumph of art over the scoundrels who traded in death and ugliness. Commercialism had no right to be a patron of the arts.

The fact that Ángel Santiago wanted to sleep with her again meant he didn't know her very well. They had spent a few hours together, a quickie on a mattress, and he had talked her into going back to school. In her empty world these trivial events constituted the most intense relationship she had ever had, perhaps in her entire life.

So, before this incipient love got ground to bits by mutual disgust, poverty—the squalor of the parts of her life that he still knew nothing about, the stigma only her dance could redeem—then thrown into the garbage bin along with that crumpled napkin on top of what was left of the chop suey, they should love each other fully today, and then tomorrow say farewell!

"And the fourth wish?" she said softly.

"A farm. A big farm. With all kinds of animals. Really, a zoo: cows and donkeys, but also peacocks and black-necked swans."

"I, on the other hand, see myself living in a big city. Paris, Madrid, New York."

"They already blew up New York."

"And nobody will ever forget it. Just like I don't want to forget what happened to my father."

"I understand. I know what it is to be obsessed by something. But I am just one step away from living my dream."

"How?"

"I will finally convince a great man named Nicolás Vergara Gray to become my partner."

"In what?"

"In a single, unique, and extraordinary adventure that will be forever remembered in the annals of history."

"A robbery?"

"No, Victoria Ponce, a work of art."

THOSE WHO LIVED near Plaza Brasil were enchanted with the horse; they fed him artichoke stems, and he thanked them by switching his tail back and forth. This action delighted the children, who took turns placing their heads in its path so it would muss their hair.

"How have you been, my dearest friend, apple of my eye?" Ángel greeted his beast with this Cervantine flair before he and his girlfriend mounted and road off slowly to the nearest station of mounted police. The *carabineros* gave him permission to tie the chestnut horse up in their corral and come get him the following day.

Elsa, now working as the hotel receptionist, saw the couple arrive and turned off the little television behind the reception desk in the hotel lobby on which she had been watching the latest reality show.

"We're looking for a room for a few days," Ángel said, placing some bills on the counter.

"Is the girl legal?"

"She's been my girlfriend for years."

"How old is she?"

"Twenty."

"Let's see, dear, what you're wearing under your coat."

"With this cold?" Victoria protested.

"Do it or leave."

The girl unbuttoned her overcoat.

"But she's a schoolgirl. You want them to shut us down?"

"First, she's seventeen. Second, I'm her brother."

"That's makes it even worse, son."

"And third, Vergara Gray recommended that we come here."

Elsa put on her glasses and looked for a moment at the blank television screen as if it were still on. She opened the guest book and pushed it toward them so they could write down their names.

"We are part of Vergara Gray's team. You understand we can't possibly give you our real names."

"I already figured that one out."

"I just thought I'd mention it so you didn't consider asking for our IDs."

"This fox has spent too many years in this lair, cutie-pie."

Ángel Santiago placed the guest book next to Victoria and pointed where she needed to sign.

"Just put down any name," Ángel told her.

"How about my art teacher's?"

"Perfect. What is it?"

"Sanhueza. Elena Sanhueza."

"I'm going to give you the room next to Vergara Gray's. But try not to get too enthusiastic during the night, or you'll disturb the maestro's sleep."

The receptionist made a move to hand them the key, but instead rested it on her lips.

"You have to swear to me that if there's an inspection, you'll say you came in illegally. I registered a Mr. Enrique Gutiérrez and a Ms. Elena Sanhueza, who left for an unknown location after doing their dirty deeds. Agreed?"

"Agreed. The key?"

Instead of handing it to him, she placed it in front of her nose and breathed in deeply. "Something big?"

"What?"

"What you're planning with Vergara Gray."

"If it weren't big, I wouldn't be working with him. You think I'm a small-time player?"

"Not at all. But if it is something really big, I'd like to help. Tell Nico that Elsa, at the front desk, said so."

"You tell him yourself. I'm nobody's messenger boy."

She lifted her eyebrows, looked offended, then hung the key up in its box. "Okay, then go screw each other at the Salvation Army."

Ángel Santiago saw that Victoria was inching toward the door in shame and placed a hand on the receptionist's shoulder. "Okay. I'll try to put in a good word for you."

"Because if it's a question of favors, he owes me quite a few."

"I'll tell him."

"Second floor, third door on your right."

"ASK ME ANOTHER," Victoria ordered him at two in the morning, just as he was tracing a line on her inner thigh with his tongue.

"Aw, let's take a break."

"Please, anything."

"Physics?"

"Okay."

"What did Stephen Hawking write and what theory did he propose?"

"We reviewed that yesterday, didn't we?"

"You should remember."

"Hawking wrote *A Brief History of Time*, and he says that time has no beginning and no end."

"Perfect."

He pulled back the sheet and continued to savor her, moving around behind, up, and over.

"That's enough for now, you . . . !"

The young man continued along his path, unperturbed, wiggling his nose in between her legs.

"What happened in 1989 in Tiananmen Square?"

"There was a massacre in Peking with the army and tanks."

He lifted his head to her chest and drew circles around her nipples. "What would happen to our bodies if the atmospheric pressure suddenly changed?"

"We would explode."

"Perfect. What was Saint Ignatius of Loyola's motto in life?"

" 'For the greater glory of God.' "

"Correct. What was the name of the first architect of the Egyptian pyramids?"

"Imhotep."

"What is a miracle?"

The girl buried her fingers in the young man's curly hair, which was impervious to any brush or comb, and tried unsuccessfully to untangle one of the most rebellious of his black locks.

"An event that happens against the laws of nature, perpetrated by supernatural intervention of divine origin."

"What is the scientific name for sweet acacia?"

"*Acacia farnesiana.*"

"What is the organic compound that produces gout and rheumatism when it accumulates in the human body?"

"Uric acid."

"That's amazing, Victoria. You haven't missed any."

"Did you know all that before?"

"No, I've learned it with you."

The girl took his penis in her hand and pushed down his foreskin, then brought her face up close, breathing his scent in deeply.

"I couldn't control myself that first time."

"What are you talking about?"

"I came so quickly and all."

"Don't be silly. Those are just chauvinist myths. Women don't care that much."

"Well, I cared."

"I could tell you were pretty upset about it. But since then . . ."

"You really came just now?"

"Couldn't you tell?"

"The magazines say that women can fake it."

"My God, Ángel Santiago. Don't you realize we're soaked?"

"You're right. What is parthenogenesis?"

"Reproduction of live individuals without the presence of male sperm. By the way, shouldn't we be using condoms?"

"You—"

"Never mind, I don't want to talk about that now. Geometry."

"What does the Pythagorean theorem state?"

"In any right triangle, the area of the square whose side is the hypotenuse is equal to the sum of the areas of the squares on the other two sides."

"What is bile?"

"Pancreatic secretion."

"The names of the sons of Oedipus?"

"Eteocles and Polynices."

"Symptoms of a black widow spider bite?"

Victoria ignored Ángel and mounted him. Once he was inside her, she gently began to ride him.

"What are you doing?"

"I don't know."

"Yes, you do."

"I'm too shy to say it."

"But not to do it?"

"Language is sacred. Think of all those words racing around the world. They excite me."

"You don't have to be so academic. You could just say 'they turn me on.'"

"Yes, my love."

"Careful. The word 'love' has just made its debut."

The girl clenched her teeth, then contracted her pelvic muscles along the length of his penis until her whole body began to convulse almost violently.

"You made me come again, you beast," she said, collapsing onto his chest.

A CCORDING TO FRESIA SÁNCHEZ, proprietor of the bakery on the corner of Salvador Allende and General Schneider streets in the town of San Bernardo, the man who passed by the door at dawn, hugging the adobe wall as if trying to vanish into the last strokes of night's darkness, was Rigoberto Marín himself.

She later recounted that there were a dozen stray dogs following him, sniffing the ground and the air, as if trying to detect the source of the danger. The strays seemed possessed by some kind of ethereal silence, their attention focused on deeds much loftier than squirting on trees or electric poles.

It was the hour when workers straggled to the corner to wait for the buses that would take them to the construction sites downtown, and the contrast between them and Rigoberto Marín was like night and day: they were beginning their day while Marín was ending his night.

I'm glad he didn't come into my shop, the baker thought.

Nor did she envy anybody who opened a door for him. The man attracted death the way carrion attracts vultures, as if wherever his steps happened to fall, strife reigned, knife battles broke out, maybe a bullet that would bring the police to round up eyewitnesses and cart off the dead.

It was common knowledge that Marín had been sentenced to death and that only a merciful presidential decree had commuted his punishment to more than one life sentence without possibility of parole. If he had escaped from prison and was looking for refuge in San Bernardo, Fresia Sánchez thought, as she took the golden *marraquetas* out of the oven and emptied them into an enormous basket, the outlaw had acted astutely. In the first place, nobody dared squeal on him; in the second, there were numerous women of all ages who had benefited from his prodigious virility and would take great pains to protect him. They claimed he made love with passion combined with violent tenderness that both confused and excited them.

She herself had once heard the secret confessions of a widow, who had recounted with photographic precision how Marín had spent an hour caressing her and crying after he had done everything he wanted with her. In addition, none of his murder victims had been women, even if in this case the victim had been the woman's husband. Which didn't stand in the way, after the funeral, of the widow and Marín having a good, long screw in the Conchalí Hotel, amid the funeral flowers and half-burnt candles, "Because I love you and respect him," the woman had told Marín.

Marín's ardor led men to somewhat less lyrical expressions of irony. They said that the bastard was so hot he could iron his shirts with his hands.

According to Fresia Sánchez, the fugitive was heading to the same widow's brick house. As irrefutable proof, a large number of dogs were stretched out on the street from the dear woman's front door to the facing sidewalk, scratching their fleas, getting in the way of the carts carrying fruit to the market, and stoically withstanding the bucketfuls of cold water the neighborhood women dumped on them to get them to disperse.

STILL RIGOROUSLY DRESSED in mourning, the widow kept a shelf in her dining room exclusively dedicated to Saint Anthony of Padua, and on the small round table covered with an oilcloth and decorated with Chilean pastoral motifs, a glass held two daisies. Marín pushed it aside to make room for several dozen clams and two lemons, which he dumped out of a bag onto the table. He broke the first one open with a blow of his fist, squeezed a few drops of lemon juice on his victim to make sure it was fresh enough to wiggle, then placed it on the widow's tongue.

"For ten years I've dreamed of a breakfast like this," Marín said.

"Of Chilean seafood?"

"Of you. But you've been untrue to me." Marín pointed with a somber gesture at the saint. "You've been true to him. And you still have that picture of the dead man. But there isn't a trace of me."

"You don't leave pictures, Rigo; you leave wounds."

The woman walked over to the stove and brought back a kettle of boiling water to pour into the two cups of Nescafé. The man chewed another clam with relish and pointed the knife at the widow as if it were simply the extension of his index finger.

"From the very first moment I was free, my steps led me to you."

"Did you escape?"

"Sort of."

"What do you mean, Rigo?"

"I'm on parole."

"The newspapers said you were given two life sentences and five years and one day. You can't lie to me. You escaped."

"I did it for you. Nobody squeezes it like you do."

The woman placed her hand on the felon's unshaven cheek. She caressed it with tenderness, then lifted his upper lip and looked affectionately at the space between his two front teeth.

"I'm not going to turn you in."

"Nobody in the world can know. If anybody finds out, I'm a dead man."

"Did anybody see you come here?"

"I crept through the shadows."

"I don't like people blabbing about how my husband's murderer is staying at my house."

"If he'd really loved you, he'd have gotten you out of this stinking hole."

"He had his moments, Rigo. But wine and unemployment sank him. This house is his, and I demand respect. If you don't like it, get out."

"Your wish is my command."

He picked up the empty shells, shook them in his hands, and let them roll over the oilcloth as if they were dice. "You know how to tell your fortune from this mess?"

"Clamshells don't work. But I can read your cards."

"No need. I always get the golden sun." He brought the cup of coffee to his lips, then quickly placed it back down on the table with a grimace of pain. "Shit, I burned my tongue."

The widow gave him some cold water, then stirred the coffee and told him to take another sip. Marín obeyed without looking away from the woman's large black eyes.

"The truth is, they let me out to kill somebody."

"Who?"

"A poor bastard who doesn't even have a record and whose only crime hasn't yet been committed."

"I don't understand."

"He's a handsome kid the warden threw into a cell with some sleazebags so they could baptize him his first night there. The warden took his turn, too. Now the boy is free and the warden is sure he's going to kill him."

"How does he know?"

"The kid told everybody, and the day he got out he swore he would do it, right to the warden's face."

"Kids that age are braggarts. Whatever they lack in experience, they've got in gab."

"Not this one. This one does what he says he's gonna do."

"And you?"

"The warden gave me a month. He planned it all out; everybody inside thinks I'm in solitary. Nobody'd suspect me."

"Why did you agree to do it, Rigo?"

"Thirty days, thirty wild nights. The first one with you."

The woman placed her hand on his knee, then moved it up his thigh. The flame of the heater began to fade under the bright morning sunlight filtering in around the edges of the crepe curtains.

"What happens if they catch you?"

"I told you, I'm dead."

He spoke these words as if conjuring up a curse, then walked over to the window and edged open the curtain. The dogs were still there, their noses in the dust, waiting for him.

"Dogs have followed me around ever since I was a kid. They come up to me, sniff me, then follow me wherever I go."

The widow placed her hands above the heater, then on her cheeks. The bed was unmade, just as she had left it when she jumped up to answer Marín's knocks on the door.

"Go to bed. Sleep will do you good."

"I don't want to sleep, woman. I've got to take advantage of every minute of freedom."

She climbed onto her knees on the bed; with a little effort she lowered her panties until her strong copper-colored bottom was waving, naked, in the air. With one hand between her thighs, she cleared away the tangled mane that covered her pubis and, opening her lips, delighted in the palpitations and abundant secretions of her own vagina.

Rigoberto Marín let his pants fall around his knees and, without even taking off his worn-out brown tweed jacket, he walked over to the bed and approached the widow just the way her body was begging him to.

He jabbed it in her from behind.

Like she wanted.

Like a dog.

T HAT NIGHT, VERGARA GRAY took a walk along the
Mapocho River, its waters brown like the city's refuse that
filled its banks. Old tires, scrap lumber, fecal matter, tin cans,
rotten vegetables, branches, dead dogs, crushed pigeons, and, every
once in a while, a human cadaver. After the military coup, people would
stand on the bridges and point down at the dead floating by, their skulls
and chests crushed by soldiers' bullets. There were days when the families of the disappeared would sit on these banks, hoping that the bodies
they hadn't found at the police stations or the morgue would float by so
they could give their loved ones a proper burial.

Now the city had been modernized and the Mapocho tamed by
civil engineers. They diverted its course to build freeways, straight
as arrows, that took the city's wealthy citizens from the exclusive
suburbs to their banks downtown. The river was no longer the refuge of street urchins and young hooligans; now it was a kind of
backyard to Santiago's financial center. Along its banks rose four or
five tall steel buildings that aspired to being skyscrapers; Chileans,
with their self-deprecating sense of humor, had unofficially baptized that pretentious, stuck-up neighborhood *Sanhattan.*

Vergara Gray thought he could exhaust his cares by walking until he collapsed. In his present state of mind he might have thrown himself against the paving stones along the banks below, but the idea came and went in seconds. Suicide was an undignified act. Only somebody with no sense of modesty would expose himself to whomever happened by, his clothes torn up by blackberry brambles and sharp branches, his eyes devoured by rats, sockets staring empty out of a dead face.

Finally, at daybreak, when the hint of light transformed his anguish into plain and simple sadness, he turned his steps toward Las Tabernas Street and his room. My grave, he told himself. My tomb.

According to one of his favorite tangos, this was the hour when those who know they're dying bid farewell to the world. As he climbed the stairs, he loosened his tie and undid the top button on his shirt.

When he opened the door, he was sure it was the wrong one. There, in the middle of the room, above a table covered with a white tablecloth and beaming over a steaming pot of coffee and a basket overflowing with rolls, hovered the supremely clean smile of the young Ángel Santiago, accompanied by a helpless-looking schoolgirl as thin as a ballerina.

"Breakfast is ready, maestro. Would you mind if we joined you?"

"What is that girl in a school uniform doing in this brothel? If they discover her in my room, I'll go straight to jail. My freedom will have turned into a curse if I go down as a sex offender."

The boy jumped up and pulled a chair out for the man; after making sure he was comfortable, he encouraged him to shake the hand the girl was holding out to him over the table.

"This is Victoria Ponce. I'm helping her cram for an exam she has to take next week."

"In this dive the word 'cram' seems especially appropriate."

The boy pointed his finger directly at the girl's forehead. "What is the main characteristic of an amoeba?"

"It is only one cell," she answered quickly.

Ángel Santiago rubbed his hands together, then spread his arms out as wide as he could to bring everyone's attention to the delicacies on the table.

"Help yourself, maestro. Two *marraquetas*, two *colizas*, three *hallullas*, three *flautas*, four cold *tostadas*—because the stove had a short circuit—three onion rolls, and three slices of kuchen with raisins and candied fruits. Happy birthday, Don Nico."

"Today is not my birthday."

"Details, my dear professor. I bet if you go to a funeral you make them show you the body, and if you go to a baptism, you have to see the baby. Just enjoy your breakfast without so much fuss and bother!"

Vergara Gray let them pour milk into his Nescafé and spread butter on his *marraqueta*. He continued to study the girl as he took his first bite. She responded to his stares by moving the sides of her nostrils in and out like a rabbit.

"What are we really celebrating, Mr. Santiago?"

"The beginning of the execution of the Dwarf's plan."

"Oh, really?"

"Yesterday I was in the maintenance area of the Schendler plant. I went to the cafeteria where the elevator mechanics eat. It's the least secure place in the world. They leave their jackets with their identity badges just hanging there and go sit down."

"I'm pleased to see that you entertain this girl with your fairy tales."

"It's no more a fairy tale than there are three halves to a whole."

Moving from words to deeds, he took a blue plastic bag off the bed and pulled out two jean jackets, holding one up in each fist, like a fisherman showing off his giant catch.

"And what does this have to do with the Dwarf's plan?"

"I already told you we were celebrating the beginning of its execution. We still need you to do your part."

"What are you talking about, you fool?"

The boy brought the jackets over to show him the Schendler Elevators identity badges on each one. The faces of the rightful owners had been exchanged for those of Ángel Santiago and Vergara Gray.

"Just take a look at the details!" the boy bragged.

"Where did you get those pictures?"

"I took mine on Matte Street. Yours, I downloaded from the Internet. Your entire career is posted online. Now it's just a matter of checking up on sources and writing a novel about your life."

With furrowed brow, the man chewed a *marraqueta* spread with butter, then turned to Victoria, who looked back at him as she silently drank her coffee with milk, waiting for what he would say once he swallowed the bread that was slowly dissolving in his mouth.

"What is the epidermis?" he finally mumbled.

Victoria cast about in her chair, looking silently at Ángel for help. The boy deliberately rubbed his hand against his skin.

"No cheating, young man!"

"The epidermis is the collection of materials that make up the border between the organism and the external environment," the girl said emphatically.

"And where did you get the seal of Schendler Elevators to stamp our pictures with?"

"That was a cinch, maestro. In every elevator in the city there's a tiny window with a piece of paper where Schendler's seal is stamped to indicate when the last safety check was done. I broke one with a little hammer and put the rest together on the computer, shrank everything in a color photocopier, two snips of the scissors, glue, plastic cover, and ready to go."

Vergara Gray took the credentials off the jackets and with perfect aim chucked them into the wastepaper basket next to the window.

"No, maestro," the boy exclaimed as he jumped up. "That's no way to treat a work of art!"

The man turned to the girl and stretched out his hand. She held it for a few moments.

"From epidermis to epidermis, I wish you the very best of luck on your exam, dear girl."

"If I don't pass, they'll expel me from school. I have to learn all the material that has been covered so far this year."

She pulled her hair up into a bun and got up from her chair. She picked up the schoolbag and gestured to Ángel Santiago to accompany her out. In the dark hallway, she let the boy put her coat on over her uniform, and as she hugged him she whispered in his ear.

"There are still a lot of things about me you don't know, Ángel Santiago."

"Like what, for example?"

"Things that aren't good."

"You'll tell me in good time. Right now the worst thing that could happen to us is that you are late for school."

"I have to pay my dance teacher tomorrow. Can you lend me anything?"

"I spent my last pesos on that breakfast."

"The teacher won't let me in."

"We'll pay a day or two late."

"I already owe her for *three* months. She's got to pay rent and heating."

"She should be on her knees in gratitude that she has a student like you. Nobody has ever done so many pirouettes so gracefully. You should be dancing at the Municipal Theater instead of in that basement."

"I'll never dance at the Municipal Theater, Ángel. That's where the swans dance; the rats dance in my neighborhood."

"Just focus now on your exam. Amoebas, epidermis, where you put the accents."

"Ángel."

"Yes, Ángel, for example. Do you have money for the bus?"

"I've got enough to pay the student fare."

"And the return?"

"I'll work it out."

"What does your mother say?"

"She's still depressed."

The boy rubbed his face hard, as if wanting to erase it. "Everything will change soon. You see, I've already started to execute the plan."

"I don't think it's going to happen. Did you see how the old man reacted?"

"It's only natural for him to be scared. He was in jail for five years and everybody suspects he's planning something. Everybody's dying to work with him. But only I, and I alone, am his partner."

The girl wiped the tip of her nose on the sleeve of her coat and descended the stairs.

WHEN ÁNGEL RETURNED to the room, Vergara Gray was making inroads on a slice of kuchen spread with a thick layer of jam. He chewed it carefully, indicating with a pointed finger that the young man should have a seat on the edge of the bed.

"The first commandment in this jungle is, 'Thou shalt not get involved,' and I'm not about to do so with you or even somebody less immature."

"You'll rot in this room, maestro."

"Nor with somebody as insolent as you."

"Pardon me, maestro. But you are not treating yourself with the respect you deserve. Any professional of your stature would be proud of your curriculum."

"You mean my record. Don't come to me with your euphemisms."

The young man smiled and opened a liquid pineapple yogurt. He drank it in one gulp, painting a white mustache over the boyish stubble on his upper lip. He didn't wipe it off.

"I know exactly what a euphemism is, Don Nico. Allow me to explain it to you in purely business terms. You, stuck in this hotel full of whores and broken hearts, listening to corny boleros and tangos, are not investing your most valuable resource, your capital, your genius! You're throwing your life away without sorrow or glory."

"Relax. Monasterio owes me a lot of money and one day my wife might take me back."

"Congratulations."

"Anyway, I will never again commit any crime. In jail I lost my wife, my son, my money, and my dreams. I'm sick of being a pariah."

"A man with your reputation could never be a pariah. There are many who would sacrifice their balls to be in your shoes."

"One thing is fantasy, the other reality. People picture us in limousines smoking Cuban cigars, but they've never smelled the stench of their own urine when the guard is drunk and doesn't open your cell door to let you go to the bathroom. They've never counted the cockroaches you have to smash in the summer, when the sun turns your metal bed into a red-hot grill."

"This dump isn't many steps above that."

"It is a temporary abode."

"Everybody knows that Monasterio isn't going to pay you. Not because he doesn't want to, but because he spent all your money paying off Pinochet's goons."

"He spent his half; mine is intact."

"So why hasn't he given it to you?"

"I understand he has cash-flow problems."

"Why not face the truth, maestro?"

"Because if I did, I'd have to kill him. And I don't want to go to jail."

"Well, I'm proposing an alternative, so you can kill two birds with one stone *and* keep out of jail."

"The Dwarf's plan."

"The Dwarf held on to this like it was a precious jewel, until they gave him some twenty-odd years. The fact that he isn't still holding on to it is proof of his love and admiration for the great Vergara Gray. You can't be so arrogant and just reject it."

"I'm not rejecting it out of arrogance; it's prudence."

"The second bird you kill, maestro: the safe we'll open belongs to the chief of the ex-dictator's security services, General Canteros."

"But they've already got him behind bars."

"They built him a five-star hotel, that's what they did. They gave him five years and now he's strolling down the street laughing at the fools. He made all his money through his security business. He hired all the torturers who had worked with him during the dictatorship and who were left unemployed when democracy came. He dresses them up in guard uniforms and promises businessmen that his men will watch over their interests. And those who don't agree, get stung."

"You're ranting. Let go of the past."

"You can, if you want, you can forget your past, because you've got such a long one. Mine is short and my father made it shit."

"Tell me about it."

"I don't want to. But I would love to relieve that pig Canteros of his dough."

"If you succeed, I'll be very happy to read about it in the papers."

"Without you there's no coup, maestro. You know it, the Dwarf knows it, and Ángel Santiago knows it. A lot of people are depending on your decision."

"A lot? Like who?"

"You, me, your wife, your son, Victoria Ponce, her dance teacher, and even the Dwarf, who could be eating steak instead of beans."

The young man untied the red string tied around the rolled-up graph paper and spread the Dwarf's plans out on the bed, holding down the edges with a pair of Vergara Gray's scuffed-up shoes.

"Put that away, son."

"I just want you to tell me one thing."

"Take that off my bed."

"Independently of whether or not you participate in the coup, if you were to judge it objectively, how would you grade it? I am simply asking for an expert's opinion. Is it good, bad, or just okay?"

Vergara Gray poured what was left in the pot into his cup and drank it, grateful for the flavor that penetrated his taste buds after so many hard times. "An objective judgment?"

"Precisely. An expert opinion. No strings attached."

Vergara Gray cleared his throat and rubbed the back of his hand over his mustache to remove any traces of coffee. Hiding his enthusiasm carefully behind his sober expression, he said, "Genius. Lira's plan, in the absence of a thunderbolt from the hand of God Himself, is totally and absolutely genius."

The boy tossed the man's shoes up to the ceiling, then threw his arms around him, planting exuberant kisses on each of his cheeks.

Monasterio entered the room without knocking. And without saying a word, he began pulling the sheets off the bed.

"I hope you're not going to say something like, 'It's not what you think, partner.'"

"What are you doing in my room?"

The man walked over to the closet, opened the doors wide, and looked at the empty glasses on the tablecloth.

"Three things, Nico. First, I want to remind you that strictly speaking this room is mine. Second, I was informed that you gentlemen brought a minor into this room. I don't want them to shut down my only source of income and have them accuse you of sex with a minor at my place of business. Third, I don't appreciate shoes being thrown up at the floor of my office. And fourth," he added with a sudden inspiration, "I would be very sorry to learn that what I just saw meant that you had gone over to the other side."

Ángel Santiago pulled back his fist in preparation for a blow to Monasterio's jaw, but Vergara Gray held his arm with an iron grip.

"I will not allow some old gangster to doubt my virility!" Ángel said.

"Don't look so outraged," said Monasterio. "They didn't call you the Cherub for nothing. Your ass had more traffic through it than the Alameda."

A wave of vertigo swept over the young man, twisting his gut, swelling his eyes with pumping blood and rising tears, and though he struggled to release a roar from his throat, he found that his lungs were devoid of air. His hands started to shake and his heart pounded with feverish violence. With a strength that rose from deep within, he freed himself from Vergara Gray and threw himself on Monasterio, sinking his thumbs into either side of his Adam's apple. Ángel kept up the pressure until Monasterio fell to his knees, gasping for breath and unable to beg for mercy.

Ángel wanted to accompany the throttling with the onslaught of words and insults boiling up in his throat, but he had reverted to a primitive state, a state prior to the acquisition of language: he had to kill, though he couldn't utter the words *I'm going to kill you.* This was the realm of pure instinct, before memory, before thought.

Summoning up strength he didn't think he still possessed, Vergara Gray managed to dislodge Ángel from his victim, push him over to the window, and throw him out. The young man landed on the pavement, blood pouring out of his nostrils and dripping down the backs of his hands. He stared incredulously at Vergara Gray, who was ordering him to get the hell out of there immediately if he knew what was good for him.

"I'll say I did it," he told him. "Everyone knows he stole my money. Now get out of here, son."

"Where should I go?"

"Far away, and with a one-way ticket."

"Did you hear what he said to me?"

"That's still no excuse for losing your temper. It is ill-advised to be so temperamental with a plan like that at your disposal."

"So what should I do?"

"For the moment, make yourself scarce."

"Okay, maestro."

When the boy turned and looked around, he realized he was surrounded by curious bystanders: the shoeshine boy, the newsboy, the flower girl, and old Santelices, who raised his eyes to the second floor, then grabbed the boy's lapels.

"Did you fall, son?"

Vergara Gray had moved away from the window. Ángel Santiago looked up and took a deep breath, trying to swallow the blood that was pouring from his nose.

"Do you want me to call an ambulance?"

"Don't bother, my friend. I've been a nose-bleeder since I was a kid."

"But this is a hemorrhage."

"It's nothing; bleeding just reminds us we're mortal. How much do you make taking care of these cars?"

"About eight thousand pesos a day."

"Could you do me a favor and lend me a couple thousand to take a taxi?"

"But I don't know you from Adam."

"I work with Vergara Gray."

"What's that to me?"

"That the two thousand you lend me now could mean a fortune for you tomorrow."

Santelices adjusted his gray hat with a government logo on the visor. He moved from hand to hand the yellow rag he used to dust off cars and signal to drivers to park in the spot he pre-tended to have reserved just for them, then stuck his hand in his jacket pocket. The sound of metal clinking against metal could be heard.

"All I've got is some change."

"No problem."

"You sure you don't want me to call an ambulance?"

"Not a chance, man. A cop car always comes with an ambulance."

"You don't like the cops, do you?"

"No way."

The young man held out his hand, and the valet placed one-hundred-peso coins in it, one by one, until he'd counted out two thousand. When Santelices finished, he sidled up to Ángel as if they were old chums.

"You didn't fall out of that second-story window, young man. I saw Vergara Gray push you."

"Yeah, he always does that."

"Did you have a fight?"

"No, just an argument," he said, spitting out a clot of blood. "A friendly argument."

THE AMBULANCE ARRIVED ten minutes later, for Monasterio. They carried him to his room, gave him a shot of muscle relaxant, and put an oxygen mask over his face for about half an hour. His neck was decorated with a couple of bruises the size of oranges, which Elsa anointed with homeopathic cream. Vergara Gray refused to leave him until he had recovered and thereby took full responsi-bility for the boy's actions. When Monasterio appeared to be com-pletely recovered, his ex-partner asked him to tell Elsa to leave the room, then brought a chair closer to the bed, an attempt to re-create the closeness between two friends who had trusted each other before the great betrayal.

"I'm sorry about what happened, Monasterio, but you were very rude to the boy."

Lying in bed, Monasterio sipped his *yerba mate* tea and wrinkled his nose derisively.

"He almost broke my jugular vein, plucky little *faggot*."

"He's nothing of the kind. They *baptized* him in jail, and he doesn't particularly like to be reminded of it."

"Well, I wasn't as rude as I could have been."

For a moment Vergara Gray stroked his mustache, then moved on to his graying sideburns.

"It's time you and I talked. You still haven't said a word about what you owe me."

"I know, my friend. I've been waiting for things to turn around, but they're only getting worse."

"Let's go step by step. Where's my money?"

Monasterio placed the pot of *yerba mate* on the bedside table. "Keep in mind that your accomplice just tanned me, and at my age I might not survive another beating like that."

"You know I am not a violent man."

"I know. First I put my half in the stock market. The bank gave me all kinds of guarantees and everything looked rosy until the Asian crisis struck. Everything crashed. Then came the attack on New York and the international markets went under. Our dream turned to dust, Nico."

"*Your* dream and *your* money turned to dust, Mono. Where's my money?"

"We've been sending Teresa Capriatti a check every month."

"You haven't sent her anything for six months. Anyway, I'm not talking about those crumbs. I'm talking about the million dollars that are mine."

"It wasn't that much. Just under nine hundred thousand dollars, that's all."

"Whatever it is, I want it."

"Well, I had to invest it to get income. This place, the hotel, bribes for the inspectors. It didn't make sense, with you being in jail, to just hold on to the money."

"You used my share without my permission."

"Without your permission, but to your advantage. While you sat peacefully in your cell, we religiously sent Teresa Capriatti her monthly allowance."

"Do you know what happens to people in our line of business who do what you've done?"

"I know it by heart. But you just said you aren't a violent man, Nico. You have a heart of gold and everybody loves you for that. Me, on the other hand, even the shoeshine boy despises me. I'm a perfect nobody. Nico, I must confess, I really envy you."

Vergara Gray squeezed his hands between his knees to prevent them from finishing what the boy had begun.

"Let's go one step at a time," he said in a sugarcoated voice. "If you bought the bar and hotel with my money, then both of them are mine."

Monasterio made as if to rearrange his pillow, but he was really checking to make sure his Browning .45 was within reach.

"Technically, yes. But you would have to subtract some costs and other intangibles."

"Like what?"

"Administration costs, passive capital, inventory, furnishings."

"Okay. But all of that comes out of the profits."

"There are no profits, Nico. That's why we haven't sent your wife anything for the past six months."

"So if there aren't any profits, Monasterio, why do you keep going with it?"

"You'd never understand."

"It's my money, I'll make an enormous effort."

"If I shut down, everybody'll be out of work. Unemployment is very high in Santiago. The cashier, for instance, she wouldn't have anywhere to go."

"Your lover."

"The bar girls are used to the place. They get treated badly everywhere else. Then you've got the bartender, the waiters, the janitor, the doorman, the housekeepers who clean the rooms."

"So you are the Good Samaritan, eh, Monasterio?"

"I know I'm no angel, Nico. But I do have a good heart."

"For everyone except me, you bastard. You've got me living in a dump, and my wife and son despise me."

"I know. I'm sorry, partner. These are difficult times everywhere. There's even a recession in Germany."

Vergara Gray walked over to the window and opened it. He was hoping for a breath of invigorating air to clear up his confused and tangled thoughts, but all he found was the humid gray of the winter smog. Monasterio made himself sound like a martyr, but it was *his*, Vergara Gray's, money he had squandered. The man had never visited him in jail, never even sent one of his messengers with a turkey or a bottle of wine on Christmas, and now he was trying to pass off his thievery as deeds of charity.

"What are you going to do, Nico?"

"I'm thinking."

"As far as I know, you've never killed anyone."

"No, not yet."

"You're not going to start with an old friend. I was loyal to you until the cord got stretched too thin."

Monasterio poured a little more boiling water into the *yerba mate* and stirred it with the metal straw.

"I love to drink *mate*. It calms my nerves and clears my head."

"I'm glad; you're going to need to be very clear-headed for what's coming."

"When I was young, I sang a song for an advertisement for *yerba mate*. It was a great success. Did you ever hear it?"

"Never."

"I sang it on Radio Rivadavia in Buenos Aires. You Chileans still haven't really discovered *mate*."

"*Maté, mato, mataré*," Vergara Gray muttered, conjugating the verb "to kill" in Spanish. Then out loud he said, "How did that song about *mate* go?"

"You really want to hear it?"

"I'd love to."

"Now, a cappella? Without a guitar or anything?"

"Just shoot. In cold blood."

"You sure?"

"I'm dying to."

"Okay. Your wish is my command. I'm going to sing it fast, 'cause it sounds better that way."

> *Toma mate y aviváte,*
> *que la cosa, ché, hermano,*
> *es muy sencilla:*
> *mate dulce, mate amargo,*
> *con bombilla o sin bombilla,*
> *es la octava maravilla*
> *de la industria nacional.*

"What do you think?"

"Sell!" said Vergara Gray in a hoarse voice.

"I don't understand."

"You sell everything: the hotel, the bar, the beds, the safe, the neon sign, and you pay me what you owe me."

Adjusting his position in bed, Monasterio slid his hand under the pillow and curled his index finger around the trigger.

"There's nothing I'd rather do for you, Nico. But it simply isn't possible."

"Why not?"

"Everything you see and everything you still haven't seen, it's all been mortgaged. The bank has us by the balls and everything else. We're living on credit, my friend. The tango isn't in fashion anymore, but we've still got the *chan-chan* at the end."

Vergara Gray looked out the window and just as he took in a deep breath of the poisonous air, he felt his heart contract.

He collapsed at the foot of the bed; very purposefully, Monasterio picked up the phone and dialed.

"Tell the ambulance to get back here," he ordered.

THE CARABINEROS WERE in high spirits when the young man arrived to pick up the chestnut horse. They had just received a bonus to purchase winter clothes, and their families had come right away to pick up the money. After their shopping spree, they'd be back at the station to share with their men a nice hot stew and show off their new coats and rubber boots. There was no longer any need to read the weather reports: winter had settled in, along with the frost on the windows and the stench of paraffin from the filthy wicks on the heaters, which poisoned the air. The corporal had been kind enough to throw a blanket over the horse; Ángel removed it before returning it to its owner.

"Start looking for a stable, man. If this champion catches cold, he won't be able to run the Grand Prix at the Hippodrome."

"He does one minute sixteen on the twelve hundred."

"That's what they do in the classics out there in the provinces. You should take him to La Serena."

"How are your horses?"

"Slow, but brave. They have to put up with the rocks from the students and the Molotov cocktails from the Communists. They've gotten used to it. Nothing scares them. How long have you had that horse?"

"We grew up together in the countryside."

"Whereabouts?"

"Near Talca."

"Out there, life is healthy. Here there's work, but too much sadness."

"That's where I'm headed, Corporal. I just can't find my place in the city. My dream is to own my own ranch."

"Play the lottery."

"I have bad luck at games."

"And at love?"

"So-so."

"Got a girl?"

"Yeah, I got one."

"What's her name?"

"Victoria, but she likes people to call her *La* Victoria."

When the carabinero saw the horse blow a dense cloud of steam into the penetrating cold, he returned the blanket and adjusted it on the horse's back.

"You know what, pal, I'm going to give you that blanket."

"You're kidding!"

"No, really. I'll go right now and remove it from the list of station assets."

"I'm really grateful, Corporal . . . ?"

"Zúñiga. Any problems you have with the police, I'm here to help. If they give you a ticket—"

"I don't have a car."

"They might give the horse a ticket! Just tell them he belongs to the Carabineros of Chile," said Corporal Zúñiga. "The blanket is proof enough."

"Thank you, Corporal."

"Behave yourself, kid."

Ángel Santiago trotted off on his horse to La Vega Market, and as he wove his way through the fruit and vegetable carts, merchants stuffed artichoke stems and other goodies in the horse's muzzle. At noon, Ángel got hungry, but he was too proud to beg; he made do with half a carrot he pulled out of the animal's teeth.

If Vergara Gray refused to participate in the coup, Ángel's own prospects would sink drastically. He couldn't return to the maestro's hotel because his damned partner would have him shot, especially after Ángel had engraved those heroic and well-deserved fingerprints on his neck. It looked like he was condemned to being a homeless beggar, a ghost of a horseman living off petty thievery—starvation wages, he thought—an occasional crust, alms for the poor, then curling up in some stable stinking of manure and covering himself with straw and empty flour sacks to survive the night and the sharp wind sweeping down from the Andes.

Without the maestro, of course, he could dress up as an elevator repairman and reach General Canteros's safe, but once there he would come up against that mass of steel and his own complete ignorance about how to open it. The guards would find him staring in wonderment at the locks and handles, and they would carry him back to the slammer, where Lira the Dwarf would slit his throat for having blown the crime of the millennium in the stupidest possible way. That is, if Canteros's goons hadn't already treated him to a sampling of their finest torture techniques—honed to perfection during the dictatorship—then thrown him into a secret jail.

Did he have any reason at all to keep living? Apart from the coup, he had three or four things he could dream about. In order of importance—he told himself as he galloped toward Victoria Ponce's school—first came the execution of Warden Santoro. Even that pig Monasterio had found out what had happened to him in prison and thrown it in his face. He hated being called Cherub. Rather than exalt his beauty, it defined him, within that world, as someone who had allowed himself to be sodomized, even enjoyed it. If his face could mirror what seethed in his soul, he would have a hooked, sharp nose like a crow's beak, the bloodshot eyes of a madman, and the savage scars of a mercenary soldier; his thick, curly locks would be the tangled, matted hair of a savage, and he'd have the fangs of a tiger. One look at him and people would run away in a panic.

But even when he did his best to make brusque, harsh movements and harden his face into a cynical scowl, Ángel Santiago was unable to disguise his delicate profile, lithe body, aquiline nose, proper speech learned in good schools, and his righteous desire to right the wrongs done to him personally as well as those committed against the most vulnerable. He had an account to settle with the warden, but also with this country full of gold and shit that didn't have the guts to mete out justice to killers and rapists, yet had sentenced him, as a child of eighteen, to many years in prison for having stolen, out of love, out of the simple and mad love of adventure, a beautiful black horse that happened to belong to a brutal landowner.

They caught him one summer night while he was eating watermelon in the moonlight near an oak tree while the pitch-black colt drank from the Piduco River, surrounded by crickets and fireflies, the Milky Way, and the sporadic hooting of owls. He had the sensation that the horse had turned to him to say good-bye as the peons and the sheriff led it back to its owner.

His own father, a tenant on the land, had the stubborn convictions of a man with two or three crude principles. In the presence of his patron and landlord, he testified in court, asking the judge to give his son "a sentence that will make a man out of Ángel, because ever since he got out of school he's done nothing but wander around the countryside like a little rich boy, his head in the clouds, reading books that fill his head with crazy ideas and snubbing his nose at farm labor: even the fruit of the trees fall rotten to the ground because the boy's back is too weak to bend down and pick it up."

Á NGEL TIED UP the horse in an abandoned lot where several trucks were parked and, brushing off his jacket, he entered the school when all the students were in class and the courtyards were empty.

A plump woman with eyes the size of hundred-peso coins approached him, pointing her index finger right at his face.

"What is a handsome young man like you doing in a girls' school? You're going to cause quite a sensation coming in here looking like that."

Ángel Santiago looked humbly at his shoes, then lifted his eyes. "It's just that I have an urgent message for my sister."

"Who might that be?"

"Victoria Ponce."

The teacher clapped her hands together joyously and, grabbing his elbow, led him behind an ancient palm tree.

"I know that student as if she were my own flesh and blood."

"Who are you?"

"Her art teacher."

"Oh, yes. She talks about you with a lot of respect. It's thanks to you they agreed to take her back."

"I put in my two cents. But the most important thing that happened is that she changed. She got back the will to live."

"Or to dance. She wants to be an artist."

"Girls her age all have the same silly ideas in their heads."

The teacher noticed that the boy kept ironing the lapels of his jacket with his hands, and she contributed to his grooming efforts by placing the corner of his shirt collar outside his green sweater.

"Victoria doesn't have any brothers. Who are you?"

"I'm a friend. I'm like a brother."

"Boyfriend." The woman's enormous eyelashes fluttered with complicity.

"Well . . . 'boyfriend' sounds so formal."

"Lover?"

The boy dropped his head as if it were about to fall off his shoulders.

"So handsome and so shy! You turned fuchsia."

"That's a color only an art teacher would think of. You embarrassed me."

"But that's no reason to turn crimson. You can rinse your face in the fountain. I recommend you wait for Victoria out on the street. I'll give her your message."

"Thank you, teacher."

"Tell me something, young man. Do you love her?"

"What?"

"Like in the movies. Like Clark Gable loved Vivien Leigh in *Gone with the Wind*."

"I think the two of us are too poor to love each other like that."

"Are you using anything?"

"Excuse me, ma'am?"

"To protect yourselves. When you're in bed . . . How can I say it? Do you wear a *hat*?

"You mean a condom?"

"You said it. I never say things so straightforwardly."

"I think we're too poor for that, too."

The teacher took out of her bag a package of Éxtasis condoms with a picture of a smooth obelisk and placed it in his hand, which closed up tightly around it.

"I'm Catholic, but can you imagine Victoria dancing with a balloon for a belly? That would be the end of all her dreams. I must assume you love her a little and wouldn't want to cause her so much harm."

"I promise you, teacher."

"She's a very sensitive girl, but unfortunately very sad. Her favorite painter is Edward Hopper. Do you know him?"

"No, teacher. I'm not very up on painters."

"Well, Hopper . . . Put those away in your pocket, you're making me nervous."

She led the young man to the double doors and pushed him gently out to the street.

"Hopper is a sad artist. If he paints a house, it is the loneliest house in the world. If he draws an usher in a full movie theater, that usher is the most abandoned woman in the world. That is, he disperses melancholy with a fan."

The recess bell rang and with it came the students' shouts as they spilled into the hallways and the courtyard. Ángel rubbed his cold nose and happened upon a rather surprising speech at the tip of his tongue.

"But just because someone likes sad things doesn't mean they're sad. For example, Victoria is choreographing a dance to a poem by Gabriela Mistral: '*From the frozen niche where men have put you, / I will lower you to the humble, sun-drenched earth.*' It's sad, but when she dances it, she has a smile on her face."

The art teacher placed her glasses on the bridge of her nose, then looked over them so she could look directly into the boy's eyes.

"Do you know how that poem of Mistral's ends?"

"No idea, teacher, I'm not too good at literature, either."

" '*For to those hidden depths no hand descends to dispute me for your fist of bones.*' Do you know how Victoria's father died?"

"Sort of. She's also told me about her mother."

"Victoria is a very sad girl. And very fragile. The littlest thing could break her. If you can't protect her, get away from her."

A few minutes passed before the girl came out to the street. Ángel approached her.

"I didn't get the money to pay for your ballet classes, Victoria. I'm really sorry."

"It's okay. I'll talk to the teacher. Maybe she'll give me another month."

"How did you pay before?"

"I had some savings. Why did you come?"

Standing on that busy street, traffic all around him, Ángel Santiago felt as if he'd just been stripped naked, brutally exposed to the noise and exhaust, the shrill blows of the traffic cops' whistles, the shouts of the street vendors, the students walking by singing the latest hits in English, the irritating drizzle on his face. It might have been the most innocent question in the world, but hearing it after everything that had already happened that day, the precariousness of his situation became implacably clear.

Until that moment, Lira's coup and Ángel's association with Vergara Gray had constituted a life project. As that prospect dissolved into a swamp of humiliations, he was left with nothing to offer the girl besides his revoltingly available and apparently wholly dispensable presence.

"Why did you come?" she repeated.

"I was on my way out to the countryside," he said, desperately trying to tie together a few shreds of meaning in order to stave off his sadness. "I have to let the horse loose. A horse that doesn't gallop gets sick."

"I understand."

"And I'd like you to come with me."

"Me, go to the countryside?"

Victoria stared off into the gray clouds and the peaks of the cordillera poking through.

"It's just that, like I watched you dance, I want you to come with me and be with me in the countryside."

"I don't understand what one thing has to do with the other. Dancing is doing something, creating. Being in the country . . . that's all it is: being in the country."

The girl's logic was irrefutable, and he felt he was the most awkward and insignificant of mortal beings. When he left jail he had stood tall, a man on top of the world; now he was slumping and felt he was the lowliest creature on the planet. He impulsively hugged the girl and whispered in her ear.

"Come with me, Victoria. I beg you."

TERESA CAPRIATTI PLACED the picture on the café table. The man in it had a dark-complexion, his cheeks were taut, and his lips thin. At the bottom was a name and an ID number with seven digits.

"Where did you get it?"

"I looked through his jacket pockets when he came to the house to talk to Pedro Pablo. Do you know him?"

Vergara Gray brought the picture up to his face as if to smell it. He lifted it up, examined its edges, and even turned it around, searching for a clue.

"What made you think to do this?"

"Do what?"

"Steal his picture."

"He seemed like a man from some other world. His age and his general manner, he had nothing in common with Pedro's other school-mates or teachers."

"What else did you notice?"

"His clothes were all new. From the shirt to the shoes. And everything was a little too big on him, as if he had stolen it all without trying it on."

"Did he give you a name?"

"When he came in he said he wanted to congratulate me for having a son as bright as Pedro Pablo. He said I was lucky that with such a famous family he was such a good student."

Vergara Gray rummaged around in his pants pocket to count the number of bills he was carrying. He figured he had enough to pay for another round of lattes, so he called the waiter over and placed his order.

"You need a man at home, Teresa. It's time you let me come back."

"I don't see why. Nothing has improved since the last time I saw you."

"But I'm on the right path."

"It doesn't show. I've been six months without any money. Why do you think Pedro Pablo is talking to this guy?"

"I didn't want to say anything until I was sure. But if you really press me, I should tell you that I've got something very good coming up."

"When?"

"Soon."

The woman put two teaspoons of sugar in her coffee, then threw the spoon down on the table with disdain. "Legal or the usual?"

"Why do you care?"

"Because the answer to that question is the difference between freedom and prison."

Now it was his turn to throw down the spoon. "How considerate of you to worry about me! I've been free for a couple of weeks and you haven't even seen me."

"Yes I have, and I'm seeing you now."

"You know what I mean, Teresa. I love you, and you don't even let me enter my own apartment."

"You saved that apartment from the disaster because you put it in my name and I forced you to sign a prenuptial agreement before we got married."

"What does any of that have to do with love?"

"A lot, Nico. For me there is no love without dignity and security, the two things you can't give me."

"I agree, I'm no saint. But do you feel *anything* for me?"

"These conversations drive me crazy. It sounds like we're singing a bolero. Listen, Nico. I wanted to see you because our son is involved in something shady, maybe something illegal to get the money you no longer give us. Look at this picture. Do you know this guy?"

"His hair is combed differently, and it's shorter, and he probably covered up a scar on his cheek with some makeup. And this is a very recent picture, taken for a new fake identity card. But he can't hide that look in his eyes."

"Who is it?"

"It can't be who it is because who it is has a life sentence without possibility of parole. But it sure looks like him."

"So it can't be who you think it is. He can't be free and in prison at the same time."

"Logic doesn't always work in this world. Nor does loyalty."

"Are you referring to me?"

The man stirred his coffee. "You let somebody off the street into your house and you won't even let your own husband in."

"Please, get a grip on yourself."

The man placed his hands palms down on the tablecloth and sat in silence. Teresa Capriatti placed her own hands on top of her husband's and kept her eyes lowered. He realized that it had been exactly five years since anyone had offered him a gesture of tenderness. He leaned over the table and passionately kissed his wife's hands, then pulled back so she could remove them discreetly.

"Who's the man in the picture, Nico?"

"I have to do some checking. Before you hear from me, you probably shouldn't know his real name."

"Don't you trust me?"

"It's not that. It's for your own protection."

He picked up the photograph again and studied it as he furrowed his brow.

"So what should I do?" she asked.

"First of all, don't question the false name he gave you. He's Alberto Parra Chacón, period. If you see him, call him Don Alberto. 'Nice to see you, Don Alberto.' "

"What do you think is going on between him and our son?"

"If he is who I think he is, it would be very strange for him to hook up with a kid from the university. Some dealers try to become friends with young people so they can get drugs into the classrooms. They give a little to a kid in a bar or a soda fountain, and the second time they give them a little more, maybe even a little advance on a sale they might make."

"I don't think that's what Pedro Pablo's involved in. He's a good boy, he likes sports, he studies hard."

"That's good to hear, but neither of us has given him any money for months."

The woman leaned back in her chair. "That's not my fault!"

"But I suspect this has nothing to do with drugs. Something tells me this guy wants to reach the father through the son."

"What?"

"He probably doesn't know where I live and he's going wherever he can pick up a trail. The most natural place to start is my last known address, that is, my house."

"Why does he want to find you?"

"Some have some skills and others have other skills. I'm famous for being good at certain things."

"Nico!"

"I'm not proud of my defects, Teresa. Since I got out of jail I haven't broken a single law."

"Nor will you."

"I'm not so sure anymore, my love. What have I gained with my freedom? You won't have me, my son has rejected me, my partner stole all my money, and poverty is gnawing away at me." He crossed his legs, showing a hole on the bottom of his shoe.

"So how are you managing?"

"I fix the hole in my shoe with newspaper and Scotch tape. But the one in my soul, nothing. The important thing right now is that neither you nor Pedro Pablo tell Alberto Parra Chacón where I'm living."

"There's no worry there. We don't even know."

"Better that way. Do you have a gun in the apartment?"

"You always told me to avoid them."

"If you don't know how to use one properly, it's better not to have one."

His wife leaned over and pulled off a piece of thread hanging from his tie. "Are we in danger, Nico?"

"No, not at all. Did you notice anything else about the man?"

"The clothes are new, but he really looks like someone from the slums. Like a beggar."

"Scum?"

"Exactly. Scum."

"Anything else?"

"I don't know if this will help."

"Tell me anyway."

"He smells like a dog."

A T ABOUT THREE in the afternoon, the dark gray sky lightened slightly, the clouds parted, and the sun's hazy light peeked through. Ángel Santiago took this tiny respite that barely thawed the air as a good omen. He led the chestnut horse across the stream, then up the gentle slope of a hill. From the top they could see a field of wheat and, right down the middle, a cart pulled by two oxen and from which two children were tossing out grain.

He left the horse next to an oak tree and took Victoria by the hand down a path that ended in a pine forest. They made their way through the trees, the boy pressing the girl on with his enthusiasm. It wasn't long before they reached a spot in the forest that opened out onto a large pond.

He led Victoria over to two tree trunks that had been carved and sanded into seats. She took off her jacket and straddled one of them. Ángel sat down and leaned his head against the other and looked up at the sky.

"Who owns this land?"

"It's a reserve. It belongs to the government."

"I love it."

"I knew you would. Here nobody is allowed to shoot birds or harm any animal that comes to drink. It's how God imagined the world, don't you think?"

"How can you know what God imagined? Nobody can be in God's head."

"Not even the pope?"

"The pope is just a man, like all the others."

"But he has a special in on what's going on in God's head."

"You say that because you haven't studied philosophy."

"So why don't you explain it to me?"

"Look, God—"

"Stop there, there's no more to say," Ángel said, and smiled as he imagined that the two rapidly moving cumulus clouds were competing in a race across the sky.

"God can't think!"

"You're nuts! God is omnipotent, and if He's omnipotent, He can think. Better than you, than me, than the pope, better even than Vergara Gray."

"I don't care much for philosophy," Victoria said, "but I like to imagine that everything is God. I mean, the stars, the wind, the tides, human beings, mountains, rivers, trees, animals . . ."

"That would mean that the horse is God, too?"

"If you are a pantheist, then you believe that the whole universe is God. And if you hurt somebody, then you are hurting God, who is infinitely good."

Ángel Santiago jumped up, stood on the fallen tree trunk, and stared long and hard, taking in the totality of the scene.

"If you had to take revenge on somebody, somebody who did a terrible thing to you—"

"Like the man who killed my father?"

"I don't want you to get sad. But . . . would you wait for God's infinite goodness to forgive him?"

"No. My only problem is that I don't know who killed my father."

"It was the dictatorship."

"But the dictatorship can be everybody and nobody at the same time. You get on a bus and the guy sitting next to you could be the murderer."

Suddenly the young man tensed. He listened carefully to the sound of barking coming from the direction of the cordillera.

"They must have sensed that somebody was here."

"Will they come here?" Victoria whispered.

"They could."

"What should we do?"

"Nothing. They won't hurt you. Are you going to be tested on philosophy on the exam?"

"Yes, I'm going to be tested on everything, remember?"

"What is philosophy, anyway?"

"It's something only human beings do because we have consciousness. Take the river, for instance. It doesn't even know it's a river, but it acts like a river."

"In Talca, there's an enormous river, the Maule."

"And what did you think about when you sat on its banks?"

"Nothing. I just sat there."

"You never thought about what it means that the river is flowing?"

"To tell you the truth, no."

"Then I guess you're not a philosopher. Philosophers observe the world and then invent ideas that explain why things are as they are. Close your eyes and imagine, for once, that there's nothing of nothing."

"I can imagine that there is nothing of nothing, but if I am thinking that there is nothing of nothing, then I *am*, because in order to think that there is nothing of nothing, there has to be somebody to think it."

"See, that's how philosophers think. Now try to imagine that man didn't exist. Would the world exist?"

"Of course it would."

The barking got closer. Santiago lifted his finger and pointed to two meadowlarks playing on the water.

"You see? Even if man didn't exist, there would be rivers and seas and clouds, and sky and horses and birds. It's incredible."

"Victoria, I don't really see, but if everything you know helps you dance, then I think it's fantastic."

Three dogs ran toward them at top speed, crunching the fallen leaves under their steps, then stopped right in front of them. At that very instant, they stopped barking to smell the invaders' feet. One of them was a brown Labrador, who stared at Victoria. The others wagged their tails and calmly drank from the pond.

The boy pulled a twig off a tree and started breaking it into small pieces. A colder wind now began to blow from the cordillera, and the clouds became denser, blocking out the sun.

"I want to ask you a question, Victoria."

The girl stood up and, with a shiver, tightened the belt on her coat. The dogs threw themselves down on the leaves, their fur covered with brambles from the mountain and moss from the pond.

"For the exam?"

"Not this time. You told me that I don't know you very well."

"I'm not going to talk about myself at this moment, in this place. It would be like throwing garbage all over this sanctuary."

"Okay, so just let me ask you a question that is more about me than you."

"Go ahead."

"What are we?"

Victoria burst out in joyous laughter, grabbed him around the waist, pushed him down on the trunk, and lay on top of him, burying her nose in his temple.

"Is this a philosophical question about our place in the universe?"

Under his back the boy felt the dampness of earth verging on mud, the elemental softness of the forest floor, the rough brush of the stones, the movement of ants as they carried sprigs of grass to their nests. Above, in the spaces that opened up between the locks of Victoria's hair falling over his face, he saw the low, crushing winter sky, which urged him to find refuge. Not a hut, not a cavern among the cliffs in the mountains, but rather an emotional respite. He imagined his mother dressed in a tailored suit and a felt hat, waving good-bye to him at the port in Valparaíso. When she left, had she already decided not to return? If she despised his father so much, how could she leave her only son in his hands? At some moment, like in a fairy tale, would she come from some Eastern land to find him and give him refuge?

A refuge in herself.

"I'm not joking, Victoria. What are we? I mean, what is our relationship? Are we . . . ?"

"You mean like boyfriend-girlfriend?"

"I'm speaking seriously."

"Why are you asking? What's wrong with you? You asked me to come with you and I came. Aren't you happy?"

"Happy, yes, I'm happy."

"So?"

"It's just that I'm happy in a different way than when I'd come to a place like this alone. I always used to feel like it was enough for me to be near a pond, surrounded by birds, breathing in and out, and that was all there was. I was satisfied. But now . . . now I'm happy, but it hurts to be happy."

The girl wanted to understand him, but it was getting colder and her ears were beginning to throb.

"What's our relationship, Victoria?"

The girl rubbed her nose into the boy's chest, then glued her eyes on his and said confidently, "You and I are together."

VERGARA GRAY HAD two reasons to go to his former prison and pay a visit to Warden Huerta. After greeting him affectionately, Vergara Gray would urgently—no, desperately—ask Huerta to write him a check substantial enough to allow him to survive for a few weeks.

His return to civilian life had turned out to be more difficult than he had imagined. Monasterio was hanging on by a thread, and there was very little chance of recuperating his share of the loot, unless there was an unexpected upswing in the world economy, that is. Those much-needed pesos from Huerta would help Teresa Capriatti and his son pay for the basics: electricity, telephone, water, and gas; he had no personal expenses other than his cigarettes and a little dye for his graying mustache.

The second reason was stranger, though he intended to be perfectly frank with the warden, as was appropriate between old friends who had struggled on different fronts, "a situation that sharpens and deepens one's feelings and affections," as Huerta put it. "One respects loyalty from a rival more than from wolves in the same den."

Could Huerta, through his prison contacts, find out if the prisoner Rigoberto Marín was still behind bars? Or had Marín possibly escaped without the press discovering the disaster and besieging Warden Santoro? Might he have been the beneficiary of some new-fangled amnesty from the Ministry of Justice, or was something strange, very strange, going on?

Mr. Huerta had no problem at all sliding his old Parker fountain pen over a check from Banco Santander and soberly handing the document to Vergara Gray, no questions asked. The recipient, in turn, assured him, with more conviction than he really felt, that within one month he would return the sum—he knew all too well the size of public servants' salaries, and he held his friend's self-less sacrifice in high esteem. Huerta had the good breeding to pretend he didn't even hear Gray's comments and instead showed great interest in the second issue he raised.

By Huerta's reckoning, this could be addressed head-on or by setting in motion certain criminal networks within the prison system. Huerta admitted to not having many snitches he could count on: the annex under his jurisdiction was for the more distinguished professionals "like you, Nico," and not for brutal murderers and common criminals. A phone call from warden to warden would be the most direct way, but if something strange was going on—and there was every chance there would be in this slippery, ambiguous, promiscuous New Santiago—he would thereby alert Santoro that an administrative irregularity was suspected in his realm, an irregularity that might occasion some danger to Vergara Gray, or to Teresa Capriatti and Pedro Pablo Vergara Gray.

"Pedro Pablo Capriatti," the father corrected him with a pained smile. "The fool changed his last name, in my honor, of course."

"We'll take the most discreet path," Huerta announced, patting his favorite ex-convict on the shoulder.

Vergara Gray carried the check out of the prison and stood on the sidewalk for a while looking it over carefully. Huerta's manners were scrupulous. He had even had the tact to not indicate a payee so as to avoid Vergara Gray the embarrassment of being asked for his identification, hearing his name shouted out in front of a long line of customers, then being referred to a manager who would subject it to scrutiny before finally giving him the money an hour later.

As he approached Las Cantinas Street, he stopped to chat with an old newspaper reporter, someone who had followed his life for years and who attempted to jot down some notes as they spoke. Vergara Gray was very frank with him. He told him just a fraction of his misadventures, including his failed attempts to win back Teresa Capriatti, this after being assured by this veteran of the lino-type that the next day's headline would not read: "Gangster Vergara Gray Dying of Love."

Once that hurdle had been overcome, his instinct warned him that he would encounter another at the corner in front of the hotel. And there he was: the young Ángel Santiago awaiting his arrival with impatience.

"We've got nothing to talk about," he told him before the young man had time to suck him into an exchange.

"Oh, yes, we do, Professor!"

"In any civilized society, even this one, it is the elder who decides if a dialogue will take place. Even the Araucano Indians obeyed their chiefs. I have approximately a forty-year advantage over you."

"Okay, okay," Ángel conceded, running alongside him. "I'm not going to burden you with the reasons I'm emotionally devastated. I just want you to give me back those Schendler jean jackets."

"With pleasure. I will be delighted to do anything if it means ridding my life of crime and, above all, your presence, for the indefinite and infinite future."

"Thank you, maestro."

"Let's enter quietly so Monasterio doesn't see you. Even though, I must confess, I wouldn't be too troubled by your demise, I wouldn't want to be the means of giving that lying bandit the pleasure of bringing it about."

"Why don't you just kill him?"

"Pure arithmetic, my son. How many years of jail will that one minute of happiness while I am strangling him cost me? And what for? Before, while I was doing time, I at least had the hope of recovering my capital and my family. After killing Monasterio, the only entertainment I'd have would be to check off the days until I died."

"You sure are pessimistic, maestro. Nothing I suggest excites you very much."

The man opened the door to his room and invited the young man in. The wardrobe creaked as he opened the door, took out the jean jackets, and laid them on the bed.

"They're all yours."

Ángel picked them up, stuffed them under his arm, and began to rummage through the garbage can.

"What are you doing?"

"Looking for the ID tags."

"You won't find them. They take the garbage out daily."

The young man kept rummaging, then let out a melodramatic sound of discovery. "I don't think so. Here is Sunday's *El Mercado*. And here are the tags." He wiped them off on the front of his shirt and stuffed them into his pockets.

"What are you going to do with those?"

"Look, Don Nico. If you are asking me a question, that means we have established a dialogue, and you just told me you didn't want to have one with me."

"Drop that pedantic rhetoric and tell me what you're going to do with them."

The boy raised his eyes and with a grave look on his face, stated flatly, "The coup."

"Who with?"

"Alone."

"So why do you want both jackets?"

"So I'll have a spare."

The man pushed the wardrobe door closed with his foot; this time it made a shrill screech. "You know very well that you can't do it alone."

"What do you want me to do if you refuse to collaborate? Lira sends it to you on a golden platter and you reject it out of pure arrogance."

"I told you it was a brilliant plan, and that I'm turning it down because no plan, no matter how brilliant, will guarantee you stay out of jail."

"Look, sir, I know they call you 'Silk Fingers.' You have never carried a gun and you have never killed. But I wouldn't take any chances. If there was any problem at any moment, I'd have one bullet for me and another for you. What do you think?"

"You would really be capable of shooting me if we were in trouble?"

"In cold blood, no, because I love you and admire you. But if you asked me to, I could. In jail I read a book where one friend says to another, 'It's always good to have someone around who would kill you if the moment arose.'"

"I thought the only thing that interested you about books was the graph paper used to cover them."

"Not at all, maestro. I've gotten a very good education recently helping Victoria study for her exam. Do you know anything about Being?"

"I've never heard of Being."

"Victoria had to learn it for her exam. It's the opposite of Nothingness. You see?"

"Whatever you say."

"Ask me the key question."

"Which?"

"Is there Nothingness?"

"How could there *be* Nothingness?"

"Because if there's nothing, Nothingness is and has Being."

Vergara Gray went over to the sink and splashed some water on his forehead. He felt like this kid could give him a fever in a matter of minutes.

"Take your jacket and go."

"Okay, I'll take the *jackets* and go."

"Who will use the other one?"

"I can't say."

"You don't trust me?"

"I trust you totally. But I don't know how my partner would feel about you."

"Ángel Santiago, I know every veteran in this world. Give me his name so that I can tell you if your coup has even the minutest possibility of success with him."

"Okay. His name is Toño Lucena."

"Toño Lucena?"

"Yes, sir."

"That's the name of a Spanish singer. When I was a young man, someone named Pepe Lucena performed at the Goyescas Cabaret. He used to sing '*Castillito en la arena, que el viento se lo llevó.*'"

"This Lucena is also Spanish, but he doesn't sing. He's a professional picklock. He does have an ear to hear the melodies of the combinations."

"As long as he doesn't have Beethoven's ear!"

"You're jealous, Professor Vergara Gray."

"I'm not jealous, you fool."

"But your face has gone fuchsia!"

"Fuchsia? Where did you get such an adjective?"

"From an art teacher."

The man rubbed his eyes as if trying to wake himself up from a nightmare. The impertinent young man was right. Not only was his face fuchsia, but his heart was skipping beats all over the place. He needed air.

"Come with me."

"Where are we going, maestro?"

"To cash a check."

"A great big whale of a check?"

"No, my son. Just a little guppy that will barely keep us afloat."

WHEN THEY FINISHED at the bank, the man invited the boy to a soda fountain. They ordered ham and avocado sandwiches, tea with milk, and two packs of cigarettes. When the order arrived, Vergara Gray put one pack of cigarettes in Ángel Santiago's pocket. The boy accepted it with a smile. After taking his first sip of tea, the maestro leaned back in his chair and, wiping his hands off on the napkin, spoke with great solemnity.

"You told me before that you were emotionally devastated, and then I see that you are still prepared to demolish Canteros's empire. This appears to be contradictory, if not outright schizophrenic."

"Not really. I always find a way out, Professor. If I'm feeling down, I go to the countryside and there, among the birds, my problems drift away. Did I tell you that I am a pantheist?"

"You hadn't told me, nor do I have any idea what that is."

"Neither did I, but I had it explained to me. I believe that God is in the world."

"Rather than, say, on the balcony?"

"Exactly."

"So?"

"Nothing. I like believing that."

"So what caused your emotional devastation?"

"Do you remember the girl I brought to your room?"

"How could I forget? Miss Epidermis."

"The very same. Well, Victoria is a dancer. She takes dance classes at night in an academy on Manuel Montt Avenue, and last night the instructor didn't let her into the studio because she hasn't paid for three months."

"What a monster!"

"She's not a bad woman. It's just that a lot of people in Santiago are going through hard times. Recently they cut off her electricity. The students dance to the piano and a portable radio that runs on batteries. When they run out, the instructor is going to have to whistle the tunes."

"What did you do?"

"I took her to her mother's house to make sure she got some sleep. Today, she has to take an exam that will decide if they let her back in school. When we separated, she said to me, 'I'm emotionally devastated.' "

"Just like you told me."

"We're together."

"I understand."

"In a few hours, she's going to take her exam."

"You should be with her now and not gossiping with a boring old man."

"I have a wonderful time with you, Professor. It's just that it would be good for everybody if you decided to do the coup. For you, for me, for Victoria, and indirectly, for your wife and son."

"Don't bring them into this."

"What we're planning is an act of justice. They've stolen everything and all we want to do is get back a tiny part of what belongs to us."

"Look, bambino. I read *Robin Hood* when I was twelve years old. At sixty, fairy tales bore me."

"Why do you call them fairy tales?" Ángel exclaimed, lighting the man's cigarette. "You know very well that Lira the Dwarf's plan is as real as this table. Your own verdict was that it was genius."

"For somebody else, but not for me. For your flamenco singer, for example."

"There's no singer, no nothing, Professor. I said that just to provoke you."

"Well, you failed. What you need, kid, is a plain old run-of-the-mill job that would allow you to help that schoolgirl and nurture your pantheistic spirit."

The young man grabbed his head, then frantically stirred the sugar into his tea. "Unemployment rates are sky-high. Where am I supposed to find work?"

"At a government employment office."

"Those jobs for idiots? For five hundred pesos a day I'm supposed to sweep leaves out of gutters?"

"I'm not talking about the minimum work plan. You could get something you're qualified for. You went to high school."

"Yeah, but it didn't do me any good."

"Why?"

"Because I had the bad idea of stealing a horse whose owner was a fascist and demanded that I get a five-year sentence, and the judge, who was his brother, gave him what he wanted."

"That was it?"

"Doesn't seem like much, does it?"

Vergara Gray couldn't help himself from reaching out his hand and tenderly stroking the boy's hair. "Son! If that's your whole rap sheet, as far as society goes you're as clean as a whistle. You could get a very good job!"

"I doubt it."

The man stood up and told Ángel to put on his jacket. They walked toward the Plaza de Armas. There they hired a photographer with a tripod and dressed in a white apron—which might have been starched and bleached a decade ago—to take their portrait. Behind them loomed the statue of Pedro de Valdivia, the conqueror, and kitty-corner to it, by decree of the Illustrious Municipality of Santiago, historical balance had been restored: a statue of the brave Indian warrior Caupolicán represented the other component of Chilean blood.

The pictures came out well. Vergara Gray paid two thousand pesos for each, and as they walked away toward the Mapocho Station, making their way through throngs of unemployed Peruvians trying to sell little medallions and alpaca sweaters, they waved the pictures through the air to dry them off. When they reached General Mackenna Street, the man stopped in front of the employment office.

"Go in here and I guarantee you that when you leave you'll have a job like any other honorable citizen."

"You don't want to go in, too?"

"Frankly, I don't think that at sixty I can start in the mailroom. But you can!"

"Me? In the mailroom? I prefer prison, Vergara Gray."

The man offered him his lighter and suggested he straighten out his hair with his fingers.

"Offer the interviewer a cigarette. If he accepts, light it quickly, decisively. Sit up straight in your chair and with dignity. Show motivation, enthusiasm. Everyone wants to help a motivated and good-looking young man."

"I don't like to be called good-looking."

"Sorry, but in this case that defect can serve you well. What would you say to a job as a flight attendant?" Vergara Gray placed his hand like a visor over his eyes and pretended to observe the view from an airplane.

"Flight attendant?"

"What a perfect job for a pantheist! Just imagine yourself in the sky; stretched out below you, oceans, mountains, rivers, forests, jungles, deserts, cathedrals, men and women like little ants, pulsating throughout the universe, and you up there smiling as if you owned the world."

"I've never flown. I mean, in an airplane."

The man led him over to the building's large double doors and wished him luck with a pat on the shoulder.

"I'll wait for you at the café on the corner."

THE CLERK HOLDING his hand out across the desk—which reminded Ángel of elementary school—was only a few years older than him, and he looked immensely more optimistic than the people sitting in the waiting room. Makes sense, Ángel thought, this one's got work and the others don't. Following the professor's advice, Ángel offered him a cigarette and lit it. Clearly he hadn't hit rock bottom because he still had money to buy cigarettes and the lighter still had fluid.

As Ángel told his life story, the clerk took notes in a government notebook with a gray cover. Then he leaned against the back of his chair and flashed a sympathetic smile.

"If I may give you a preliminary diagnosis and prognosis, Mr. Santiago, your case, please excuse my frankness, doesn't look very promising."

"But why, sir? As I was telling it to you, I had the feeling that it really wasn't that bad."

The clerk began to sharpen his pencil with a razor blade. Ángel could tell that this was what he did with all the applicants. There were pencil shavings all over the table and the bare floor.

"It's just that there's much more of 'should have' than 'did.' Out of a grand total of twenty years, you've spent more than two in jail."

"I had a bad stroke of luck. I committed a childish prank and faced a strict judge. But besides that, I finished high school and got decent grades. Except for that mishap, I would have gone to the university."

"With what money?"

"That was the problem. Since I didn't have any money, I stole the horse."

"To sell it?"

"No, just to ride it."

"Any potential employer who takes a look at your history would see that since you left school you haven't earned a single peso."

"I didn't need to. But now I urgently do."

"Why?"

"I want to get married."

"In this country we have hundreds of thousands of unemployed, some of them with technical or university degrees. Some even with university degrees *and* work experience! With what you've got, you could sell peanuts."

"Peanuts?"

"You get a little capital and you buy a cart, a tiny oven to keep the peanuts hot, and you go make the best of the winter in the Bellavista neighborhood. Sundays are especially good because parents take their kids up Pío Nono to the zoo."

"I'd rather sell peanuts on the street than have a job like yours. All you do is hit people when they're already down."

"I do my job in the spirit of public service."

"Help me, then. I have lots of skills and frankly I have higher ambitions than pushing around a peanut cart."

"But you must maintain those ambitions within the boundaries of what is legal. A stint in jail in the current situation is like committing hara-kiri."

"You can't offer me anything else? Gardener, janitor, electrician?"

"I have nothing of anything. I could turn my pockets inside out and I still wouldn't find anything."

"So what's the point of your job?"

"We're waiting for the global economy to improve. Then there'll be more jobs. But there's a crisis in Germany, Asia, the United States. Chile is doing everything right, but if the other countries don't grow, what can we do?"

"So you can't do anything for me?"

"The only thing I can offer you is a certificate that proves that you've been here and that we have nothing to offer you."

"What good would a certificate like that do me?"

"Nothing, to tell you the truth. But you could show it to somebody to prove that you made an effort. There are people who value a young person who makes an effort."

"Okay, go ahead and give it to me."

"With pleasure. I know some young people your age who sing in the subway and beg and show off the certificate. That softens up the passersby."

"Beg?"

"Not ideal, but if you're desperate . . ." The clerk filled out the preprinted form and stamped it twice. "I wish you the best of luck, Mr. Santiago."

"I am grateful to you."

"What do you think you'll do with the certificate?"

"Just what you said, sir. Nothing."

The young man stood up, gathered some of the shavings off the desk, and placed them in the palm of his left hand. "Nobody has ever invented anything better than a Faber number two pencil. Don't you think, sir?"

"It's the one they recommend at school."

"And if you sharpen it very well, you can have very elegant handwriting. I see you don't use a pencil sharpener?"

"Just a razor blade."

"Why is that?"

"It does two things: sharpens the pencil and calms the nerves."

ATE OF THE First Punic War; when did Hannibal invade the Iberian Peninsula after crossing the Alps; what year did Julius Caesar die; what is the difference between an aristocracy and an oligarchy; give the name of a saturated hydrocarbon; give the name of the ester whose formula is CH_3COCH_3; who translated the Bible into German; name three novels by Blasco Ibáñez; who was the mother of Emperor Charles V; who said, "The imagination could never invent so many and diverse contradictions as exist naturally in the heart of each person"; what is, according to Husserl's phenomenology, *epoché*; who said, "It takes more than an hour to conquer Zamora"; what chemical compound was used in 1948 to make the first transistor; what year was the treaty signed that permanently divided North and South Korea; who was the priestess who gave Apollo the Oracle of Delphi; what are the two classes of flowering plants that have one cotyledon covering the seed; what's the relationship between Gandhi and the Amritsar Massacre; what do the Egyptian Anwar el-Sadat and the Israeli Menachem Begin have in common; what region is called the Horn of Africa; what are the basic units when subatomic particles absorb and release energy; insulin can be extracted from what animal; how can one observe the effect produced by the increase of carbon dioxide in the atmosphere; what novel begins with the sentence, "Would I find La Maga?"; what is a megathere; what is an inflammation of the mucous membrane surrounding the urethra called?

THE QUESTIONS AND their answers were like stones under Victoria Ponce's pillow. And under her eyelids the memories of the humiliation she had suffered at the ballet academy fluttered like sharp metal splinters. She had stood there watching from outside the window and the lesson had continued exactly as usual without her. Her banishment was suffocating her. Ángel tried to cheer her up: tomorrow he'd get some money, and since there was no evil from which something good didn't come, she could use those hours to focus on reviewing the questions for the exam. Once the school problems were cleared away, they'd figure out, together "the best way for you to dance at the Municipal Theater." Then she'd gotten onto a bus with a broken muffler, and the exhaust mixed with the night's cold wind and poisonous smog had set her cheeks on fire.

Her mother wasn't surprised to see her arrive so early. After a few minutes, she served her pea soup with bacon and sat down with her at the table, stroking her black embroidered shawl. Every once in a while she took a sip of red wine, then passed her tongue over her lips. Once, she turned to look at the television set and stared at the blank screen for a few minutes, as if she were watching a show. The girl said there had been a cold draft on the bus and that maybe she had caught a cold. Her mother brought her a glass of tap water and an aspirin.

It was cold in every room in Santiago. There was something

strange about that city, the way the walls seemed to suck all the warmth out of living bodies and expel it outside. The plastic-covered chairs were freezing, and the rugs were the same temperature as the concrete under them.

Victoria piled all the textbooks on the sofa and leafed through them, attempting to recover a bit of enthusiasm. She tried to picture the teachers who would gather tomorrow and subject her to the final exam; when an image of them sitting there facing her came to mind, she shivered, then closed her eyes and pictured a scene from the ballet *La Bayadère*.

She saw herself escaping a hundred, a thousand times through the streets of Santiago after the ridicule her dance teacher had subjected her to. How had she suddenly gotten unused to such rudeness? Is it possible that a couple of weeks with a boy who was an expert at doing foolish things, and a trot out to a pond with him for a day full of birds and dogs were enough to revive her desire to live?

Ángel Santiago had witnessed her disgrace at the door of the ballet academy and done nothing but look pleadingly at the instructor. Then he had put his arm around her and led her to the bus stop, not allowing her to run off wildly, blinded by sorrow. In a hoarse voice, with tears running down her cheeks, she had reproached him for not fulfilling his promise. Twice he told her that he would find a way to pay what she owed and get the dance teacher to let her back.

She clasped her hands over her chest in a gesture of prayer, a gesture she had made since she was a child. But just like every other night, she didn't pray to anybody, didn't ask for divine intervention, didn't invoke her guardian angel, said nothing to the small effigy of the Virgin Mary standing on its little pedestal. Ángel Santiago had shouted out to her from the sidewalk as the bus pulled away from the curb that tomorrow first thing he would come by the school to give her the money for the teacher. Would he manage it or would it end up being another empty promise?

If he found the money, hope might lift her chin and put some color in her cheeks before she had to face those teachers. But if not, if he didn't get there in time, what would help her stand up to the disdain of the math teacher, Berríos, who couldn't even look her in the eyes, who felt, as she overheard him say, "wounded in the depths of my academic being" that a student like her, categorically ignorant of even her multiplication tables, should be given the Academic Aptitude Exam.

The night passed. She heard every howl of every cat on every rooftop, the creak of every door in every neighboring house, the far-off roar of a motorbike without a muffler racing over the cobblestone streets, the sirens of ambulances and police patrols.

The knowledge devoured so furiously during the last few days seemed to be sitting like badly digested food in her stomach. Her mother moaned every once in a while from the neighboring room, then came a dense silence, the most unnerving sound of all.

She managed to sleep for an hour or two before the alarm went off. Her eyelids felt heavy, and it was painful to crawl into the rawness of her room from under the heavy wool blanket from Chiloé. To avoid any temptation to return to the warmth of her bed, she rushed into the bathroom, filled the sink with cold water, held her breath, and dunked her head.

She heated water on the stove and drank a cup of tea without sugar; when she opened her closet she felt a moment of tenderness for her mother, who had ironed her blouse and slightly starched the collar. Even though she liked to feel the cloth on her breasts, she decided to wear a brassiere; she wanted to give the impression of being a disciplined student, the perfect Catholic schoolgirl, as if she had no ambition besides passing that test and devoting herself, after graduation, to working as a secretary in a government office.

She would tame the artistic rebel within. She would douse, in one fell swoop, the fire in her veins, her constant thoughts about the best possible movements if she were ever, for example, to play the protagonist of *La Bayadère*. The teachers would see her as a pale, submissive ghost, shy and with a bad cold, a pathetic stray cat asking for a saucer of warm milk and a bit of affection.

She stopped for a moment at the door to the school, trying to suppress the chills that suddenly racked her body. It wasn't the normal winter chill that filled the whole gray city, rather a frost that emanated from her bones. Her joints hurt, her temples were taut, and she felt as if three cracks had opened up across her forehead. If, until now, the questions and answers had been a game she played with Ángel Santiago between kisses and caresses, they now felt to her like a catalogue of undecipherable signs.

The exam would take place in the library from eleven o'clock to noon. Her classmates would spend their extra free hour chatting in the patio, or—which frightened her to death—poking their noses into the exam room to witness her muteness.

Victoria didn't want to attend her morning class. Nor would anybody consider it a serious breach of the rules if she devoted herself to spiritual renewal before such an important exam. Her real purpose, however, was to wait for Ángel Santiago. She imagined him jumping off the bus, a wad of bills tied with a rubber band in his hand, running up to give her a hug.

With joy and devotion he would hand her the money to pay her ballet teacher; then she would enter the library—calm, cool, and collected—and stroll through the test by fire without even singeing her feet, thereby taking the first huge step toward reaching the stage of the Municipal Theater. Those heavy velvet garnet curtains would open and there she would be, silhouetted against the fine beam of the spotlight, in ready position, waiting for the conductor to lower his baton.

Then, yes, madness. Just as the music erupts, she grows beyond herself, *becomes dance.* The entire history of her life merges with her body at the service of the music. Without vanity, with humility, full of a spirituality as fine as Saint Teresa's, her soul would find peace through movement, movement in the stillness.

No matter how many times she paced between the street and the doors of the school, no matter how hard she hoped for it, the boy didn't appear. Then she sat on the bench under the plastic roof, feeling the passing minutes erode her faith.

At eleven in the morning, wishing she were in Africa rather than the library of her school in Santiago, Chile, she sat down in front of her teachers. Her art teacher gave her the thumbs-up, and her physics teacher asked her the first question. It was about quantum mechanics, and Victoria answered; she was asked about amoebas, and she shone; they shot her a question about pancreatic secretions, no problem; the Pythagorean theorem rolled off her tongue without her even forgetting the measures of the legs, the squares, or the hypotenuses; in the blink of an eye she spewed out the names of Oedipus's sons, Polynices and Eteocles; in one breath she defined parthenogenesis, summed up Stephen Hawking's theories, knew that *Acacia farnesiana* was the scientific name of the sweet acacia, and that Imhotep was the architect of the Egyptian pyramids; she asserted to the approving teacher that Anwar el-Sadat and Menachim Begin shared the Nobel Peace Prize; she knew that "it takes more than an hour to conquer Zamora" came from Cervantes. With a nod to the rivers and the sea, and a stroll through the founders of the Chilean nation and stoic philosophy, all as smoothly as if she were wearing silk gloves, warmth rose from her belly to her heart, and the math teacher (seeing that she was passing with flying colors, that the girl was shining in answer after answer and that she was gaining points, that she knew that insulin was made from the pig, and that Martin Luther had translated the Bible into German) abstained for the moment from asking any questions and gave his turn to the Spanish teacher, who, rather than ask her the fine points of grammar, questioned her about "The Coplas on the Death of His Father," by Jorge Manrique, at which Victoria Ponce's face lit up because this was her favorite poem in the history of world literature, Neruda notwithstanding.

> *O let the soul her slumbers break,*
> *Let thought be quickened, and awake;*
> *Awake to see*
> *How soon this life is past and gone,*
> *And death comes softly stealing on,*
> *How silently!*

But that light in her face quickly faded when Victoria Ponce's Spanish teacher told her to stop reciting Manrique's couplets, and in a hoarse and bilious voice exhorted her to move on to an analysis of the "aesthetic contribution of this poem," completely transforming the mood of the exam, which from that moment on—according to the art teacher, Doña Elena Sanhueza—went exactly as follows:

"Miss Ponce, how many metaphors, alliterations, metonymies, and hyperboles does Manrique's text contain? Also, identify the rhyme scheme and the nature of the address. Is it apostrophic, enunciating, horizontal, or vertical?"

"I don't know, Mrs. Petzold."

"You don't know anything I asked you?"

"Unfortunately, no, Professor."

"Would you be able to tell me if the poem contains any images that might be a polysyndeton, an anaphor, or a synecdoche?"

"I wouldn't know, teacher."

"But at least you could tell me who the lyric speaker is."

"The poet."

"How quaint! So you can't distinguish between the author of a work and the lyric speaker, the system of symbols created to sustain a discourse?"

"I can distinguish very well, Mrs. Petzold. There is a man of flesh and blood, Jorge Manrique, whose blood and tears are poured into his verses, word by word unleashing images in his work."

"What ignorance, what arrogance, what innocence!"

"Ma'am, it is Jorge Manrique himself who speaks about the death of *his* father, Don Rodrigo. Do you remember when he says 'But he was mortal; and the breath, that flamed from the hot forge of Death, blasted his years'?"

"Who is taking this test, young lady, you or I?"

"Forgive me, ma'am."

"Don't you know that the quality of a poem depends on how the meter is carried out? If it is iambic or trochaic, for example. How many great works in our language owe their immortality to the simple fact of being written in hendecasyllables?"

"I'm sorry, Mrs. Petzold, but I have been mourning the death of my father for years, and my sorrow is not soothed by knowing about metaphors, iambic meters, and much less metonymies. When Jorge Manrique finds out about his father's death, he leaves the court and locks himself away in the castle, where he writes his poem out of the depths of his sorrow."

"My dear girl, that is all fine and dandy, but it is pure historiographical gossip! I am asking you for a literary analysis."

"I'm sorry, teacher, but I'm not going to do any bullshit analysis of the lyric speaker. The poem is too beautiful for that crap."

AS NOBODY HAD ever shouted the word "bullshit" in the school library, let alone "crap," the words seemed to bounce off the walls then remain suspended in midair.

Nor did the bright red sheen on the cheeks of the Spanish teacher, nor the secret mutterings of the math teacher as he scratched his nose, nor the noise of the students in the patio that sounded like a buzzing behind the curtain manage to dissipate the silence that had settled among the other teachers present.

A long pause ensued, during which everybody refrained from clearing their throats, and Victoria Ponce wiped her suddenly sweaty palms on her knees.

"That will be all for now," the principal declared, closing her grade book.

Relieved, the staff rose, and the least polite among them placed cigarettes in their mouths, ready to light up as soon as they left the room. That was the moment the art teacher, Elena Sanhueza, raised her hand.

"Permission to speak, Ms. Principal."

"No, Ms. Sanhueza."

"According to the teaching statutes—"

"Don't push it, Elena."

"I just wanted to say—"

"Whatever you say will be off the record. The session has been suspended."

In spite of her voluminous body, the woman ran to the doorway and spread herself like a crucifix across both doors, trying to prevent the teachers from leaving.

" 'The height of folly,' " she proclaimed with grave intensity, " 'is to learn what one must then forget.' Erasmus of Rotterdam, not I, said that."

The principal looked scornfully at the woman's splayed arms and said in an authoritarian voice, "Excuse me."

"We have just sacrificed someone to the gods of obscurantism and pedantry."

"Enough already, Ms. Sanhueza. Lower your arms."

The woman, defeated, obeyed, watching her fellow teachers cross the threshold. She then walked over to Victoria Ponce and placed both hands on her cheeks.

"You were doing so well, young lady."

The girl slowly started picking up her papers and placing them in her knapsack; when she finished, she sat there in a deep reverie. Although she didn't want to focus her gaze on anything in particular, her eyes were drawn to a portrait of Gabriela Mistral: short hair, upturned nose, eyes that beckoned you to sink into them. Around her, piles of elegantly bound books. Next to her portrait hung the heavy clock from the turn of the last century whose minute hand, in a few seconds, would strike noon.

"HEY, KID, THE cathedral bells have already struck twelve."

"I'm sorry, maestro. There were a lot of hungry dogs and not a scrap to toss them.

"Don't talk to me about dogs! How did it go?"

"Fantastic, Don Nico."

He handed him the certificate covered with ornate, official stamps. Vergara Gray read it, then listlessly placed it on the table next to the empty cup of coffee.

"But this is a total failure. You didn't get anything."

"Nothing at all," the young man exclaimed, leaning back in his chair and scratching his neck.

"So what are you so happy about?"

"Don't you understand, Professor? We've got no choice but the coup."

The man gestured for the waiter to bring him the check.

"Forgive me for not offering you coffee. I've had five since you left. My blood pressure must be sky-high."

"Didn't you at least read your fortune in the grounds? In jail there was an old Turk who used to do it. Let me see yours."

Without waiting for permission, Ángel brought the cup to his nose and, shaking it up, considered how he might frame a persuasive argument.

"I see a whole lot of money in your future."

"For the fifth time today, don't count on me, Ángel Santiago."

"I see you in another country, smoking a Cuban cigar, walking with a beautiful woman on your arm."

The waiter held out the check, and Vergara Gray told him to keep the change from the bill he gave him.

"What else do the grounds say, Aladdin?"

"That you are going to lend me thirty thousand pesos," the boy mumbled with humility in his eyes and a sly smile on his lips.

The man had stood up. He placed on his head a gray felt hat with a green feather, then wrapped a black cashmere scarf around his neck. The boy had a sullen expression on his face.

"It's so cold out there it'll freeze your liver. Don't you have a coat? A scarf?"

"I do, I do."

"So use it. Or do you want me to have to come visit you in the indigents' ward at the public hospital?"

"Would you do that for me if I got sick?"

"You are an adult and you should take responsibility for your actions. The Chilean winter requires a scarf and coat."

"I always wear a leather jacket. Winter and summer. What do you say about the loan?"

They had already reached the street, and Ángel suspected that Vergara Gray didn't know which direction to take. His suspicions were confirmed when the older man took out a cigarette and, shielding the lighter's small flame under his scarf, took a deep, calm drag.

"Why do you want the money, son?"

"Victoria has to pay for her ballet classes today. If her teacher locks her out again tonight, she'll kill herself or just die."

"I must confess two things to you."

"Yes, Professor?"

"First, to borrow this money my self-respect took a beating, from which I have yet to recover. I don't relish the thought of it evaporating out of my hands."

"I'll return it to you with interest."

"Second, I don't believe you that it's for the ballet classes."

"You mean you don't trust me, maestro."

"I trust you, but I wouldn't tie my own dog up within reach of a steak. I'd love to make the schoolgirl happy, but without intermediaries."

"What do you mean?"

"Take me to where she is and I'll give her the money myself."

Ángel Santiago wrapped his arms around Vergara Gray's neck and planted an enthusiastic kiss on each of his cheeks.

The man pushed him away and looked nervously from left to right. "Would you stop kissing me? What will people say?"

"That we are father and son, Don Nico!" the happy boy cried, planting another kiss right on target in the middle of his forehead.

"Can we leave now?" Vergara Gray asked, trying to hide the blush on his cheeks behind his scarf as he took off walking toward the Alameda.

His companion followed him for four or five blocks at a steady pace until, sidling up to him, he said, "Professor, if you add another five to the thirty-thousand, I'll pay for a taxi."

"How much farther to the school?"

"By foot, a couple of hours; in a taxi, about fifteen minutes."

"We haven't got much money. We must be frugal."

"Like in La Fontaine's fable of the ant and the grasshopper."

"Exactly. It's just that for us it's already winter and we've got nothing in the cupboard."

"Don't take it so much to heart. Just think of the fable as a metaphor."

"I don't know what you're talking about."

"Let me explain: the work the ant does is like the experience we gain. We have, how should I say it, collected who we are. We are our own cupboards. We just need to open the door and all the miracles of the universe will pour out."

The old thief stopped and bought two bags of roasted peanuts from a peanut vendor with a white apron. He bit into one, spit out the shell, then chewed three more nuts without taking off their red skins.

"They're nice and hot."

The young man rolled a shell between his fingers, then popped the two nuts into his mouth.

"What do you say about my metaphor, Professor? Did you get the moral of the fable?"

"All your stories end with the same moral: we have to do Lira the Dwarf's coup. And all my responses have the same elegant monotony: no. Or, if you prefer in good scatological Chilean slang: *ni cagando.*"

"Okay, okay, Professor. I don't want to upset you when Victoria needs you more than ever."

"That's what we're about. We're helping somebody and, on the way, shrinking this belly by taking a brisk walk."

"I'm just a little worried that we'll get there too late. Because of you, I wasn't at the school before her exam—"

"Because of me?"

"Because of your insistence that I go to that place to look for work. You know what the clerk said?"

"What?"

"That I should get a peanut vending cart."

"That's a great idea. You just saw that I paid sixty pesos for two little bags. Just imagine if you could sell at least twenty bags an hour for eight hours. That would come to forty-eight hundred pesos a day, or ninety-six thousand a month, not as much as a minister makes but without the risk of them putting you in jail because of some scandal."

The young man stopped abruptly and impetuously threw his bag of peanuts at the man's feet.

Vergara Gray humbly picked it up and placed it in his pocket. "Now I'll have something to eat with my whiskey tonight."

Vergara Gray hailed a taxi. Having to choose between the open door of the vehicle and a humiliating retreat, Ángel chose—in the name of love—to get into the car, where he sank into his seat and buried his head between his shoulders.

"How do you think your little bobbysocker did?" Vergara Gray asked him.

"Good," the boy snorted. "She had to; she's got no other choice."

"You can say such drastic things at your age. But whenever there's no way out the main door, one can always find a crack to slip through."

"You seem so happy with so little, maestro. But neither Victoria nor I are so pusillanimous."

"So what?"

"Pusillanimous."

"Luckily, I don't know what that means, but my intuition tells me that I should break your nose with my fist. Where did you learn such extravagant words?"

The boy squeezed his nostrils as if checking for a nosebleed, then stared at the little statue of the Virgin Mary hanging from the taxi's rearview mirror.

"I once had a teacher who told us that we Chileans have a vocabulary of one hundred words maximum. He made us read books and every time we'd come across a word that we didn't understand, we'd have to write it down one hundred times and look it up in the dictionary."

"He must have forgotten about Neruda."

"That makes one Chilean."

"And Gabriela Mistral."

"That makes two."

"There are sports announcers who are pretty eloquent. The other day one of them described a goal made by the Colo-Colo team as ingenuous."

"He should have said ingenious."

"And when Herrera was about a yard away from the goal and didn't score, he even spoke in Latin."

"What did he say?"

"*Herrera humanum est.*"

As they got farther away from downtown, Santiago's neighborhoods seemed to recede more and more into the past. They passed wave upon wave of run-down shacks with rusted metal roofs, some livened up with yellow paint and purple windowsills. The city seemed to become more and more intimate the uglier it got. These were the slums, Ángel thought, but not his destiny.

When they got near the school, they hung around at the bus stop, the corner store, even the mini-mart, trying to figure out what to do. Vergara Gray suggested they pretend they worked for the post office and were bringing the girl a money order for thirty thousand pesos from some relative in the south. Ángel thought it was a good idea, and they managed to infiltrate the teachers' lounge carrying the three bluish ten-thousand-peso bills as safe-conduct passes.

The only person in the dreary, wintry room was the art teacher. She was sitting right under the chandelier, totally focused on what she was writing. They walked up to her, and Ángel Santiago flashed her a broad smile.

"Do you remember me, teacher?"

The woman lowered her frameless glasses onto the tip of her nose and studied the two men as if she had just been awoken from a deep trance.

"You, I remember, but not the other handsome one. He certainly makes a good first impression, looks like Federico Luppi, the Argentinean actor, with that sexy graying at the temples and the mustache. What's your name?"

"Nicolás," the man responded curtly as if to protect his identity.

When the teacher realized that Ángel wanted to see what she was writing, she pushed it toward him.

"Read it. It's my letter of resignation."

"What happened, teacher?"

"Nothing happened to me. But they ground your poor girlfriend into the dust."

"During the exam?"

"I'm afraid so, dear boy."

"But that can't be. She knew everything!"

"Yes, everything that mattered, not the bullshit!"

The boy looked pleadingly at Vergara Gray, as if he had the power to contradict the teacher's words. All Gray did was spread out his hands in a gesture of impotence.

"Where is she now?"

"Somewhere in Santiago, drowning like a poor swallow. Or has it stopped raining?"

"On and off. You can't give me any idea which direction she might have taken?"

"I'm afraid it could be anywhere, someplace she could hurl herself off of, maybe a bridge over the Mapocho River, the telephone company building—"

"And you didn't do anything?"

"What do you mean, *I* didn't do anything? I can see you don't know whom you're dealing with, you snot-nosed brat. I am writing my letter of resignation before they fire me for insubordination."

She stood up and threw the pad of paper on the rug. The years had almost completely erased the Persian tiger from the weave, and bleach stains made it impossible to make out the eyes of the damsels admiring him.

"How will you make a living if you quit?" Vergara Gray asked.

"I'll find something. At the unemployment office, or maybe outside Santiago. And what do you do?"

The man searched for inspiration in the portraits of the directors hanging on the walls, then confidently lowered his eyes. "I'm a loan broker."

"Do you make a lot of money?"

"For the moment, I am loaning and not collecting."

"You must have a good chunk of capital!"

"Not really. I'm short on money, but long on patience."

Ángel Santiago looked at him askance, then pointed his index finger at him. "Patience that never spoils him, Ms. Sanhueza. Like a worm gnawing away at a buried cadaver."

"What do you want me to do, son?" Vergara Gray asked with genuine concern.

"I don't know what you're going to do, but I'm going to comb Santiago until I find her. Do you really think that something terrible could have happened to her?"

"The only thing that reassures me is that she has dance, and it's as good a reason as any to keep on living."

"She *had* dance, teacher. Let's get moving, Don Nico."

The young man kissed Ms. Elena Sanhueza's cheek, and Vergara Gray gallantly took her hand and brushed his mustache against it. She collapsed into the chair just under the skylight, perhaps hoping that the sky would open up and a ray of sun would filter through. When the young man got to the door, he had the feeling that this room had gotten bigger and colder, and he wished he could simply whisk the teacher away from there.

And offer her what? he thought. The streets of Santiago? His debts? His doubts?

He called to her gently before leaving the room. She adjusted her glasses to bring him into focus and cupped her hand around her ear to hear his words.

"Sitting there like that, teacher, you look like you're in a painting by Hopper," he told her.

THE SHOPPING PASSAGES in downtown Santiago are labyrinthine. Tiny caves of businesses, facades that hide something much more sinister. There, the city is a no-man's-land, a constant trafficking of trivialities and mediocrities. Everything is ordinary, everything is sexualized. Homeopathic pharmacies and shoe repairs. Lottery and racetrack betting agents. Shop windows full of women's underwear. Picture windows full of Asian spices. Toys from Hong Kong. Plastic airplanes with elephant trunks. Potties with Mickey Mouse smiles. Insecticides next to fans. Videos with samurais on the cover. Notions wrapped in ribbons. Beggars on the street selling tissues for runny noses. Miniskirts bursting at the seams over round buttocks. Young bums standing around, smoking cigarette after cigarette, waiting for somebody to drop a coin or a bill after buying a newspaper. Florists selling cheap flowers. Hustlers tossing their three coins, stepping on one, then asking the passersby to bet on heads or tails. Bicycle tire repairs. Pharmacies with herbs for the liver, to treat gonorrhea, kidney stones, and the benign swelling of the prostate. And in the middle of it all, down carpeted staircases, which in some other decade might have been elegant and plush, are the theaters that show movies continuously from one hour before lunch until late in the night. Shows for lonely hearts and the unemployed. For fugitives and the toothless. For fans of movie screens filled with martial arts and insatiable Swedish women mounting African men in a tourist's paradise on the Mediterranean.

They entered the hair salon in the arcade right in front of the movie house and asked if anyone had seen Victoria. Nobody had, or so they said. In these parts everyone tended to be discreet, minding their own business, but we can wash away the gray for two thousand pesos, and for you, young man, a really *cute* cut with spiky ends and lots of gel for only fifteen hundred pesos; in the back we've got two kinds of massages, simple and *full service*, with girls from twenty-five to forty years old, the age determines the price; we even have masseurs for men.

Vergara Gray let the talk flow while he tried to find some clue about the girl's whereabouts. He knew that going straight to the point could silence potential informers and that many people felt an aversion toward smart-aleck kids who asked too many questions. In the meantime, Ángel Santiago looked at the movie posters. *Sex in the Jungle* promised sex scenes with coconuts and bananas, a virile gorilla that made King Kong look like a dwarf, and gangs of Dutchmen who kidnapped damsels for export to Arab countries and the harems therein. He told Vergara Gray that he wanted to go in to see if he could find the girl. That he should give him at least five minutes, until his eyes got used to the dark, and that would he please wait, for he was counting on him to pay for the ballet classes. "A promise is a debt," stated the maestro as he wandered over to a used-magazine stand.

The cashier let Ángel in and told him to sit down in the last row, then look around later for a better seat.

It was even colder inside the theater than on the street, maybe because of the ceiling fan turning to disperse the rancid odors. The movie screen was old, one of those square ones with scratches that fit in with the static of the soundtrack. Inside a torch-lit cave, a blond woman with enormous breasts and thick locks of hair held a snake and pretended to guide it inside her. Two young men dressed in shorts, with curly hair and their hands over their genitals, played at opening and closing their flies and exhibited clear signs of arousal at the movements of the actress, who, while she handled the snake in one hand, gestured with the other for them to approach her, crotches first.

The screen emitted very little light. It was a dark print, and as the young man began to realize what was going on in the theater, he understood that this was probably deliberate. In the front rows he saw several couples embracing; single women moved from one seat to another, always sitting down next to a man or another single woman. One of those women skirting along the aisles came and sat next to Ángel and, without taking her eyes off the screen, held a small package in front of his chest.

"Want some gum?"

"Okay," said Ángel. He took one and the taste of Adam's spearmint spread over his tongue.

The woman placed a hand on his knee. "This your first time here?"

"Yes."

"You know the prices?"

"No."

"I let you grab my tits and stick your finger in my pussy for three thousand pesos, okay?"

"Right here?"

"I'm not wearing anything under my coat. My bra and panties

are in my purse. I always bring mint gum 'cause sometimes the guys have bad breath. The customers here are big drinkers."

"To tell you the truth, I didn't come for that."

"Don't tell me you're a film buff."

"It's just that I'm looking for someone."

"Who?"

"My sister. She said she was going to the movies and I'm not sure if she meant this one."

A heavy man came and sat down at the end of the row, the seat squeaking under his weight.

"Only whores come here, kiddo. Go look for your sister in church. It's just around the corner."

"I have to find her and tell her that our mother is very sick."

The woman lit a match and in the tenuous light of the small flame examined his features until the match burned her fingertips, then she threw the ember on the floor.

"Wow, you are a looker."

"Don't say that, please."

"What, you don't like women?"

"Me? I adore women."

"So, go for it, sugar. I'll let you kiss me and bite my nipples."

"I'm totally broke."

The woman leaned away from him as if offended, making tinkle a stack of bracelets piled on her wrists. "You just think I'm too old."

"Naw, I haven't even looked at you."

"Just look at the big tits I've got. Not like that bitch in the movie; hers are like grapes, is all." She grabbed the boy's hand and led it around the breadth of her voluminous breasts.

"They're nice."

"You see, and they're firm."

"Uh-huh."

"I'll let you suck them for two thousand. For as long as you like."

"I told you, I don't have any money. I'm broke *and* unemployed."

She stood up, passed her tongue over her lips, and pinched his nose, as if to rebuke him. "The theaters for faggots are in the Cathedral Passage. Don't come back here."

She went over and sat down next to the big man, and Ángel Santiago could overhear bits of the same, ritual dialogue as she offered him the same mint gum. He went to sit on the aisle seat of the row opposite, hoping from there to methodically scan the twenty or thirty people in the theater, a few solitary folks, some office workers taking an early siesta, and the couples. Everywhere he looked in the damp, dull darkness, he saw the same embraces, the same kisses.

His eyes finally landed on a silhouette five rows ahead of him. First he saw the head fall languidly against the back of the seat, then he saw the hair, *her* hair, fall over the back of the seat. Then the person next to her, wearing a beret, buried his head in her lap. Even from that distance and through the darkness Ángel could tell he was kissing her breasts and burying his nose in her belly.

"What the fuck do I care?" he said to himself, brushing away the tears that started flowing down his cheeks. "What the hell do I fucking care?" he said to himself again, turning in his seat as if somebody had taken a mallet to his liver.

But when he leapt out of his seat, he knew that if he had a gun, he would shoot; and if a knife had magically appeared in his hand, he would slit a throat. As he approached, he saw everything he had already imagined but in a much more powerful dimension than any image on any screen.

In a split second he was on her. Neither had seen him coming, not the man with his eyes still closed, concentrating on his ecstasy, nor the girl now bending over him, speeding up her movements to finish her deed.

He grabbed Victoria by the hair with the force of someone strip-ping off his own skin and dragged her into the aisle; as he did so, the shout that had been building up inside him erupted like the roar of a wounded beast.

It was more than indignation and disgust, much more than love and betrayed tenderness, infinitely deeper than the profound hatred for the world and all its monsters, eternally fiercer than the anger of his wounded male ego, much more blinding than the blood that pounded in his temples.

He would have rather been blind and not seen, deaf and not heard, as cold and indifferent as an iceberg; he would have rather never left jail, and in the midst of his confusion he thought he now understood that meeting Victoria Ponce by accident was a death sentence, sealed and signed by an authority that had found the per-fect equivalent of the firing squad, the needle with the lethal injec-tion, the thousand volts that would have fried him in the electric chair, and this breath that carried to his lungs a ton of gas in the death chamber. Death doesn't hurt the dying as much as life hurt him at that moment. As his shout rang out, the other moviegoers sank deeper into their chairs, afraid of being caught by the police, the drug squad, the anti-pedophile patrols, the sanitary services, the creditors of their bounced checks, the detectives their jealous wives had hired.

Perhaps they feared that his shout was announcing the arrival of the Angel of the Apocalypse, a knight with a lance like they'd seen on this very screen, who could smash through his enemies' shields and armor and tear open their hearts.

Ángel staggered up the stairs; once he reached the street, and with another shout that quickly dispersed the curious hairdressers who had congregated in the hopes of seeing the victim, and with his last ounce of strength, he dragged Victoria to Vergara Gray's feet.

"YOU ASKED TO see her *in person*, maestro, and here you have her. *In person*, Miss Victoria Ponce. You may give her the money *in person*."

The girl fell to her knees and covered her face with her hair to hide from the stares of the bystanders, her head bent as if in prayer. The man knelt down and tried to lift her chin.

"Goodness gracious, dear girl, what happened to you?"

"I have to wash myself, sir," she said in a barely audible voice.

"Get up and let's go into the salon. They'll give you some water there."

"I want to go far away from here, Don Nico."

"Stand up and lean on me."

"I don't want anybody to see my face."

"It's okay. Keep your hair over your face and let's get out of here."

The girl obeyed and took refuge under the man's arm. He gestured to the onlookers to move aside, silently asking for compassion for the young girl in trouble. In this way, almost like two cripples, they proceeded to Santo Domingo Street, followed at a certain distance by Ángel Santiago, his hands buried deeply in the pockets of his leather jacket.

The sun's pressure had dispersed the layer of clouds, and it now shone with a hue more irritating than warm. Once out in the light of day, Victoria Ponce seemed to gain a more acute consciousness of her own body. She began to shake and scratch herself.

"I have to wash."

"We're on our way. We'll soon find a place."

"No, you don't understand. It's urgent."

She scratched her cheeks, and as she pulled her hand away there was a thin trickle of blood.

"Just try to calm down now. A little more patience."

"I want to wash. Please, help me."

"Just keep walking with me, dear. I'm looking for any kind of faucet."

"If I don't wash myself, I'll die, Don Nico."

"You already said that."

"Where are they?"

"Who?"

"The people in the arcade."

"We left them behind."

"They aren't following us?"

"Calm down, we're alone."

"Where's some water, Professor?"

She stuck a few fingers in her mouth and tried without success to make herself vomit.

"What are you doing, dear girl?"

"Trying to throw up."

"Go ahead if you can."

She gagged, managing only to spit up a few drops of yellow liquid.

Vergara Gray left her alone so as to give her a little privacy, and at the very moment the light changed on the corner of Miraflores and Santo Domingo, the girl took off between the cars and buses and ran in the direction of the cordillera.

"Wait," the man shouted after her. "I brought you the money for your classes!"

Victoria obviously couldn't hear him through the din of the traffic. She was now weaving her way through the pedestrians; she crossed through two red lights, paying no attention to the honking of the buses or the whistles of the traffic cop.

At the corner of the Palacio de Bellas Artes, she ran up the stairs and turned to see if either of the two men were still following her. She could see the old professor from afar, his hand over his heart, but Ángel Santiago was closer, gesturing for her to stop. Victoria kept running across Santa Lucía, right to the middle of the Parque Forestal. The tears began to flow as fast as her feet were running, blood burned her cheeks, and her school loafers kicked up the dust onto her back.

She had to reach the Alemana Fountain. There she would find the waterfalls and the spring: from that lavish sculpture with its bronze boat would fall that precious liquid in generous drops, in the clear and crisp crackling of rising waves.

Running, jogging, tripping, she now caught a glimpse of the ocean in the middle of downtown Santiago, the astonished seals of polished steel, the bird of good omen behind the rowing gods, its wings urging on the company of emigrants and colonizers, pirates and saints, rebels and kings, still and quiet in the fountain that was so close, within arm's reach, so close to her, that gorgeous fountain, the beauty of rain and bronze, the most fertile of winter's cold fog, in an afternoon of grays and lazy students exchanging kisses and promises on the benches of the Parque Forestal, within reach of her hands, her breasts, her hair, her besmirched throat, her tongue full of rage and anger, full of anonymous spilled sperm, what a vision of grace that incessant water tumbling down just for her, how confused now with all the other fountains she had dreamed about, the Trevi, the Fontana dei Quattro Fiumi in Piazza Navona, the Cibeles, Margot Fonteyn at the Royal Palace, l'Opéra of Paris, La Scala in Milan, the wonderful languages she would learn as soon as she set foot in unknown lands, running and reaching it, the same death as Manrique, Professor Petzold, the same cursed death as her father, the same death that was stalking her lover, sniffing him out like a dog, her lover with such a tremendous desire to live, so determined and loving, her lover her father, so different than the death that awaits me and I deserve, faster rather than slower, wider and deeper than a vein slit by a razor blade, but water, now, here now finally here, there to touch, the bird of rain is tangible, that music she sinks her fingers into and splashes her face, the call to a new life, baptism, now yes here, now finally her hands rubbing her face, washing off the gelatinous clumps in her hair, finally splashing her neck, furiously opening up her coat, tearing off a button, and with her two hands washing her breasts, furiously rubbing them, sinking her nipples into the water, rubbing them with that friendly water and washing and cleansing and wetting and expanding and pressing and rinsing and transforming that water of pity into a downpour, and she pours the water over her body, cupping her hands, and now she stops for a moment because she hears next to her the voice of Ángel Santiago, who is saying to her, "Stop, Victoria, for God's sake, stop already, Victoria Ponce, stop," but she can't hear him anymore because she has entered the fountain.

"WARDEN?"

"Yes, sir."

"It's me."

Santoro put the phone down, walked over to the door, peered up and down the long hallway, and, not seeing any guards in the immediate vicinity, went back to his desk and unplugged the answering machine.

"Is it done?"

"Not yet, chief."

"You've had fifteen days, you sonofabitch!"

"You gave me a month."

"I never should have done it. I can't sleep, and when I finally manage to doze off, I have nightmares."

"I'm sorry, Warden, but it's hard for me to work when I don't exist. I don't know if you catch my drift."

"What do you mean?"

"Santiago is a big city, and if I can't contact my people, how am I going to find the pawn?"

"I gave you the other's home address."

"He doesn't live there, chief. They don't want to know nothing about him. The wife, though, she's ready for eating, bones and all."

"Get a grip on yourself, you animal. One single violation, and I will personally kill you."

"Calm down, I've got plenty of places to wave my wand."

"And what if they recognize you?"

"When I get the urge, I don't go where I've been before."

"That's how it should be. If anyone recognizes you, I'll be flogged, fired, and thrown in prison, maybe even in this prison. Can you imagine the number of assholes who'd like to get hold of me and slice off my wiener?"

"In your jail, I know at least two."

"Who?"

"You-know-who and another."

"Who's the other?"

"As long as you've got him inside, you've got nothing to fear, Warden."

"Tell me."

"The little job you gave me doesn't include ratting."

"Okay, fine. Why did you call me?"

"The information you gave me last time we talked is correct. The pawn is planning something with Vergara Gray."

"Go on."

"They've been seen together on Las Tabernas Street."

"You can't go there. Even the lampposts will recognize you. That's why I told you to find him through his family."

"The son just doesn't give. He's duller than a slow dance with your sister. And his mother doesn't trust me; she keeps her legs tightly crossed."

"So why did you call?"

"Because I got a bright idea, Warden, really bright. If the pawn is planning something with Vergara Gray, it must be the size of the *Titanic*."

"Nico doesn't get mixed up with small-fry."

"And if we, with a little help from Lady Luck, manage to put two and two together, wouldn't it be better to hop on the victory cart than kill the horse?"

"Explain yourself."

"The old guy is tops, and he can whistle a tango like nobody else, but you-know-who has got to be the guy with the plan and the balls to carry it out."

"Agreed, because the plan and the balls to kill me, he's definitely got."

"But he's got no money. And he knows that Vergara Gray does."

"Your reasoning is perfect. But you forgot one thing, you unrecognized genius: the old guy hung up his gloves."

"There isn't a single champ who's made that announcement and won't go back into the ring for a cool couple million. Like Muhammad Ali. What does he care if they punch the daylights out of him, as long as he gets the dough?"

"What are you suggesting?"

"That you find out from Warden Huerta what plan Superman came out of his jail with."

"I should talk to Huerta? That bastard is a socialist!"

"Even if he were a Muslim! Listen, Warden, you're better off than me because you're on the right side of the law. But if you'll allow me to speak frankly, neither of us lives in the lap of luxury. If we get hooked up with whatever the old guy is planning, we can take our cut, and with the money, you can get your teeth fixed and send your daughters to a private school."

"I sure would like to get them away from that crowd they're hanging out with."

ANTONIO SKÁRMETA

"You see, Mr. Santoro, sir, talk to Huerta and squeeze something out of him."

Santoro decided it was time to put an end to this little chat. It
was more than likely that Rigoberto Marín was trying to get him
interested in this fantasy so he could squeeze a few extra days out
of his free ride and spare himself the danger of killing the Cherub.
That pampered little horse thief could never partner with Vergara
Gray, with his skill and intelligence; he might be his assistant, but
he could never be his accomplice.

"Warden?"

"I was thinking. Just take care of you-know-who as quickly as
possible and get back home."

"You're asking me to kill the goose that lays the golden eggs."

"At this moment, I'm more interested in saving my own very real
life than getting some very hypothetical money."

"But Vergara Gray is in on it!"

"If everybody knows, then the cops must be following every step
they take."

"Call Huerta, Mr. Santoro. Listen to me."

"I might. But first, take care of the pawn for me."

"How much time have I got?"

"A little over two more weeks."

"You're going to regret it, Warden."

"Don't believe it; when all the dogs want the same bone, they end
up gnawing on each others' teeth."

"Funny you should mention it, sir. I live surrounded by dogs."

"Don't let their fleas get into your rags."

"Hey, watch what you're saying. I'm wearing a brand-new suit!"

"Where did you get the money?"

"Women always lend me a hand."

"You must be well endowed, man."

"Nature works in strange ways. Gives a little here, takes away a little there."

"Well, you can say good-bye to what it's given you if you-know-who is still alive in fifteen days."

Santoro hung up the phone and walked over to the heater, rubbing his hands together in front of the hot grate. When his fingers had thawed out, he leafed through his address book, then dialed the phone. Huerta himself picked up on the other end.

"This is Santoro, your fellow warden."

"How could I ever forget you?"

"So kind of you to say so."

"I didn't mean it as a compliment. After the coup, I was your prisoner for six months."

"Come on, let bygones be bygones, for God's sake. I was twenty-five years old back then."

"You were a sergeant, and you collaborated with the new authorities."

"Just like almost everybody else. You know Chile was in chaos; we needed a firm hand."

"Funny, that's exactly what you gave me. How did you ever manage to become a warden once we returned to democracy?"

"The civil service is exempt from political considerations."

"I didn't know that torture was a political consideration."

"Don't make such a big deal about it, Huerta. They were just a few light punches."

"I still don't hear well out of my left ear and sometimes I lose my balance. In my case it was one brutal punch to the side of my head."

"That wasn't me, and you know it."

"Not you personally."

"But that's what the armed forces are saying. That there's personal not institutional responsibility."

"Yes, yes, I've been hearing that for the past twenty years. Why are you calling me?"

"I'd like for us to work together, colleague."

"You and I?"

"Why not? We all want there to be peace and order in Chile, don't we?"

"Yeah, but some use laws and others use guns."

"Neither of us is the same as we were back then. Nowadays, I wouldn't touch a prisoner with a rose petal."

"You've become very poetic, Santoro. What are you getting at?"

"You released Vergara Gray a few weeks ago, right?"

"Yes, he received a pardon."

"Exactly. So tell me, colleague, what's he up to?"

"He's retired."

"But he's only sixty."

"He might well be, but he doesn't want to play anymore."

"What's he living on? Everyone knows his partner cheated him out of his share of the loot."

"He's borrowing from friends."

"For now. But what will he do later?"

"Get to the point, Santoro."

"There are rumors that the old guy is involved in something big."

"So?"

"It would be a good idea if we talked him out of it. As public servants we owe it to our country. People won't look kindly on the fact that under a democratic government, pardoned criminals relapse with a nod from the authorities."

"Vergara Gray will not commit any more crimes."

"Oh, really? Would you bet on that?"

"Go ask him yourself. And then you can blackmail him, all on your own."

"What are you talking about, Huerta?"

"You're just looking for a cut."

"You deeply offend me."

"You are more than welcome to hang up the phone."

"You first."

"No, sir. I am a gentleman and you were the one who called me."

"Remember, I suggested we work together and you refused. If Vergara Gray is doing something and the press is after him, they're going to go to you to find out about it."

"I don't see why or how."

"Your phone might be bugged."

Huerta rubbed his cold fingers over his weary eyelids. "Do whatever you want, Santoro."

"I wouldn't do anything to hurt you, but I sure as hell would like to see you a bit more cooperative the next time I call you."

"Have you got something to tell me?"

"Like what?"

"Some secret?"

"For instance?"

"Nothing. I was just asking."

T HE DIAGNOSIS OF the patient, Victoria Ponce, left
much to be desired: she had a streptococcus infection
in her throat, a systemic viral infection, an average fever
of 104.4 degrees Fahrenheit, and on top of that she was suffering from severe depression. The young doctor on duty, Gabriel
Ortega, concluded that he had done all he could and that she
needed much more attention than he could possibly give her under
the circumstances.

In very simple but no uncertain terms, he made it clear to the
girl's *uncle*, Don Nico, and to her *older brother*, Ángel Santiago, that
he had already injected the nymph of the Alemana Fountain with a
gallon of antibiotics, an arsenal of acetaminophen, and that there
was no single spot on her aquatic body—he said jokingly—where
they hadn't applied a compress. The patient was underweight, but
she had good muscle tone and superb reflexes. With a little song and
dance, they might even get a smile out of her, and in about three
days she'd be swimming in the pool at the National Stadium. He
strongly recommended that the girl's relatives make a huge effort
to heal her spirit. "Any doctor can give her pills and injections to

deal with the bacteria, but the blues this girl is singing are, to put it mildly, dismal, even morbid. It appears that Ms. Ponce holds to the philosophical concept, espoused by existentialists and Argentinean musicians, that life is not worth living. I don't know your relative's story, dear sirs, but it seems she has, so to speak, thrown in the towel. In other words, and as sad as it may sound, she's lost the will to live.

"The other issue, of course, is one of resources. Ms. Ponce's illness is most likely the result of having dived into the Alemana Fountain fully dressed, coat included, and having remained there until the ambulance came to rescue her. As a result, she is occupying a room that could be used by that child out there who was run over by a drunk driver; the guy with his eyes dug out of their sockets in a street fight; a domestic servant, victim of her young master's lust, after a self-induced abortion; a case of advanced appendicitis that requires immediate surgery; a fit of insanity that requires strait-jackets and encephalograms. Shall I go on?

"Bottom line, Victoria Ponce's affliction is child's play compared to what awaits me out there. And to make matters even worse, I had plans to watch Real Madrid play Juventus on cable tonight, but I'm on duty here until dawn, if I can keep awake, that is. I've already had seven cups of coffee, one every half hour.

"So, what can we do with the girl? Does she have medical insur-ance? Any kind of health plan? Could you put her in a private clinic for a few days? When they admit your niece, Don Nico, you give them a blank check and pay when she's released. You say you don't have any checks? So, take her home. I'll show you how to give her the injections. I'll give you cotton, alcohol, needles, everything you need, but take her out of here, please, sir, there are patients dying in the hallway. She's a very nice girl with the sensitivity and beauty of a true artist, but she needs too much attention. You've got to surround her with positive energy. The two of you have to rip this depression out by the roots. If she continues with this sadness, she's going to let the fever devour her. She must drink lots of liquids, but inside her body, not on the outside! No fountains, rivers, not even oceans!

"Take her home. Doesn't this girl have a mother? She has a mother? Then take her to her. She should take care of her, raise her spirits. Or take her to your house, young man! What? You don't have a home? Neither of you? That's difficult to believe. Everybody has a home. People like you are very unusual. Oh, so you're from Talca. So, take a taxi and put her on the train to Talca. That will be great: nature, birds, mountains, weeping willows, ducks, cows, chickens, anything would be better than this hellhole. Do you understand? Do you both understand? Okay, then let's get her out of this room and then she'll just have to wait her turn while I sew up somebody's forehead, give that guy who ate rotten meat out of a dumpster an enema. . . . Everybody wants a piece of Dr. Gabriel Ortega."

The two men carried Victoria's cot out into the hallway and got in line behind a drunk old man with blood pouring out of his wrist listening to old tango songs on Radio Carrera—"Nothing remains in your native town the same." There were two signs on the wall: one forbidding smoking and the other asking people not to smoke. Vergara Gray wanted to find a telephone to call Teresa Capriatti. The day had taken an unexpected turn. He wasn't sure how or why he had fallen into the quicksand of other people's dramas, when he had, after all, several of his very own.

"What are we going to do, maestro?"

"We've got to find the girl a place to sleep. What about her mother's place?"

"Her old lady is deeply depressed."

"The cure will be worse than the disease."

"And your wife's apartment?"

"I'm not even allowed to show my face around there, how do you think they're going to feel about taking in some half-drowned waif I fished out of a fountain?"

THEY WALKED TO the corner of the Alameda and Portugal and ordered two beers. Ángel Santiago watched many people come and go through the bar, eat sandwiches, drink a soda, talk with friends, then go back out into the street and down the stairs to the Catholic University subway station, where they'd then transfer to buses that would take them home. Some of them probably lived in little more than shacks made of tin and mud, with leaky gas pipes and the stench of paraffin, surrounded by piles of garbage and illegal goings-on, but when all was said and done, it was something they could call home. Come to my home, they would say to a friend, even if the walls were eaten away by termites and stained with squashed cockroaches.

Vergara Gray picked a piece of tobacco out of his mustache.

"I've already taken money from Monasterio's lover and Warden Huerta. Teresa is about to have her gas cut off, and winter is only just beginning. I can't think of anybody else. What about you?"

"I got some cash out of an ATM machine after a lady forgot her card, and I borrowed two thousand from the guy who takes care of cars on Las Tabernas Street."

"What did you do with the money from the ATM?"

"It was near the racetrack. I bought a horse."

"Sell it."

"I'd rather die."

"Are you crazy?"

"I always pictured myself galloping across my own land on a

horse. The minute I got out of jail, I decided I was going to make my dreams come true. So I started with the most practical thing."

"The horse."

"I got it for a song. It can do better than one-fifteen on the twelve hundred. He's no good for the races, but on my little ranch he'll do just fine."

"Where is this champion?"

"Around."

"Around! Same as you, same as your little dove. Around!"

"Well, it's your fault, Professor. If you had signed on to the coup, we'd be happy, and the joke would be on all the people who've stood in our way."

"Even this misery, kid, is better than jail."

"No, it's not better, maestro. The bad thing about this is that it's *real*, with a capital *R*. Jail's still just a possibility."

"A very real possibility!"

"Yeah, but *remote* with a small *r*. You yourself said that little Lira's plan was genius."

"Hold your horses. I meant in the Chilean context."

"Anywhere in the world, maestro. Why diminish Dwarf Lira's stature even further? Just imagine an elevator that leads right into a safe. Between the two lies a doorway covered with a metal sheet that can be removed with a pocketknife. Then you turn the knobs, cut the electronic alarm, and we fill the elevator with dollar bills."

The man drank another half a glass of beer and savored for a moment the refreshing bitterness on his tongue.

"Everyone would suspect me."

"But the genius of it is that besides Canteros and his mafia, nobody will even find out that such a robbery took place."

"What do you mean?"

"It's as clear as water."

"Don't mention that abominable word. Just talking about water gives me the hiccups."

"The money Canteros keeps in that safe is what he collects from his so-called security services, the bribes businesses pay him for having defended their interests during the dictatorship. That money doesn't officially exist, he doesn't pay taxes on it, and nobody gets a receipt for having paid it. That money isn't really there. That's why, when it disappears from his coffers, he won't have anywhere to go to complain. Canteros is a fox every dog in Chile would like to dig his teeth into."

"You're right. Lira's plan is shrewd even down to that detail."

"I'm very glad you are beginning to see the light."

"I saw the light a while ago. But since you only think about yourself, you haven't realized that once you've carried out the operation, you can just vanish into a most delightful fog of anonymity. Nobody is going to think some donkey thief was the brains behind a coup of this magnitude. And where does that leave me, son?"

"You sure are thick in the upper story. I just showed you why the police will never get involved."

"The police, no. But Canteros and his goons, yes! Who are they first going to think of when they find their safe empty?"

A shadow stole over the boy's previously enthusiastic face. He took a sip of beer straight from the bottle and wiped the foam off his lips with a brusque sweep of the hand.

"You, Professor. I surrender in the face of the evidence."

"In the supposed case that we would be totally successful, you could buy yourself a nice little piece of land in the Amazon jungle and off you go, good-bye and good luck; but before slitting my throat, Canteros's goons would crush my very own, very macho balls."

"What if you came with us?"

"Who's *us*?"

"With me and Victoria?"

"Don't tell me you're going to carry that dear demented girl around with you your whole life."

"We're together, maestro!"

When he dug his hand into his pocket and brought his money out onto the table, Vergara Gray realized that the expenses he had hereby incurred rendered him incapable of paying the whole check. With a gesture that was already getting familiar to Santiago, the man pressed the bridge of his nose and made a sound between a sigh and a snort.

"I don't have enough to pay," he said. "All I've got left are the thirty thousand pesos I promised Victoria for her ballet classes. But spending that would be like giving her the coup de grâce."

The boy wanted, with his entire being, for his voice to sound confident and indifferent, but before the words came out of his mouth, they went gurgling down his throat.

"Don't worry, maestro," he mumbled. "In the ambulance, Victoria gave me the money she made in the theater."

And he placed on the table three blue bills that added up to thirty thousand pesos.

TEMPERATURE AT 104.3, 104.5, 104.7, change the compress, bring over more ice, something stronger than acetaminophen, 104.9, 105, I can't understand what she's saying, the doctor's got to come back, he's got to see her again, just touch her, can't you see she's burning up, she's on fire, can't you see, it's going up, over 105, no, the doctor's gotta come, I don't care if he *is* operating, bring him here now, I can't, Don Nico, you're just going to have to somehow, what do you want me to do? I'm only a nurse, I don't have the authority, I don't know what to do anymore, they're calling me from everywhere, I'm on my way, just a second, I've been changing her compresses for half an hour, look, and I take them off her hot, like an iron, bags of ice are better, bring that bag of ice over here, but there isn't any more ice, so just put some cold water in a hot water bottle, that's right, you see? and the thermometer in her mouth, poor dear, look at her lips, you see that whitish layer on them, poor thing, so weak, again it's up to almost 105, you see, now 104.3, put that pill in her mouth, force her to drink, a little orange juice, my dear, you're going to be just fine, and if we can get it down to 104, we'll save her, otherwise she could get encephalitis, you know what that is? It's an inflammation of the brain, God forbid that should happen to her, but look, Don Nico, what is she saying, I can't understand what she's saying, as if she were speaking a different language, poor dear, 104.1, hurry up with that cold water bottle, hold her hand, young man, so she'll know she's not alone, who are you to her? Her boyfriend, friend, brother? Look at the poor dear girl, how she moves her little hands, calm down, my dear, ssshhh.

LET'S GO, A one, and a two, and a three, and a four, and *grand rond de jambe en l'air*, good, like that, yes, excellent, chin up, my little one, and two, and three, very good, and now, *et alors*, let's do an *arabesque croisée*, head up, leaning your body toward the audience, very good, yes, yes, *très bien*, and now the pirouette *en dehors*, raise the arms to the chest, yes, yes, and turn, *très bien, et maintenant le pas de chat*, keep your body straight, lean forward now, from the hip, drop your shoulders, stomach in, lift your diaphragm and move slowly into a *demi-plié, très bien*, now into a *jeté en tournant*, turn in the air and extend both arms, more energy in the left leg to give you the impetus to turn, yes, very good, but stretch both legs as far as you can, from the hips to the toes, now I want you to prepare for the *grand jeté*, up, *très bien*, now watch how you land, on your right foot and tighten your glutes so you can land gently, that's right, on the left foot *demi-plié*, on your toes before your heels, okay, and a one, and a two, and a three, and a four, with the *emboîté en tournant*, half turns from one foot to the other, switching your legs in the air and moving to the right, very good, excellent, now for the *sauté*, a little jump on two feet, stomach in, body forward, into the *demi-plié*, good, enough practice, you are now warmed up and you can do some free dancing, the lighter you feel your body, the more ready you will be for your character, whichever you want, Coppelia, or if you like, Giselle, pull the petals off the daisy and Albrecht-Loys will come to make love to you and comfort you, or if you like, *Spectre of the Rose*, it might inspire your dance of Mistral, dance, Victoria, until you fall apart like the rose, like its ghost, dance its aroma, dance, let's go, *pas emboîté*, very good, *très bien, très près de la morte*, quite close to death.

DR. ORTEGA FINALLY agreed to put her in a room and immediately gave her oxygen. He was joined by another doctor with gray hair, small and robust, who took her pulse and listened to her heart through a stethoscope. They consulted near the head of the bed, then Dr. Ortega herded Vergara Gray and Ángel Santiago over to the darkest corner of the room.

"The poor old woman who was here died. I had her taken to the morgue so that Miss Ponce could have her room."

As soon as he could find his voice, Vergara Gray spoke in humble tones. "She's very bad, isn't she, Doctor?"

"Hovering between life and death, sir."

"Is there any hope?"

"In a case like this, there's a little more hope for somebody under twenty than over eighty, for sure."

"Will she recover?"

"Her condition has worsened; strep is a very aggressive bacteria, but if the antibiotics kick in, we'll get her to the other side."

"The other side!" Ángel went pale.

"The good side, son. The other side in this case means this side, life."

The young man looked at his hands, made two fists, then opened and closed them several times.

"Forgive us for dragging you out of the operating room, Doctor.

But I was holding on to Victoria's hand and she told me to let go of her, to stop talking to her, that she had some work to do in death. It scared me."

"You did the right thing. Delirium can lead to coma."

"What exactly does that mean?"

"It's like a sleep you don't wake up from, and it's often the final stage of an illness."

"She begged me not to hold her back. She said something about a dance of shadows."

"What time is it?"

Vergara Gray lifted the edge of the sleeve of his tweed jacket and looked at his large silver watch. "It's eight o'clock."

"Sorry for asking, but this emergency room is like a hell without limits. Is it eight at night or eight in the morning?"

Vergara Gray smiled, pulled out a pack of cigarettes, and offered him one. "Eight at night."

"Do you know who won, Real Madrid or Juventus?"

Both Don Nico and the boy shook their heads. The doctor went out into the hallway with the cigarette between his lips to ask somebody else the same question. Ángel Santiago kept staring at Vergara Gray's face, until the latter realized it and looked back at him inquisitively.

"What?"

"Nice watch, Professor. If we had sold that before noon, we could have avoided this whole thing."

ALBERTO PARRA CHACÓN, otherwise known as Rigoberto Marín, told the widow to get him an old suitcase, preferably a faded brown one with straps, and a straw basket to carry some Chilean sweets, a few hard-boiled eggs, two or three rolls, and a couple of pears.

At the precise moment night made its final retreat and the first light appeared in the sky, the couple got out of a taxi on Las Tabernas Street and rang the bell of Monasterio's seedy hotel. The time of day had been carefully chosen: at that early hour, the carabineros who had been on duty all night had returned to their barracks, convinced that everybody was too drunk to shoot straight even if there was a brawl. Those on the next shift were still carefully shaving in front of the mirror at their station before going on morning duty, and it would take them a few minutes to drink their coffee and get into their patrol cars.

Wrapped in a rose-colored shawl, Elsa was sitting at the reception desk in the lobby and working a crossword puzzle when she saw the couple through the window. She pressed the button to let them in. They were shivering from the cold, and Marín ostentatiously placed the handmade basket on the counter, a sign—one they had meticulously planned—that meant they had just arrived from the countryside.

"We'd like a room with heat," the widow said, shivering.

"By the hour or for the night?"

"For the whole day." Rigoberto Marín smiled. "I've got some promises to keep to the lady here."

"I see," the receptionist said. "Did you arrive by train?"

"It was five hours late."

"Just visiting Santiago?"

"Visiting your hotel, ma'am. Out there, in the village, everyone pokes around in everybody else's business and my love here that you see before you is a respectable married woman."

"I didn't ask for that information. If I needed to see marriage licenses, I'd be out of business, and my boss would be in the metro begging with a tin can."

"My love and I are grateful for your discretion. We bought some Chilean sweets when we passed through La Ligua. Would you like one?"

"I'd love one. I especially like the ones with powdered sugar."

"I like the ones they call *princes*," the widow said. "They're softer and they've got more caramel inside."

While she chewed, Elsa reached around into the cubbyhole for the key to room number eleven. Marín looked at his accomplice and arched his eyebrows in that direction so she would see that in the cubby next to it, attached with a piece of Scotch tape, was a note that said "Nico." The widow nodded, and the criminal patted his pocket to make sure his silencer-fitted Browning was still there.

"Would you like your breakfast brought up at any particular time?"

"We don't want to waste our time on that."

"The only thing I ask of you is that you not make a huge racket.

The other day we had a woman here who shouted out her orgasm like an opera singer, and even though it's hard to believe, we've got a couple of respectable people staying here."

Rigoberto Marín pointed to the cubbyholes, specifically to the one he had noticed.

"Like Mr. Nico?"

The cashier turned around, surprised by the question, until she remembered that she herself had placed the note there as a sign of affection; she turned to the couple, smiling.

"Exactly. Though your neighbor wasn't here last night."

"Where is he?"

"How should I know? He is a man of few words. Sorry, but we always ask for payment in advance."

"How low is the price?"

"Forty thousand for the night."

"But we're using it during the day. Look at that gentle sun shining on the cordillera."

"Seems like a summer day," the widow mused. "Yesterday's rain must have washed away the smog."

"Anyway, it's forty thousand."

"Here. And thank you."

"Thank you for the sweets."

"Don't mention it. Do you like hard-boiled eggs?"

"Love them. Don't tell me you have one!"

The widow pulled an egg out of the basket along with a little saltshaker she handed to her. "You'll have to peel it."

"That's okay. It'll keep me busy. I've worked the night shift for so many years I know all the crossword puzzle tricks. It's always the same things. The clue is *thirty days*, and the answer is *month*. *Egyptian deity*, two letters, and you put *Ra*. Or they give you H_2O and you write *water*."

"It has been a real pleasure to meet you . . ."

"My name is Elsa."

"Alberto Parra Chacón, at your service."

"Like a combination of Violeta Parra and Arturo Prat Chacón?"

"Yes, but I don't even reach the knees of those geniuses."

"What kind of work do you do?"

Rigoberto Marín ran his index finger along the scar that dug a swath from his upper lip to his left temple, and, throwing sparks out of his eyes like a naughty child, he turned to the widow and stared at her, then finally said, "Love."

THE LOVERS UNCORKED a bottle of red wine and filled two plastic cups they found in the bathroom. Marín peeled an egg and sprinkled a lot of salt on it; the widow took a bite out of a pear and a few drops of its juice fell on her black blouse. The top button was open, revealing the tantalizing edges of a well-filled brassiere.

The man took off his jacket and hung it up, but not before taking out the gun and the knife and laying them on the bed.

"I am truly grateful for your company. I wouldn't have dared go alone into the fox's lair."

"It's quite all right, my love. You know that when you go back to prison I won't see you again. Right?"

"After this, there is no more."

He undid the belts around the ratty suitcase made of cardboard that looked like leather. From inside a dirty, crumpled-up shirt, he took out a handful of bullets, then sat down on the edge of the bed to load the pistol.

"Are you going to kill him here?"

"The less I'm seen, the better."

"And if he doesn't come?"

"I'll wait. You can go if you like."

"I'm staying with you, Marín, but I don't want to be in the hotel when you kill him."

"I understand perfectly."

The man finished his task, put the safety latch on the gun, and pointed at a moth flying around the lightbulb.

"Are you gonna do the old guy and the young one?" the woman asked.

"Naw, just the young one. But since this is the hotel where Vergara Gray is staying, there'll be a lot of press afterward."

"So?"

"That's good for me. That way Santoro will find out in the best possible way that I obeyed him and did away with his nightmare."

The woman sauntered over to the bed.

"Doesn't it kind of bother you, Marín, to kill a guy who hasn't done anything to you?"

"That's the way it is when you do these things on assignment, widow. If you start getting sentimental, you're fucked."

The woman felt the heat rise from her thighs to her forehead. Lying down on the bed, she spread her legs and moved aside the triangle of cloth that covered her crotch. His hands and her vagina were equally hot. Without even bothering to take off her panties, she pulled away the hairs that covered her clitoris and, exposing it in all its majesty, gave the murderer his instructions: "Eat me like only you know how, you dog."

LL NIGHT AT the public hospital the pendulum swung
back and forth.

One heartbeat brought Victoria back toward life, the
next pulled her away. Each breath seemed an enormous effort. Her
body trembled with delirium, and all the encouraging words Vergara Gray and the young Santiago whispered in her ear did not
seem to bring her solace. Her rapid and irregular heart rate led
the men to despair and brought Dr. Ortega back again and again
to her side. Thus they made their way until dawn. The last medical pronouncements—according to Ortega—were that "the match
is under way" that "the opposition is giving its all" and that "the
results are uncertain."

It was precisely this uncertainty that unhinged Santiago: he knew
that if he remained in that room one minute longer he would collapse. He lifted the curtain, caught a glimpse of the street, and saw that
the sun was shining off the cordillera: a flame unchecked by clouds
sketched the promise of spring over the city's smogless sky.

"What do you think, Professor?"

"You heard the doctor. The match is tied."

"You should go home and get some sleep."

"Don't worry about me. Emergencies like this get my adrenaline pumping."

"Did you see what a glorious day is dawning?"

"Yes, why?"

"Nobody can die on a day like this, don't you think, Don Nico?"

"It would be an absurdity."

"If Victoria dies——"

"Don't think about it. Don't say it. Take that thought out of your head."

The young man took out of his backpack the scarf Santoro had given him. It seemed to have become even more threadbare in the intervening days. The strong fluorescent lights in that white room revealed a few bits of the garment's biography that the boy had not previously noticed: a small hole—perhaps the result of a fallen cigarette ash—a stain of red wine, a few specks of yellow on the edges, and a little tag that read CONFECCIONES AREQUIPA.

"I want to ask you one more favor, maestro."

"The coup again? No!"

"Perhaps the last favor I will ask you in my life."

"What's gotten into everybody lately that you all talk in tangos?"

Ángel Santiago raised his hand to vertical and made the man read what he had written on his palm. "This is the number of the phone in the hallway. I'm going out for a few hours and at precisely eight o'clock, I will call you."

As he said this, he looked at the crucifix hanging over the head of the bed and rubbed his hands on the scarf.

"What are you going to do at this time of day, son? The city is empty!"

Ángel Santiago pointed his chin at the suffering, emaciated Christ whose joints had weakened so much that his head fell on his chest in defeat. "First, I want to give this gentleman here time to work on Victoria. Second, I'm going to do something I don't want to talk about."

"A job?"

"Better for me to keep quiet, Professor. In two hours the telephone will ring. I will ask if Victoria is dead or alive."

"What will you do if the worst has happened?"

"You yourself prohibited me from considering that possibility."

"I want to know before I let you go."

"Okay, I'll tell you. I'll go on a rampage, maestro."

"What will you do?"

"Somebody has to pay for this!"

"I see. But who?"

"I've got a few ideas."

Vergara Gray grabbed him by his leather jacket, pulled him close, and shook him like a rag doll. "Listen, you foolish boy. Nobody is guilty of anybody else's life or death. It's destiny. Do what you will, you can't change it."

Unexpectedly, a shining smile played on the boy's lips for the first time that day. "So who's singing tangos now?"

He watched Vergara Gray's stunned expression, then left the room without realizing that he was dragging the scarf behind him. The man appeared in the hallway and heaved a deep sigh to steady himself. "Ángel Santiago?"

"Professor?"

"If you are alive at eight o'clock in the morning, would you be so kind as to pass by the hotel and bring me a clean shirt and my toothbrush? I feel like a pig wallowing in shit."

"With great pleasure, maestro."

At that moment, the boy hesitated, patted his pockets, then screwed up his face.

"I know it's rude, maestro, but do you think you could lend me a hundred pesos for the phone call?"

Vergara Gray handed him the coin and clenched his teeth in a relentless stare. "You are aware of how much you're putting on the line?"

"There's life or there's death, maestro. There's nothing in between."

"Don't be an idiot. In between is the magnificent and multicolored spectacle of existence."

The young man only pointed his finger at the bed where Victoria Ponce lay in a feverish swoon.

GO FOR IT, my chestnut horse, hoof and fire, go for it, shoe and sand, thrust and mud, onward, steed and mount, quadruped of the skies and of kisses, jade of the heavens, stud and sentry, canter, gallop, and carry me away, scatter the sand, swallow up the earth, kick up the mud, my hack of the melancholy hooves, lower your tail and lift off like a comet, with raised mane and vibrating hoof, gallop and run, run, the old woman with the scythe is chasing you, she's nipping at your heels with her toothless gums, run, she's sucking at your strap, pulling on your saddle, the ravenous old bitch wants to grab you by the hair and gallop off with you, crop and whip, horse of my soul, protect yourself from the spider's web and the broomstick, look how many the black monster has done away with, laughing with its crossed eye, run, my hack, she wants to drown you in sorrow, smash you to bits against a drunken sacristan, the old biddy, harder, my stiff-mouthed, my fresh-mouthed horse, and I'll free you from this muzzle when we can finally shout that she is alive, so make her a corona of air with your legs, cool her off with a hurtle of clouds, douse her fever in the snows of the cordillera, God, my chestnut, don't fail me, my mule, my hag, don't get stubborn or dig in your heels, don't buck or bolt, because the fleas of a thousand dogs are scratching at your hindquarters, there are the mastiffs, the howls of the skeletons that crunch when you crush them, my panting, gaping mouth, my gaping jaws, my prince, my prayer in brown, wingèd and trained by the angels, may your spine not snap, may your blood not boil over, careful of the scythe that reaps and rips, swat with your tail the wasps that cleave onto the sweat on your back, take me away from here, my mount, take me to the town where I was born, death in an ox-drawn cart awaits you around this bend of stormy clouds pouring down from the mountains, jump over it as if you were leaping over a fence, jeer at it, subject her to derision, if you run, Victoria breathes, if you spread your wings, my Pegasus, the stars will light her up, give me back the only thing I have, don't splay your legs or snort, neigh for freedom, make your silver shoes shimmer between the pebbles, dig up the dirt as if you were digging for gold, run, she's about to catch you, the travesty that is death is catching up to you, with her viscous bladder, her flaccid teats full of black milk, run, run away from her, run through the mountains, through the sand, through the swamp, through the ravine, give it all you've got, you colt of fiber and nerves, put your whole heart into it and redouble your efforts, flanks tense, ears alert, the triumphant breast of an athlete, don't lose your breath, die and be reborn with each stride, one after another, run for her, take her to a world without reins, inhale, exhale, don't stop, you bastard, no, don't fall into nothingness, chestnut of my dreams, don't let me hear your death rattle, beast, don't rear up, I command you and beg you, I, your master without rights or sovereignty, careful, we're reaching that swarm of ghosts, the bats are sucking your blood, death is rushing violently in, now it brings you gray-cloaked paladins in mourning as the goblins and their Cerberus gnaw at your hooves, your blanket is transformed into a pall, the blast of the hunters' trumpets, now you are on the threshold of tears, Victoria Ponce, so bloodless, so lifeless, so motionless, now those shrouded fools have been thrown out of the theater, those shrouded ass-lickers, those phantoms on hooks dripping saliva, don't wait, don't stop, chestnut horse, breathe deeply, my queen, fill your bones with grace, holy Mary, pray for her, my horse, win the race, no matter how long it takes you, just win.

O N THE SAND track at the Hippodrome, one of the jockeys saw Ángel Santiago's chestnut horse sweep past his horse's left flank, its rider barely hanging on to the reins. He seemed as exhausted as his horse, and the jockey thought it was strange that someone would ride on this professional track without the least regard for the minimum safety requirements. He had no helmet, no regulation saddle, no whip, and no compassion for a beast that had galloped at full speed more than five times the distance of the Grand Prix. When the horse finally came to a stop, he considered calling its rider a criminal or an assassin, but all insults remained on his tongue when he saw the strange look in the boy's eyes, as if he had recently ingested some unknown cocktail of intoxicants.

"Hey, man, you can't do that to a horse. Do you want its blood vessels to explode?"

They were now trotting side by side, and Santiago wished he had a hat with a brim to shield his eyes from the bright light of the sun.

"It would take too long to explain it all to you, my friend."

"I understand, but this track is for professionals. We're doing timed runs, and you could have caused an accident."

"I'm leaving. I just wanted to return the horse to its trainer."

"Who is it?"

"No idea. Do you know this horse's name?"

The man ran his hand along a white patch that ran up the horse's nose, then leaned over a little to examine a bump on its right rear leg.

"This is Milton. He was stolen. Where did you find him?"

"Grazing over there, near the airport."

"Charly de la Mirándola is going to be very happy to see him."

"Who's that?"

"His trainer."

"Where can I find him?"

"Go down this path and continue straight until you come to Vivaceta."

When Charly saw Milton enter his stables, ridden by a young man, he rubbed his eyes, wondering if someone was playing a trick on him. He dropped the bucket and brush he was using to groom the mane of a dapple-gray horse and walked over with a doubting smile on his face.

"They told me this horse belongs to you, Don Charly."

"Right they are. Someone stole him from me a few weeks ago."

"I found him grazing out there, near Renca, and seeing him all alone like that, I took him, thinking I'd try to find his owner."

"I'm his trainer, young man. And this stall here is where he slept."

Ángel Santiago dismounted, and the animal, out of habit, entered the stall and began to munch on some hay on the ground.

"I guess I have to believe you," said Ángel. "This animal obviously knows his way around this place."

"He's no great shakes, but he never gets sick and he earns his keep by placing every once in a while. One time, about three years ago, he won and paid out more than a hundred to one. The headlines read: 'Upset Victory in the National Hippodrome.' Milton is living proof that in the land of the one-eyed men, the blind man is king."

"Well, Don Charly, you've got your king back."

"He seems a ghost of what he was."

"I made him work very hard this morning. I don't know yet if it paid off."

"What do you mean?"

"What time is it Mr. de la Mirándola?"

"Five to eight."

"Can I borrow a telephone?"

"I've got my cell."

"Would you mind?"

The trainer undid the case and turned on the phone. The young man read the number written on his palm and punched it in, but before pressing the *talk* button, he leaned against one of the posts in the corral to steady himself.

Every ring, as if begging to be answered, felt like the referee's grim countdown over a fallen boxer. Five, seven, even nine times it sounded before someone picked up.

"Professor?"

"Speaking, man."

"Nobody answered."

"So?"

"Got me thinking . . ."

"You said you'd call at eight. It's still a few minutes to."

Ángel Santiago took a moment to swallow the saliva that prevented him from speaking. "Is she alive?"

There was silence on the other end of the line, and the young man clutched the pole, hugging it between his arms. *Don't play with me, maestro. Not now, please,* he wanted to say, but before he could get the words out, he heard a woman's voice through the earpiece.

"Ángel? It's me, La Victoria."

The boy ran to the door of the stables and stared at the sun. "How are you?" he whispered.

"Good."

"How good?"

"Good. I'm eating some breakfast the professor brought me."

"What did you say?"

"I'm eating breakfast."

The boy walked over to Don Charly, holding the telephone in his hands as if it were some priceless jewel. "She says she's good, Don Charly. She says she's eating breakfast."

"Who?"

"You don't know her. And I don't know what to say to her now."

"Ask her what she's eating for breakfast."

"Like what?"

"Like is she drinking coffee with milk, or is it tea, or something else."

The young man took long strides over the hay as slowly as each step was long. "What are you having for breakfast, Victoria?"

"Tea, yogurt, toast with jam, and soft-boiled eggs."

"Soft-boiled eggs?"

"Soft-boiled eggs."

"Wait a minute. Don't hang up."

He walked over to de la Mirándola's side and, like a good student, repeated the information. "Tea, yogurt, toast with jam, and soft-boiled eggs."

The trainer nodded, then looked at the boy, worried. "Is that bad news?"

"What?"

"About breakfast."

"What do you mean, Don Charly? It's excellent news!"

"So why are you crying?"

"Who?"

"You, you're crying."

Ángel ran his hand along his cheek and was surprised to find that the trainer was right. Suddenly he realized that he was still on the phone and that he still didn't know what else to say. "What else should I say?"

"Anything. Ask her what kind of jam it is."

"What kind of jam?"

"Yeah, you know, strawberry, peach, papaya . . ."

He dried off his tears from where they had tried to run down his nose. "What kind of jam?"

"What does that matter?"

"It doesn't matter at all."

"If you really care, it's orange marmalade. Don Nico wants to talk to you."

The boy moved the phone to the other ear, as if this ceremonial gesture were standard practice when changing interlocutors.

"The orange marmalade is bitter, son. Like life."

"We saved her, Don Nico."

"We? No, it was that gentleman hanging on the wall here who behaved so divinely."

"Well, I did my part."

"What do you mean?"

"I galloped and galloped until I outran death."

"When you get back to the hospital, you might want a doctor here to examine your head. You could use an encephalogram."

"What's that?"

"It's an X-ray of your brain that lets them see where your nut is cracked. We won the battle against the bacteria, now we've got to wage war on the depression."

"Leave that to me, maestro."

"What are you thinking of?"

"Something big. So big that not even you, my professor, god-father, and confidant, can know about it now."

"I forbid you to do anything until you talk to me."

"My respect and admiration for you is almost limitless, but as of today I know exactly what I'm going to do with my life."

"Excellent. Then I will make sure to have your epitaph ready."

"I like 'Be right back.' "

"Oh, about coming back: when you pass by the hotel, bring those two jean jackets. They're hanging in the closet."

Ángel Santiago let himself slide down the wood column until his butt was resting on a pile of hay. He heard the click at the other end of the line and, without thinking, handed the phone to Charly de la Mirándola, who looked at him quizzically, his pudgy body balancing precariously to avoid stepping in the manure.

"What's wrong now, young man?"

"Nothing, Don Charly."

"Then why the hell are you still crying?"

THE FIRST SHADOWS of the day fall quickly over Santiago. Someone enters a corner grocery store and by the time he leaves, it is already dark. On Friday afternoons, the wealthy who own beach houses leave for the coast. Wives and children wait in shops and offices, their school backpacks packed and grocery bags full of food for the weekend, ready for the two-hour drive from Santiago to the Pacific Ocean.

The poor remain downtown in swarms, swooning in the nimbus of smog. They have to tolerate broken mufflers backfiring in their faces as they make their way through the stifling gray blanket hovering over the streets. This filthy fog puts one in the mood for trysts in poorly heated bars that smell like sour wine, trysts with large-breasted women in short skirts or games of darts or cards with chums from school or the old neighborhood. Santiaguinos tend to hold on to these time-tested connections. The dictatorship converted the uncertainty of new friendships into potential thresholds of new betrayals.

That afternoon, Santoro again carried home the keys to the cell with double sets of bars where he pretended to be holding Rigoberto Marín. "Until further notice, condemned to bread, water, and silence," he had pronounced with bitterness. He smoked a last cigarette listlessly and marked his time card precisely at seven.

With his coat collar turned up, he braved the bitter cold that always follows blue skies. After a day of winter sunshine, evenings in Santiago are frigid, like the neon lights reflected in the exhausted faces of workers returning home on the bus.

After buying a copy of *La Segunda* newspaper at the newsstand on the corner, the warden boarded a city bus—a stuffy, suffocating vehicle—where he managed to read only a few headlines: government agents investigated for receiving illegal perks; Chile wins at an international tennis tournament; soccer great Marcelo Salas, El Matador, will be transferred from Italy to Buenos Aires; an ex-beauty queen might be a right-wing-party candidate for an elegant resort town.

Several of the passengers were coughing and sneezing, but nobody dared open a window. They preferred contagion in that purulent air to the freezing cold outside.

There was one *particular* passenger sitting in the seat in the very back, the long seat, the only seat behind the rear exit, the seat where six people can fit if they squeeze in tightly, the seat that receives the brunt of the impact when the wheels hit potholes, the seat where the passengers have nowhere to hold on to when the bald tires brake on the damp streets and end up rolling down the aisle if they fail to pay attention; that *particular* passenger, one of the six, the one wearing a leather jacket and earmuffs, his neck and chin wrapped in a brown alpaca scarf made by Confecciones Arequipa, that same individual who grimly watched the warden and knew how to deftly lower his eyes when he turned around, that *particular* passenger was Ángel Santiago.

With his knees pressed together so he could fit in the corner, he ran his tongue over his lips, his mouth getting drier and drier as the bus traveled west, first toward Independencia, then to Einstein Street, finally slamming on the brakes so the warden could get off at the corner with the butcher shop.

The lights on that street were old and in disrepair and only barely dispelled the darkness. The two figures, separated by a prudent distance, walked until they came to a main thoroughfare, then turned left down a small street. The two men could not have been more different. Large, and looking even bulkier in his camel-hair coat, the warden moved forward as if he were yawning. As he made his way home, he was thinking about taking off his shoes, putting on his slippers, about he and his wife toasting to the weekend with a glass of red wine, about nodding off into a protracted siesta while watching the soap operas on television. In that mood, he would wait for dinner and might even have to give permission to his teenage daughters to go to their weekend parties, adding that he wanted them back home no later than one o'clock in the morning.

The other did not move with such ease and so few cares. He sank his head down into his leather jacket and sought the line along the wall where the shadows would keep his presence a secret. He knew he couldn't drop any farther behind because the warden was going to turn at the next corner, walk down an alleyway with three trees, and in a flash he would already be putting his key into the door of the blue house. Though Ángel feared that quickening his pace might alert his victim, he decided to trust his basketball shoes and, after making sure nobody else was around, and just before the man turned the corner, he leapt upon him in one feline movement.

He yanked off the scarf and threw it over Santoro's head like the lash of a whip out of the shadows; the warden didn't have a chance to defend himself against the brutal pressure Ángel was beginning to exert on his throat. Utterly at Ángel's mercy, he lifted his terrified eyes and tried to mouth the words *Forgive me* but managed only an unintelligible gurgling.

Now he was on his knees in front of the boy, and his eyes worked hard to express all the entreaties he could not put into words. By this time the boy had let his jacket fall down over his shoulders, and his abundant, anarchic hair followed, making him look like an angel in a village church. Just as he sensed the warden was about to pass out, Ángel released a bit of the pressure, then shoved his hand under the warden's jacket and pulled out the pistol he carried in a holster over his heart. He threw it as far away as he could; the weapon clanked as it banged into the grate over a street drain. Now he could move the man, who was almost unconscious, with the same dexterity he used to change his horse's direction. Using the scarf as a leash, he dragged him over to a leafless tree and leaned him against its trunk.

Ángel slowly released the pressure on his neck once he was sure that the man was so paralyzed by fear and asphyxiation he wouldn't try anything. The first word his victim uttered was, "Mercy," in a tone and volume that he seemed to have practiced in his many nightmares. Indeed, the warden had dreamed of this very moment on dozens of occasions, in every one of which he had seen young Santiago enter a bar on Puente Street and plunge a knife into his throat until it came out the other side. There had always been a weapon, but never a scarf. Never the scarf that he had strategically, even affectionately, given him.

"I respect you, son. I never meant to hurt you. I don't deserve to die for a moment of bad judgment," he panted.

"Don't you really, Warden?"

"It was a very strange night. We were all like castaways."

"Like beasts, Santoro."

"That's life . . . that's this shitty life we lead."

"If that's how you feel about it," said Ángel Santiago, tightening the scarf, "why do you want to hang on to it?"

"Please, I've got my wife, my two teenage daughters. They need me, Santiago. It's not fair for you to kill me a few yards away from my house."

The young man grabbed the warden's face and bashed it against the tree trunk, then rubbed it against the bark until blood dripped out of the wounds. Splinters and pieces of bark stuck on the blood and sweat, and his swollen lips were trembling.

"They had to take me that night to the hospital to give me a blood transfusion."

"I went with you in the ambulance. Don't you remember?"

"The doctor on call wrote down 'multiple hemorrhages.'"

"But you recovered, son. You're strong, you're free, you have your whole life ahead of you. What do you gain by killing me?"

"Dignity."

The young man again tightened the scarf around the man's neck until the warden's eyes were popping out of their sockets. Only then did Ángel finally let go and lean against the wall, trying to regain control of his breathing.

"You hear me, Warden?"

"Yes, son," Santoro whispered, panting and massaging his chest.

"So listen carefully to what I am going to tell you."

"I'm listening."

"I haven't come to kill you."

"I don't believe you."

"I'm not going to kill you now."

"I am very grateful, Ángel Santiago. And when are you going to kill me?"

"Never."

"Are you serious?"

"Totally serious. For reasons that you would never understand, I have changed my plans. My future doesn't include a rat like you, not even to exterminate it."

A pedestrian walked past the two men and, looking worried, kept going as if he hadn't seen them. In the house across the street, an old woman peeked through a curtain and, when she saw Ángel Santiago looking at her, closed it again.

"Thank you for your mercy."

"It's not mercy, Warden. It's been decided in cold blood. It is my lucid brain that, as of today, is separating the wheat from the chaff."

"And the story of your lost dignity?"

"No longer relevant."

"It's okay, Ángel Santiago, I believe you."

The corpulent man grabbed on to the tree trunk and with great difficulty lifted himself up. He brushed off his coat and made a move toward the gun that had landed on the grate over the drain. The young man beat him to it and placed it in the pocket of his leather jacket. "I'm going to take this on loan for a while, Warden."

"What do you need it for?"

"Nothing that has anything to do with you."

"I'm asking because I'd be really sorry to see you back in my jail."

"Would you treat me like you did before?"

"No, I wouldn't, son. I'd treat you like a prince. But if you're going to use that weapon, you better learn how it works."

The two men stood there silently, without moving. A breeze lifted a few dry leaves, and Ángel grabbed one and absentmindedly scratched its brittle surface. The warden rubbed his bruised neck and went over to the boy with outstretched hand.

"If you will allow me, I'm going to say good-bye. They're waiting for me at home."

"Go on, Warden."

They shook hands, but something still held Santoro to that spot. Cleaning some mud off his brow with a few fingers, he finally got up the courage to ask, "If you really didn't want to kill me, why did you come?"

Ángel Santiago crushed the leaf he was holding in his right hand until it turned to dust. "To give you back your scarf."

FTER TEN AT night all the traffic lights on Las Tabernas Street may as well have been green. Drivers paid no attention to lights or signs as they cruised along studying the girls sitting in café windows or standing around in small groups and wearing fur coats, transparent stockings under miniskirts, and thick red eye shadow.

As he approached the neighborhood, Ángel was overflowing with happiness. He felt as light and fresh as if a thousand jets had blasted him clean, removing all the plaque that had built up around his soul, and when he realized that he was about to do a little step and a jump right there in the middle of the street, he understood the ecstasy those heroes of Hollywood musicals must feel when they suddenly break out in song and dance.

Lithe and agile, mentally alert and light of hoof, supple and transparent, he was sure the whole world would immediately understand the dual source of his happiness: whatever he felt for Victoria Ponce was, very probably, what they called *love*; and Vergara Gray's instructions about the Schendler jean jackets made it sound as if the coup had finally taken hold of him.

Since that morning, since he had galloped that horse until he had won *his* race, he had felt as if luck were pouring down on him in torrents, as if all around him a throng of angels were making miracles happen. Those illusive and ethereal beings, diligent and benevolent, were making sure that nothing bad would happen to him, that he would, for example, release the pressure of the scarf on that pig's neck, thus liberating him from the burden of murder. He was also free of the phantom crime, the one he had committed so many times during those long nights of insomnia, when he plunged a kitchen knife into Santoro's neck. Had the warden seen that same image? The exact same image as his own waking nightmares? Could it be that fear, instead of confusing us, turns us into clairvoyants? Had the victim and he, his executioner, dreamed the same dream?

"Nothing bad can happen to me," he told himself, at the very moment he walked past a cherry-colored car and was rudely awakened from his reverie by a blast of its horn. The driver's window opened, and Nemesio Santelices's head appeared.

"Hey buddy, when the hell are you gonna pay me my two grand?"

Santiago was used to seeing the self-appointed valet waving a yellow flag and helping drivers park their cars on this busy street, but he never thought he would ever see him sitting in the driver's seat. He couldn't help but smile.

"Won't be long now, my friend," he said, ready to continue happily along his way toward the hotel.

The valet swung open the back door and gestured forcefully for him to get in. After doing as he was told and settling into the back seat, Ángel recognized Elsa, from the hotel, sitting next to him.

"You remember me, son?"

"Of course, the night receptionist."

"What happened to Elena Sanhueza?"

"That was my girlfriend's false name. She's fine, now, at the hospital recovering from an accident. Why did you want me to get into the car?"

"Nobody can see us here," the valet said.

"Why does that matter?"

The little man pulled his hat down over his eyebrows as if that should have been obvious from the mere fact of his saying so. "I once saw you fly out of a second-story window and land alive."

"That was one of Vergara Gray's jokes."

"Now we want to prevent you from flying out of a second-story window and landing dead."

The boy rubbed his knees and tried to peek out of the steamed-up window to see what was going on in front of the hotel.

Elsa took out a cigarette and opened the window a crack before she exhaled her first drag. "In that hotel there's a gentleman, not a very distinguished one, who is waiting to kill you."

"Me?"

"You or Vergara Gray. I haven't dug quite deep enough to find out. You, I couldn't care less about. Not after the way you thrashed Monasterio. But you're that gentleman's best bet for getting to Nico. And that would be a funeral I'd rather not attend."

"Who's the guy?"

"He says his name is Alberto Parra Chacón, but that's not his real name."

"How do you know?"

"Bah! The first time you came to the hotel I knew perfectly well your name wasn't Enrique Gutiérrez."

"You gave me that name."

"That's the name I give everybody so I don't forget or get caught in a lie if I ever get questioned by the police. I also wrote Alberto Parra Chacón down as Enrique Gutiérrez."

"What if someone calls him on the phone?"

"That's Gutiérrez's problem and the one who calls him, not mine."

Ángel Santiago took a comb out of his backpack and looked in the rearview mirror while giving his mane a few strokes. "What made you think that guy wants to kill us?"

"A very simple deduction. Why has he not left his room? Why has he been lying on the sofa in a T-shirt holding a Browning .38? Why, when I sent the maid in to clean Vergara Gray's room, did he come bursting out waving his gun around?"

"I don't know of anyone who would want to kill me, Señora Elsa."

"You haven't told anybody what you're planning with Vergara Gray?"

"Everybody suspects I'm planning something with the professor, but he's not in the game anymore. The only thing he wants to do is retire and live with his family."

"I know Teresa Capriatti well, and I know that if he doesn't bring home some money that's never going to happen."

"What are you trying to tell me?"

"The following: Alberto Parra Chacón is someone who wants to either kill you or take part in the heist you're planning."

"What heist, for chrissake?"

"If he's waving a gun around it's because he figures you guys are planning something that requires, besides horse thieves and expert safecrackers, somebody with the balls to kill, if necessary. He must know that this is not a job for sissies."

"For saying something very similar I almost strangled your lover, Señora Elsa."

"I'm speaking figuratively. I have proof that you gave that schoolgirl the time of her life. But if that skinny guy isn't a thief, the victim he's after must be you."

"Me? The only thing on my rap sheet is that I stole a horse. Nobody's going to kill me for that."

"And Ms. Sanhueza?"

"I don't understand."

"Your little plaything. You ever think she may have somebody else?"

"Doña Elsa, all those soap operas you watch are addling your brain!"

"Or a father who wants to defend his daughter's honor?"

Ángel Santiago grabbed the door handle and opened it angrily. "I'm going to go get a few things from Nico's room."

The valet stood in the street, not letting him pass. With the press of a button on the key chain, he opened the trunk.

"All of Vergara Gray's things are in that suitcase."

"Why?"

"We didn't want the maestro to go into the hotel and walk into a trap. And you neither. If you know where he is, bring him his things."

The young man rubbed his eyes and tried to reconstruct something out of the blur his sleepless life had been for the last fifty hours. Were his angels looking out for him or should he send this lying pair to hell? He let his mouth form the words before his reason had kicked in.

"Okay, okay. I won't go into the hotel, and I'll bring him his suitcase."

Santelices lifted it out of the trunk, handed it to him, then hailed a taxi. The man's smile now revealed that he was missing his right canine tooth. Like a comedian imitating a bellhop at a luxury hotel, he opened the taxi door with an exaggerated gesture, placed the suitcase on the seat, then helped Ángel Santiago get in with gentle support on his elbow. He then placed his hand in his pocket, produced two bills of a thousand each, and placed them in his hand.

"You'll be owing me four grand now, you sonofabitch."

"D O YOU REMEMBER me, Corporal Zúñiga?"

It took a mere two seconds for the uniformed man to progress from puzzlement to recognition. He stood up, gave the young man an effusive hug, and said, "How could I ever forget the owner of that chestnut horse! Where is the beast?"

"I took your advice. I brought him to the Hippodrome and registered him for the first race."

"Good for you! He won't let us down!"

"Charly de la Mirándola has a lot of faith in him."

"What did you tell me he did the twelve hundred in?"

"One-fifteen, one-sixteen . . ."

"Hopefully it will rain, some horses do better in the mud. What's the animal's name?"

"Milton."

"Like the soccer announcer, Milton Millas?"

"Yep."

"I'll place a bet on him."

An orderly brought in his plate of fried eggs and ham, and after pouring on an abundance of salt, the corporal dug in with a hearty appetite. He offered the young man the banana on the desk.

"Help yourself."

"Thank you, Corporal, I already had breakfast."

After a few spoonfuls punctuated by a swipe of the napkin across his mouth, the carabinero leaned back in his chair with a satisfied air and gave the boy a friendly look.

"So what brings you here, young man?"

That trivial and ordinary question brought a blush to Ángel's face and made him break into a sweat. "Do you remember when you told me that if I had any problems at all I should remember your name?"

"Corporal Zúñiga, Güechuraba Police Station, at your service."

The young man swallowed the excess saliva in his mouth, tossed back his head, and lifted his chin before saying with great feeling, "Well, I need your help."

The officer understood that he was about to hear a secret, brushed off a few crumbs that had fallen on the desk, and got up quietly to close the door. "I'm all ears."

"I imagine that you, with your experience on this side of the law, may already have a few ideas about me."

The officer sat on the edge of the desk and crossed his arms over his chest. "I figure you've paid, at least, a visit to the other side."

"I'm in rehabilitation."

"Nobody's perfect around this neighborhood, much less in Chile. So how can I help you?"

"Let's see, how can I explain it so you'll understand?"

"Take your time. It's not a crime to speak. As long as it's not part of an effort to bribe," he added. "As far as that goes, the carabineros in Chile are rock-solid."

"No, Corporal, it's pretty much the opposite of that."

"So what is it?"

"A loan."

The corporal jumped off the desk, grabbed the banana, and banged it against the palm of his hand as he spoke.

"Ah, now, there you've run aground. Asking for a loan from a carabinero is like robbing a beggar's bank. We've got the lowest salaries in Chile. If it weren't for the health insurance and the office of public assistance that gives us coupons for baby formula, we'd be better off unemployed. We'd be the ones in the protest marches throwing rocks at the pigs."

The man smiled with true good humor, and Ángel Santiago, encouraged by this cheerful speech, sidled up to him and said, almost in a whisper, "The truth is it's not a cash loan. I need some help that only you can give us."

"Us?"

"Uh-huh."

"Is it a long story?"

"If you would be so kind as to listen to it patiently."

"So long as I can eat the banana while you tell it."

"A whole bunch of bananas."

"What's her name?"

"How did you know it had something to do with a *her*?"

"Police intuition. Name?"

"Victoria Ponce."

"Age?"

"Seventeen?"

"Record?"

Ángel took out a cigarette and rolled it between his fingers to loosen up the tobacco. He walked over to the window, looked out at the cordillera, and, after asking for a light, told the girl's story without omitting many details. At ten o'clock he had already been talking for fifteen minutes, and he knew the carabinero was deeply immersed in the story. When the phone rang, he brusquely answered with, "Call back later," then slammed it down.

Trusting his instincts that carried him through an inspired description of open skies, fluffy clouds carried along by the breeze, and the sound of carts' wheels over cobblestones on the way to La Vega Market, he gave the corporal a condensed version of his own life since he had left jail, omitting two points that had absolutely nothing to do with his request: Lira's coup and the scarf attack the night before against the respectable warden of the Central Prison.

During the final three minutes, his voice getting lower and lower, he entered explosive territory, outlining the specifics of his request and explaining that although he was not seeking institutional reparations for the girl—"sooner or later other generations and laws will take care of that"—he was requesting a very particular kind of assistance from Zúñiga, a simple and good-hearted uniformed Chilean, a self-effacing public servant, and the upstanding father of a family.

When the young man finished his speech, Corporal Zúñiga's lips were pursed and two of his fingers were pressed against them, a sure sign of deep meditation. His gaze was lost in the wall in front of him as if he were trying to glean some wisdom from the mildew stains. He moved around and scanned the placement of every object on his desk. When his eyes lit on the banana peel, he swept it up and tossed it squarely into the trash basket.

"So?" Ángel finally got up the courage to ask, his words sounding as if he were standing on the tips of his toes.

Corporal Zúñiga took half a minute to tighten the belt of his uniform, then said with a grim smile, "We're going to raise holy hell."

L OOKING FOR A pretext to get on Teresa Capriatti's good
side and help bring about a reconciliation between her and
Vergara Gray, Elsa borrowed Monasterio's checkbook and
wrote out a check that relieved him of a hundred thousand pesos
without verifying if there was enough money in his account to
cover it. She took a taxi to Teresa's house and, hoping to be invited
in, bought some sugarcoated *príncipe* cookies. They would go particularly well with the tea that would, according to the most basic
rules of hospitality, be offered.

Attached to the check was an invitation. Ms. Sanhueza, who had
crafted each invitation by hand, had added above Teresa Capriatti's name a sprinkle of gold glitter. Since all the other invitations,
including her own, lacked this enhancement, Elsa deduced that
Nico had let the artist in on his personal secrets.

Teresa Capriatti opened the door barely a crack and spit out a
courteous greeting. "Oh, it's you."

Elsa, not discouraged, proceeded to remove the decorated envelope from her tiger-striped bag. "Vergara Gray sends you this
invitation."

His wife glanced at it, her lips firmly set in a frown, then lifted her eyes. "Explain."

"It's good news. Your Nico has gotten work as a culture promoter. He has become a kind of agent for performing artists."

"Judging from the glitter he used to decorate my name, he's working with showgirls, the ones who dance with gold stars over their nipples and a peacock feather on their butts."

"Teresa, you know that Vergara Gray is a serious man. We're talking here about classical ballet."

"What does he understand about any of that? One day he took me to see *Swan Lake*, and I had the distinct impression that he wouldn't have noticed if they'd been ducks."

"Then this might surprise you. This is a dance inspired by Gabriela Mistral."

" '*Little feet, children's feet, blue with cold, how to see you and not cover you—dear God!*' "

"I like Nicanor Parra's version better."

"I don't know that one."

" '*Little feet, children's feet, blue with cold, how to see you and not cover you—dear Marx!*' "

"So you came all the way here just to bring me this?"

The receptionist fingered the snap on her tiger-skin purse with feigned modesty, then said shyly, "No. I've also brought you a check."

"Come in," Teresa Capriatti said, opening the door.

Once in the living room, the visitor handed the package of cookies to her hostess, who then disappeared into the kitchen to heat up some water for tea. Elsa carefully scanned the room. All indications of Vergara Gray's presence had been meticulously purged. During the good old days, one of the pale yellow walls had been adorned with an impressive photograph of Teresa and Nico on their wedding day and in the company of nobody less than the cardinal, distantly related to the bride, from whom they'd gotten a blessing, one that seemed not to have had the desired effect.

Teresa returned with two cups of tea; the ladies unwrapped the *príncipes* and ate them, letting the sugary crumbs fall on the rug.

"Teresita—"

"I hate to be called that."

"Sorry. Do you remember a few years ago when we were closer?"

"There's nothing from that period that I miss or want to remember. You mentioned a document?"

"Yes, of course," Elsa said, pretending to have simply forgotten about it. Still she did not open her purse, as if some sudden idea she preferred not to repress had distracted her. "You know that Vergara Gray loves you madly, don't you?"

"Those are words teenagers use. The most basic attribute of someone who loves is the ability to support a family with a minimum of dignity. I have begun to take in sewing. That is mortifying. Can you imagine: 'Teresa Capriatti, seamstress'?"

"You don't give him any other choice."

Elsa had been on the verge of holding her tongue, but she suspected that all her other efforts would be worthless if she didn't speak her mind. And it looked as if she was right: her last sentence had whetted her hostess's curiosity.

"What do you mean?"

"Vergara Gray is suffering from a major contradiction. When he was in jail, he dreamed about living with you; now that he's free, you don't let him."

"I don't see any contradiction. He didn't consider my needs in either case: not now, not then."

"But you demand that he support you!"

"That's the least he can do! If you've got a check, give it to me."

"You know that Nico is capable of pulling off something big, something genius. Everybody is expecting it. The only reason he holds back is because, if he fails, he would end up back in jail and you'd definitely never see him again. But if he succeeds, your money worries are over."

"For God's sake, get a grip on yourself!"

"No, I'm going to continue. Look, Teresa, Vergara Gray's only chance right now is something big. Nobody is going to give him an entry-level job at sixty years old. And, with his rap sheet, he can't even go offer himself to Canteros for his team of security guards."

"Okay. But you said he's working as some kind of agent."

Elsa pulled out the check and placed it rather defiantly in front of her eyes.

"A hundred thousand!" Teresa exclaimed. "That's not even enough to pay the rent for a month."

Elsa stood up, dropping all the crumbs that had accumulated on her lap.

"So what are you suggesting I do?" Teresa asked.

"If you give that man a tiny bit of tenderness, he'll go to the ends of the earth for you. If he does something and dies in the act, you'll never have to see him again, but since you never see him anyway, nothing changes. If he goes to jail, you wouldn't have any obligation to visit him, just like all these years, so again, nothing changes. If he succeeds, money will come to you in buckets, and since everybody knows whatever he does will have on it the signature of the one and only Vergara Gray, he would have to go into hiding, you would never see him, and again the same result: nothing changes except you've got all the money you need."

The hostess seemed torn between the discomfort of having heard unsolicited advice and the desire to find a solution to her very precarious position.

"You know that all these years I've never had another man. Not even an occasional lover."

"That says a lot about you. And Nico."

"What do you mean?"

"Finding a human being like him these days is impossible. Next to him, anybody else looks like a primate."

"He was an excellent lover. But now the party's over."

"That's your pride speaking. But who knows what your heart would say if you'd only let it speak."

"I don't know what my heart would say, but I do know what my mouth says: Leave now, Elsa."

The cashier had already started to make her way toward the door. She looked with some interest at the two *príncipes* she'd left on the table, frankly demanding attention, but then thought it would be rude to take them.

"Are you going to come see the ballet?"

"I don't think so."

"Don't tear up the invitation. Nico wanted to impress you."

"What should I do, Elsa?"

The receptionist tapped on the doorknob, for the first time showing signs of irritation.

"Get a grip on yourself, Teresita Capriatti."

AFTER BEING SHUT up in his hotel room for three days, Rigoberto Marín came to the conclusion that something was not proceeding according to plan. So when the maid came to clean Vergara Gray's room and then went downstairs to answer the phone at the reception desk, he slipped in, opened the wardrobe, turned over the mattress, looked under the bed, and felt around for a loose board that might lead to a hiding place.

The room was as empty as a soccer stadium in the middle of the week. As he passed his hand over his stubbly chin he realized that there wasn't even a razor blade or shaving cream in the bathroom.

Somebody had evacuated Vergara Gray and the Cherub without him noticing, even though he could swear he'd been as alert as a watchdog. All things considered, he thought it appropriate to reward the receptionist for her diligence and intuition. When Elsa entered the lobby after her visit with Teresa Capriatti, she recognized Rigoberto Marín from behind as he stood at reception, digging his knife into the countertop. Through the mirror she could also see that the man had already seen her enter and that any attempt to escape would be futile: a few more steps and he would stab her through the liver and leave her to bleed to death on the rug in the entryway.

"Good afternoon, Mr. Parra Chacón," she greeted him in a friendly voice, at the same time as she stared at the shapes her guest had carved into the wood: a series of small Chilean flags, recognizable by the distribution of rectangles and squares, and the stars in the upper-left-hand corners.

"Good afternoon, Ms. Elsa."

"I see you like to carve."

"Not especially, but I had to do something to keep myself busy."

"You must be very patriotic. You've made six Chilean flags."

"Doesn't really matter what I drew. It's just a way to call your attention to the tool I used to do it." He jabbed the knife into the counter, its sharp edge pointing toward her.

"In this neighborhood one learns to respect such a weapon. How can I help you, Don Alberto?"

The woman wanted to take off her coat, but reconsidered when she realized that the thick wool could blunt the impact of the blade.

"By telling me the truth about a couple of things."

"You ask and I'll tell."

The criminal pulled out the knife and started waving it around as if it were a Bic pen. "Vergara Gray lives here, right?"

"Since everyone knows that he has received a full pardon, I have no reason to deny it. I would like to correct one small detail. He *used to* live here."

"When did he move out?"

"As he is short of funds, he moved out discreetly and left me with the bill."

"He left so discreetly with all his belongings that nobody noticed?"

"You must know about the talents that have made him famous."

"But he isn't Mandrake the Magician." He moved toward her and pushed her up against the coat stand, bringing the knifepoint right up to the tip of her nose.

"What do you want?"

"I want to know where Vergara Gray is. If you're trying to protect him, you've got nothing to worry about. I just want to offer my services for whatever he's planning."

Elsa didn't need to think twice about his statement. It was imperative that she offer him something in order to place a few inches between her face and that sharp point. In this neighborhood, she had dealt frequently with whores, drunkards, pimps, con men, and drug dealers, both big-time and small, but never with professional assassins.

"What are you going to do to me, Mr. Parra Chacón?"

"Depending on the information you give me, either stab you in the heart or scratch you on the cheek."

"I wouldn't want to be disfigured by a scar. My skin is very delicate, I have a pretty smile, and at my age we women need to take good care of whatever attractions we still have. So, if you would be so kind, I'd rather you kill me."

"Where's the professor?"

"I don't know now, but once he gets a place I will know."

"Why?"

"Because he promised to tell me, and he's a man of his word."

"How big a job is he preparing?"

"More than a million dollars."

"Who's the victim?"

"He didn't mention a word."

Alberto Parra Chacón lowered the knife to the counter. He had left the seventh Chilean flag unfinished and began to dig the knife into the wood. "When will it happen?"

"Tomorrow, the next day, Tuesday at the latest."

Parra Chacón brushed off the shavings from his efforts. "What's your relationship with Vergara Gray, ma'am?"

The woman caressed her neck and tried on what she had described a little earlier as "a pretty smile."

"God asks less and forgives more."

"I understand. Do you know who I really am?"

"No, but Alberto Parra Chacón you aren't. Look at the register: I have you down as Enrique Gutiérrez."

"Why did you do that?"

"It's a name I remember easily in case I'm questioned. I figured you wouldn't mind. . . ."

"It's all the same to me. Here's what we'll do: I respect your complexion and when you get your share, you give me a slice."

"How much?"

"I'm modest. Not so much that it hurts you, not so little that it makes me sad."

"Agreed. Something else I can do for you, Mr. Parra Chacón?"

"Could you make me some soup? I haven't eaten in two days."

ON THE MORNING of the big day, many hours before his wife, Mabel, had to get up to take their two kids to nursery school, Corporal Zúñiga woke her up and, hugging her under the warmth of the rustic sheets and thick blankets they received free from the Public Welfare Office, he told her he needed her advice. She was immediately wide awake, fearing she was about to hear some kind of unwelcome confession. She made ready to listen by affectionately running her hand under her husband's neck.

"How would you feel about me doing something illegal?"

"Such as?"

"Nothing serious."

"Not a robbery?"

"Nothing like that. Just something I don't have the authority to do."

"What's this about?"

"It's difficult to explain, Mabel. It's something that's not really good, but that I feel deep in my heart I really have to do."

"You sure are mysterious."

"It's just that I don't want to influence the advice you give me."

"If you don't tell me about it, I can't give you any advice."

"Let's see if I can come at it from a different angle."

The woman made herself more comfortable by leaning her elbow on the mattress and resting her chin in her hand. Her husband wet his lips. He was wearing a flannel pajama top with three buttons down the front.

"Go on."

"Maybe it's stupid, but I need to know something I've never asked you before. Have you ever felt uncomfortable about being married to a cop?"

"What are you talking about? I don't think of you like that. You have always just been my husband, Arnoldo."

"And before that?"

"Well, before that you were my fiancé, Arnoldo Zúñiga, and before that you were my boyfriend, and then you became the father of our children, Delia Zúñiga and Rubén Zúñiga. Whether you're a cop or an astronaut doesn't make a whole lot of difference to me."

"I don't believe you."

"What are you getting at?"

"What people say. About the protests and how we sometimes use too much force. . . ."

"That only happens once in a while. Anyway, there are police everywhere in the world."

"But they haven't done everywhere in the world what they did in Chile."

"What are you talking about?"

"You know, the tortures, the rapes, the disappeared persons."

"That was thirty years ago. You weren't even born then."

"You heard what the senator said last night on TV. There is 'institutional' guilt."

"Of course there is. But the ones who have to ask for forgiveness are those who gave the orders to kill, not you. You were still in your mother's belly."

"You never had any problems because I'm a carabinero?"

"A couple of times. When they threw rocks at our windows. That time your uncle didn't want to stay at your brother's wedding party because he saw you come in."

"And what about how people look at you?"

"Sometimes a little strangely."

"Nothing ever happened that you decided not to tell me?"

"There was, once . . . but that was many years ago. . . ."

"What happened?"

"Why do you care about that now?"

"What happened, Mabel?"

"Somebody threw a bucket of shit against the door."

"Why didn't you tell me?"

"I didn't want to upset you. It was just a month before Rubén was born."

"On TV they say the country is reconciled. Do you think that's true?"

"No, Arnoldo. I don't."

"So, what needs to happen for us to be reconciled?"

"I guess the military has to show that they are sorry, make a gesture."

"And what about the carabineros?"

"The carabineros, too, I guess."

"So"—Zúñiga got up and walked over to the window just as their neighbor's rooster crowed—"if I make a gesture toward someone who suffered a lot, you wouldn't get angry at me?"

His wife responded with alarm. "What are you going to do?"

"Make a gesture."

"They're going to fire you."

"I'll look for another job."

"Half of Chile is unemployed. What are you laughing at?"

"Life—life makes me laugh. It's like a soccer game. You can be on the field for ninety minutes and the ball never comes near you. Suddenly there's a corner kick and the ball practically lands on your forehead, and all you've got to do is tap it lightly with your head to push it in. It's that simple: Goal!"

The woman took hold of his pajama top and one of the buttons fell on the floor. He wanted to pick it up, but she held on to him.

"Your buttons are always hanging by a thread! Tell me what you're going to do."

Arnoldo Zúñiga pushed her gently away and calmly said, "I'll tell you while we eat breakfast."

Mabel walked slowly into the kitchen. "I'm scared, Arnoldo."

"No, woman, don't be. You'll see, it's no big deal."

He bent over to pick up the button, took a needle and thread out of the dresser, and carried them both into the kitchen so he could sew it on while he told her all about it.

"*Son cinco minutos, la vida es eterna en cinco minutos*," sang Victor Jara in "*Te recuerdo, Amanda*," and it was this melody that Ángel Santiago whistled all afternoon. Five minutes may have been an eternity to Jara, but the partners needed ten, to be exact. That was the length of time Victoria would be onstage.

Money appeared from everywhere: piggy banks, mattresses, savings accounts, reduced grocery lists, unauthorized loans from the girl at the bar cash register, collections taken up among the valets on Las Tabernas Street, an advance on the art teacher's unemployment benefits, a visit to the pawnshop with the wedding band that Teresa Capriatti had placed lovingly on Vergara Gray's finger, the money saved from Mabel Zúñiga and her offspring not going to the Sunday afternoon movies, the blue tickets Charly de la Mirándola had saved to bet on Milton that Saturday.

The cast met at Café Poema at the Biblioteca National, where everyone sat reading with great concentration until ten o'clock at night, at which time Vergara Gray ascertained that none of his companions was missing. The venerable professor of crime had extolled the values of elegance and punctuality, and nobody had failed him.

A few minutes before ten, Gray made his way to one of the columns in the back of the room. Against it leaned Victoria Ponce, her spine very straight, her head held high, one leg in front of the other in fourth position; her face was clean, not a drop of makeup, only a tenacious paleness inherited from her recent illness.

"You feel okay, dear?"

"Fantastic, Vergara Gray."

"Don't you think that after all we've gone through together you could call me Nico?"

"Never, maestro. I like to pronounce your full last name and address you formally. Vergara Gray sounds like the name of a politician, or a philosopher. Kind of like Ortega y Gasset."

"My family is related to the inventor of the telephone, Mr. Gray. But they stole his patent off the secretary's desk."

"How much time is left?"

"Five minutes."

Ángel Santiago gave the order and they filed out the Moneda Street exit; from there they walked to MacIver, then continued toward San Antonio, turned onto Augustinas, and in the middle of the block they saw the patrol car from the Güechuraba Police Station, its lights blinking and the siren on the roof throwing red circles onto the damp asphalt.

As soon as Corporal Zúñiga joined the group, he pulled out his gun and led the way through the artists' entrance, followed by the others, who remained close to Vergara Gray. When the carabinero raised his gun and held it just inches away from the guard's nose, Ángel Santiago felt for Santoro's gun in his pocket and decided he would not hesitate to use it if he had to.

"What's going on?" the guard asked, making a movement to pick up the telephone.

"The less you ask, the faster we'll be out of here. We're occupying the theater," Zúñiga announced.

"Occupying it? What's this all about?"

"We have information that there were two terrorists in the audience tonight."

"You're kidding!"

"We think they left behind a bomb to blow up the theater. We've come to disarm it."

"How horrible, Corporal. Why would anybody want to blow up this temple of the arts?"

Ángel Santiago stepped forward and pointed to the gun by way of a reminder. "Because there are some people who think that this show is a sacrilege, that an opera about Joaquín Murieta, a Chilean bandit in the United States, written by a Communist, Pablo Neruda, with music by another Communist, Sergio Ortega, has no place here. Understand now?"

"And you, who are you, young man?"

"Detective Enrique Gutiérrez, Homicide Division." He flashed open his jacket so quickly that the guard didn't manage to see the false ID from Schendler.

"So, what do I do now?"

"You, personally, get to a safe place. Who else is still here?"

"The lighting technician, the ushers, the janitors."

"Tell them all to meet you at the exit, but don't give them any details."

"Yes, Corporal. Should I call the mayor?"

"Absolutely not. That would be playing right into the terrorists' hands."

"You mean you want to keep a low profile."

"Exactly."

ÁNGEL SANTIAGO CLOSED the luxurious heavy velvet curtains by hand; Ruth Ulloa, Victoria's dance teacher and choreographer, placed the Zenith radio on a bathtub from the set of *The Splendor and Death of Joaquín Murieta*, and set the volume so that she wouldn't have to adjust it when the *prima ballerina* was ready; Nemesio Santelices tested the lever that lit up every bulb on the lavish chandelier hanging over the audience; and as for Vergara Gray, employing the same dexterity he used to open safes, he manipulated the buttons on the control panel until he had figured out how to focus the spotlight on center stage.

The recipients of the handmade invitations took their places in the fifth row of the orchestra section, far away from where the terrorist bomb was supposed to be—Corporal Zúñiga added jokingly—and after exchanging words of mutual congratulations for the elegant execution of the ingenious plans that had allowed them to enter this temple of the arts, everyone grew quiet. Victoria Ponce had delicately placed herself in the precise center of the autumnal spotlight, and like a soprano communicating with her accompanist, she gestured to the teacher that it was time to press the button on the tape player to start the music.

Ángel remained on the edge of the stage, wishing to share the same perspective as his lover when she began her dance. Leaning against the curtains, he held his gun in plain view to preclude any possible interruptions. Vergara Gray was also absent from the fifth row. His status as coconspirator required him to stand guard at the door in case the real police or some hysterical bureaucrat attempted to interrupt the performance.

Finally, Nemesio Santelices worked the lever; the chandelier gradually dimmed until the only light in the hall was that which shone tenuously on the girl. As the piano's first chords sounded, she was on her knees, as if praying for an absent lover.

At ten forty-five the dance performance by Victoria Ponce commenced in the Municipal Theater of Santiago, Chile.

T HE NEXT DAY the following article written by special
performing arts correspondent Sigfrido von Haseanhau-
sen appeared in *El Mercado* newspaper:

POETRY AND DANCE

It all began with an innocent phone call from my
granddaughter's art teacher, offering me an opportunity to repay her for the many favors I owe her. Unable
to give me any details, she told me only that it had
to do with a "secret ceremony," something similar to
what North Americans call a *sneak preview*.

Her instructions, however, were very precise. Once
the performance of Neruda's famous opera *The Splendor and Death of Joaquín Murieta* at the Municipal Theater
had concluded, I should not leave but rather, with the
excuse of a terrible stomachache, find my way to one
of the elegant stalls in the men's restroom and lock
myself in; one hour later, I should then sneak out and
hide behind one of the many columns in the hall,
where I would see a young dancer, let us call her in
the meantime Jane Doe, performing to a piece based

on *The Sonnets of Death*, by Gabriela Mistral, by far my favorite poet of all nations and all times. If I am one day in heaven, and charged by the Lord with the task— or assigned the punishment—of purging the list of Nobel laureates, I would not hesitate for a moment to leave only the name of this poet of deep expressiveness and archaic elegance.

An audience of a dozen or so individuals was scattered in the fifth row of the orchestra section. How, why, or when this kind of benefit performance was planned still remains a total mystery to me. I was about to leave, feeling that the stomach cramps I had feigned had became a harsh reality, when the hall's beautiful chandelier—that lamp like a crystal waterfall more beautiful than the most elaborate of fireworks—began to dim, and the grace of that brief scene held me fast in the theater.

To this pleasure were soon added three chords that rose from a radio and found the dancer in center stage in a prayer position. I was deeply impressed by both the elasticity of this sacred veneration and the unmistakable air of nostalgia that infused the music of Luis Advis, whom I have admired since he composed *Canto de una semilla*, dedicated to Violeta Parra and far superior to his *Cantata Santa María de Iquique*, the mournful tale of an insurrection of oppressed miners that resulted in many deaths at the hands of the noble Chilean army at the beginning of the twentieth century.

The fact that death is something else entirely, something delicate and mysterious, unique and unmovable, subtle and profound, was proven yesterday in the enormity of solitude the dancer, Victoria Ponce, managed to evoke within her galaxy of sorrow and emptiness.

The minimum and almost haphazard—the grave nature of this Mistralian ritual among the rude chaos of the cheap sets used in the Nerudian opera—

emphasized more effectively than brass drums, horns, and trumpets the secret death we patiently cultivate throughout our lives.

I am a simple critic; I have been denied the eloquence of poetry. If today I risk setting out a few lyrical strokes of my pen it is only a result of the impossible fusion of poetry and music that was so fully achieved in that mysterious, secret performance in the Municipal Theater of Chile. The dancer's corporal expression was reminiscent of Manrique—"so quieting"—as well as all that turbulent tranquillity—please excuse the terrible oxymoron—of Gabriela Mistral.

That such a simple, unadorned body is capable of seeding a space with so many allusions is the greatest achievement of Victoria Ponce, an artist nobody has seen and perhaps nobody will ever see, and who today is perhaps paying for her unofficial appearance on the stage of the Municipal Theater in the damp ruins of some Santiago jail cell.

Did she lack technique? Did her arms and legs, as in much of modern dance, seem to belong to different people? Was the gestural range reiterative?

Dear readers, I couldn't care less. Or, as young people in Chile say today, "*me vale callampa*." If this was a minimalist piece about the daily intimacy of death, the young artist transcended her inexperience and her precarious resources to create something that should be an essential part of all great dance: truth.

I doubt if the gentle teenager, at her tender age, has the physical knowledge of the anguish of death, the daily apocalypse we confront whenever we are lucid. Perhaps she only knows death through reading Mistral and one or another romantic bolero in which "dying from love" is evoked.

Whatever the case, whatever they say, angel or beast, Miss Victoria Ponce moved me to tears, and I confess without modesty or pride that I was among those who paid tribute to her with a standing ovation—that is, among the eight or ten phantoms who jumped out of their seats when the show was over—and I felt in full solidarity with the young man who put down the gun he had held throughout the performance to bring the dancer the largest bouquet of flowers I have ever seen.

V ICTORIA RUNS HER fingers slowly over Santiago's face. Dawn rises gently over the city. Sounds retreat. Silence is almost complete. From time to time a siren sounds, a horse and its cart carry lemons to sell at La Vega Market, or the flame of the gas heater produces a tiny explosion.

She has been repeating this gesture for a few minutes, as if her touch could take her inside the young man's absence. She is happy in this silence, but she also wants to know. She somehow needs the eloquence of that silence to be expressed in words, even imprecise ones, even if thereby they'd run the risk of adulterating the fullness of that moment, compromising the compact between her and Ángel Santiago, as solemn as a wedding ring.

She wants to think and she thinks. It is as if the future had swelled the present and filled it to overflowing. The sensation of being here now is complete. Everything makes sense to her, and that's why she does not feel compelled to question what sense any of it makes. She lays the boy down on the mattress and runs her lips down his body from his chin to his belly button and there wanders around using her tongue as a guide. Her fingers explore the spaces between his ribs. His breathing becomes more agitated, and as his chest inflates, the downy hairs catch the light of the heater and take on an ocher tone.

The studio is enormous; night is intimate. The guests left their wineglasses scattered about; the bottles have fallen to the floor; the radio is on with the volume turned down; the chicken bones lie on the plastic tray among the remnants of lettuce sprinkled with red vinegar. The couple is lying near the exercise bars, and he realizes that since he left jail he has had no home other than this warehouse studio that Ruth Ulloa calls her ballet academy.

Why did Victoria want to prolong the pleasure of scouting out his sex until it had become almost painful rather than take it sooner into her mouth? She gently bit his bony skeleton, ran her tongue along the skin covering his femur bone, rubbed her nose over his heels, wet the bottom of his feet with her saliva, hit her front teeth against his kneecaps. Her breasts, swollen on the command of her arousal, appeared again and again over the waves of her caresses.

Finally, the young man grabbed her by the waist, placed her under his body, slid one of his hands below her belly, and, inspired by the dampness he found there, played with her, certain that the vertigo occasioned by this unfurling was the realest thing ever in his life. Unable to resist her spell, he lowered himself to smell and kiss her, to tangle up his tongue in her dampness, to press her gently into the opening between his teeth. The memory of her dance inspired in him as much action as control, and the softness of the saliva mixed with her fluids kept the path of desire always within sight.

But it was *she* who dictated the moment, taking Ángel's member in her right hand and leading it toward her; it was *she* who fit it in, pushing her pelvis forward, and it was *she* herself who, feeling it fully inside her, put in action her muscles and membranes to press it so tightly that his pulsations and her walls combined in a tango, a *pas de deux* that made rise from her lips the words she had not yet spoken: "Thank you."

I N THE OFFICIAL book of records, it was noted on page 203 that "Lieutenant Rubio and two other noncommissioned officers, Malbrán and Ricardi, appeared at eight-fifteen in the morning at the Güechuraba Police Station on El Brinco Street (no street address) in order to initiate disciplinary proceedings against Corporal Arnoldo Zúñiga for serious irregularities while he was on duty, as well as for the embezzlement of government property, patrol car GÜE 1, the only motorized vehicle belonging to this station where horses are the principal means of transportation. We wish to emphasize this circumstance, for it is highly likely that if there had been more than one vehicle available to Corporal Zúñiga on the night of the incidents under investigation, he would have used them as well to carry out his criminal intentions."

On page 204 Lieutenant Rubio went on to assert that the commission had been convened on site rather than in the institution's courts in order to avoid attributing too much importance to an incident that had already been on the front pages of the tabloids, and in the hopes that a short and speedy trial and summary and appropriate punishment would quickly put an end to all speculation.

On the same page, the authorities had already enumerated the following circumstances that should be taken into consideration before judgment was passed: that Corporal Zúñiga had a "clean record" on the force and more than three notable mentions for enhancing the image of the Carabineros of Chile, including services rendered to a woman who had given birth in jail, the rescue of two young children threatened by fire on Einstein Street, and the disarming—with grave risk to his own person—of an explosive device placed in the high-tension tower on Blanco Hill.

Once these facts were duly noted, the transcript of the inquest into the actions of Corporal Arnoldo Zúñiga, who remained standing throughout the proceedings—not accepting the seat the lieutenant offered him—began on page 205.

Lieutenant: Corporal Zúñiga, I'm going to ask you to respond as briefly and concisely as possible to the questions we ask you.

Corporal: Yes, Lieutenant.

Lieutenant: Is it or is it not true that on Friday night you used personnel and vehicles belonging to this police station for an operation in a borough of Santiago that falls outside of this station's jurisdiction?

Corporal: It is true, Lieutenant.

Lieutenant: Is it or is it not true that you were motivated to carry out such an irregularity after you learned that terrorist groups had placed an explosive device in the Municipal Theater of Santiago to protest the performance of a communist-inspired show at the same location?

Corporal: It is true, Lieutenant.

Lieutenant: When you left here on your way downtown, were you

aware of the fact that you were entering territory that
was out of your jurisdiction?

Corporal: I was, Lieutenant.

Lieutenant: Please explain why you continued, knowing that what
you were doing went against every regulation, that
what you should have done was pass on the information to the Santo Domingo/MacIver Station, that is,
the station closest to the scene of the events?

Corporal: With all due respect, Lieutenant, we are talking here
about nothing less than a bomb.

Lieutenant: I don't understand.

Corporal: If you've got information like this, you can't be wasting
time calling somebody else on the telephone. While
you're trying to establish communication, for example,
the theater could be blowing sky-high.

Lieutenant: Are you aware, Zúñiga, that our force includes the
GOP, a division that specializes in investigating and
disarming explosive devices?

Corporal: I am not unaware of that, sir.

Lieutenant: Please explain.

Corporal: I don't know how to explain it, sir. The information
about the bomb reached me, and I thought that I was
man enough to deal with it on my own.

Lieutenant: Might you have seen a few too many Rambo movies,
Zúñiga?

Corporal: You can find me guilty, if you like, sir, but please don't
make fun of me.

Lieutenant: Okay, agreed. Is it true or is it not true that when you
arrived on the scene you threatened the theater guard
with your gun and later kidnapped and held against
their will and without any authority a group of

	employees of the Municipal Theater in the patrol car known as GÜE 1 belonging to this police station?
Corporal:	Yes, Lieutenant.
Lieutenant:	How do you explain this abuse of authority?
Corporal:	When terrorists attack, it's not the same as when the Franciscan monks dole out soup.
Lieutenant:	What terrorists are you talking about? The investigation didn't find even a firecracker.
Corporal:	I am very happy for Chile and her temple of the arts. Because otherwise . . .
Lieutenant:	Otherwise, Zúñiga?
Corporal:	Otherwise, instead of being subjected to this humiliating interrogation, you would be paying me honors at the General Cemetery, and the Police Marching Band would be playing the national anthem, and General Cienfuegos would be consoling my widow and presenting her with a large check to compensate her for her loss.

On page 205 it was written that Lieutenant Rubio and the other noncommissioned officers asked Corporal Zúñiga to leave the room for a few moments. They then asked the orderly to bring them coffee. Ricardi mentioned the corporal's courage and the way he seized the opportunity and confronted the unexpected danger without hesitation, and Malbrán reflected that perhaps, encouraged by his previous success at disarming a bomb, he had wanted to repeat the feat in order to gain promotion to noncommissioned officer, that is, lieutenant, so "we are almost judging one of our own." Rubio, on the other hand, remained engulfed in a turbulent silence.

When the inquest resumed, the lieutenant offered the accused a seat and a cup of coffee, into which the accused poured a large quantity of sugar, then drank in its entirety. He apologized for sitting down in front of his superiors, thereby giving the impression of exemplary modesty "that really fits in perfectly," Malbrán whispered sarcastically into Ricardi's ear, "with his reckless behavior." The truth was, even before the accused had returned to the room, they had shared the joke that, given the circumstances and the insignificance of the case, it would be better to recommend he be given a promotion rather than a demotion or expulsion. Nevertheless, "regulations are regulations and the press will want to see blood," concluded Lieutenant Rubio, "and instead of decorating him with laurels we've got to throw mud in his face."

On page 206 the transcript of the inquest continued:

Lieutenant: In your opinion, Zúñiga, what punishment do you think you deserve, given the seriousness of the case?

Corporal: Whatever you decide to do, please don't reduce my salary. I have a wife and two children, Lieutenant.

Lieutenant: So what kind of a punishment would that be?

Corporal: I have thought of one that would be so degrading it would surely please the general and the press.

Lieutenant: Go on.

Corporal: Put me in charge of the patrol animals. Rising at dawn, feeding them, brushing them, sweeping out their stalls. Mosquitoes, bees, stench. Hell.

The lieutenants exchanged looks, shrugged their shoulders indifferently, finished off their coffees, and asked the secretary to officially enter the decision that Corporal Sepúlveda would take over from Zúñiga as the principal authority of Güechuraba Station.

When the secretary and the other two had left, the lieutenant remained in the room examining the texture of the desk and occasionally patting the written pages. He opened the upper-left-hand drawer and took out a banana, a nail clipper, a jar of hair gel, a pack of cigarettes, a violet-colored lighter, and a copy of *La Fusta* newspaper, which listed the complete program of races the following day at the Hippodrome of Chile.

"So this is your little world, Zúñiga."

"Not really, sir. I mentioned my family. And my friends."

"And Victoria Ponce."

"The dancer?"

"Do you know her?"

"Well, I read the article about her in *El Mercado*."

"Are you interested in ballet, Corporal?"

"Ballet and horse racing."

"What ballets have you seen?"

"*Coppélia, Les Sylphides, Cinderella, Romeo and Juliet*. I think that's all."

"And *Swan Lake*?"

"Of course."

The lieutenant walked over to Zúñiga and, without looking him in the face, fingered a button that hung by a thread from his uniform.

"How old were you when the central command of the carabineros and the armed forces kidnapped and killed Victoria Ponce's father?"

"I, sir?"

"Don't play the fool, Zúñiga."

"I was in school. I was about fifteen."

"That means you had nothing to do with that crime; at that age you probably never even dreamed that one day you'd join the carabineros."

"You are absolutely right, Lieutenant."

"If that is the case, why the hell did you take it upon yourself to compensate the poor orphan?"

Zúñiga's superior officer had turned his eyes on him, staring with an unfriendly frown on his lips. The corporal wiped the drops of sweat off his cheeks with his sleeve.

"I wanted to make a gesture, Lieutenant Rubio."

The officer yanked off his subordinate's hanging button and angrily shook it in front of his nose. "The next time you do something like this to me, I'm going to pull off your balls instead of your button."

He threw it on the table, where it spun around until it landed lifelessly on its edge.

"I'll leave it here to help jog your memory, Zúñiga."

FTER A FEW days of Elsa's watery, tasteless soup, Rigoberto Marín decided it was time to pack it in. He kicked
away the three dogs that had joined him on Las Tabernas
Street and got into a taxi, asking the driver to take him to Delicias de
Quirihue Restaurant. He wanted to punish himself with a bucketful
of tripe and another of innards: a portion of sweetbreads, two blood
sausages, juicy grilled short ribs, half an order of brains and udder.
He would be moderate in his consumption of wine so as not to
completely lose his mind. He'd start off with a bottle of red Casillero
del Diablo to wet his lips, along with a carafe of Cachantún mineral
water. He was also going to allow the *garçon* to bring him a green bean
salad, a Chilean salad of tomatoes and onions cut up very, very small,
and even two sliced avocados to lighten the bomb-blast of beef.

Afterward, as sober as a priest, he would hail a taxi and demand
that it drive express to the widow's bed. Fortified by a carnivorous
repast of such proportions, he would surprise his lover with an
erection large enough for the Father, the Son, and the Holy Spirit,
and would allow her to savor it in her mouth before he thrust it
headlong into its final destination.

While he ate lunch, which he drowned in green salsa and Chilean *pebre*, he forgot about his mineral water, and after he'd finished a second bottle of red wine, a wave of bitterness swept over him and caused him to be rude to the waiter. When Marín flashed a switchblade, the owner, accompanied by his son, asked him at the point of a gun to leave the premises.

Though quite drunk, he realized with his few remaining shreds of lucidity that he really should get out of there. Which he did, accompanying his steps with a hoarse rendition of *"Tengo un corazón que llegaría al sacrificio por ti."* In a brief flash of prudence, he stabbed his knife into a tree on República Avenue and left it there, to the amusement of a group of university students who watched him bouncing off the parked cars and the walls of their institution.

"Don't call the police, kids," he pleaded, slurring his words. And without anybody asking, he added, "My name is Alberto Parra Chacón. Parra like Violeta, Chacón like Arturo Prat's mommy."

He stumbled into a construction site tucked away and littered with cement bags and scaffolding, and made his way into the skeleton of hallways until he found a kind of interior patio where two stray dogs were sleeping on burlap bags. He lay down between them and, placing his arms around one of them and resting his head on her teats, he fell sound asleep.

∽

WARDEN SANTORO SPENT the weekend feeling greatly relieved. In spite of the cold weather, he left his living room windows open and, warmly dressed in a sweater of indigenous design, read the Saturday newspaper, mostly the police reports and the sports and entertainment pages. He had rubbed a numbing ointment on his neck, which efficiently lessened the pain of the bruises hidden under the old, recovered scarf he stroked with affection. Spending the day in the bosom of his family, his adolescent daughters wandering around in their lovely baby-doll pajamas between the kitchen and their bedrooms—those little girls are going to drive their admirers crazy with their little upturned buttocks and perky tits, he couldn't help thinking—carried him back to a more innocent time, when he lived a dignified life, with evenings at the movies and even once in a while dining at a restaurant or dancing at a downtown *boîte*.

For the past decade, while the country was "returning to normal" after the dictatorship, he had felt what little power he once had slipping away from him. Those who had aided and abetted the top brass of the day had been denounced by those deemed free of the stain of atrocities, and certain benefits, such as paid vacations, "company" cars, and tuition assistance for the girls had been removed from his benefits package. He had had to return to riding broken-down buses, and his girls had descended from a good private school to an urban public school with unheated classrooms and few lightbulbs, where the students wore ponchos and blankets over their uniforms in winter, and began passing out from the heat at three on a summer afternoon.

They hadn't reduced his salary, but those "special" checks, drawn from a separate fund and accompanied by a pat on the back from the superintendent who coordinated the death squads, no longer made their appearance. He had never, however, used that extra money to install a telephone at home, and when the first cell phones came to Chile, they were too expensive for him to ever hope to afford one.

Slowly, everybody started using these gadgets, and his girls demanded he buy one on credit. As far as he could remember, he had used it no more than twenty times. His daughters, however, needed it constantly, even while they were sleeping; they gave it a place of honor on their pillows in the hopes that their admirers would break the rules of civility and call them with declarations of true love—and possibly sex—at any hour of the night.

So, after reading about the economic woes of his favorite soccer team, which had already gone bankrupt, he ate a big breakfast—a delicious spicy sausage nestled between two pieces of well-buttered *marraqueta*. He wiped the edges of his mouth with a paper towel and decided to put an end to the most unrewarding episode of his life by calling the hotel where Rigoberto Marín was staying under the false name of Alberto Parra Chacón. He would leave him a simple and discreet message: "Order canceled. Come back."

While the girls were showering, he took the miraculous cell phone in his hand and punched in the number for Monasterio's hotel.

ON THE OTHER end of the line Elsa, like a good student, was cutting out the article in *El Mercado*. She was planning to paste the clipping onto a piece of elegant black vellum, which she would then insert in an elegant gray folder. She would present it to Victoria's mother at five that afternoon at a tea party, which would be attended by the other women in the group, including Elena Sanhueza and Mabel Zúñiga.

She was going to wait until everyone was sitting in front of their steaming cups of tea to recite the words that would flow smoothly off her tongue, for they will have come from the certainty of her heart: "This article will be the passport that will open the borders of every country in the world."

After taking a sip of tea, Mabel Zúñiga would carry out the difficult assignment of encouraging the depressed Widow Ponce to pave the way for the crowning glory of the whole affair by granting permission for her talented daughter to enter into holy matrimony with

Ángel Santiago, a decent young man with a lot of promise and, as the latest hit song proclaimed, "a heart he would sacrifice for her."

"These," as her concluding statement would go, "are not merely the lyrics of an ordinary bolero that you hear on the buses or on TV, expressing the romantic promises any drunken Casanova can make to the woman he lusts after; we have conclusive proof that the young Santiago was at the princess's side as she struggled between life and death, and when our sleeping beauty returned like Lazarus, king of the darkness, he organized the event in a venue no less grand than the Municipal Theater, putting his own life at risk, and thanks to which Victoria Ponce now stands on the threshold of international fame." As a grand finale, she would offer up the gray folder containing the black vellum and the consecrating article.

In other words, as she moved the scissors with precision, Elsa's mind had wandered far afield. She was thinking that at seventeen she would have liked to face such a future with love, a vocation, and talent.

Even though the croupier had dealt her bad cards, she refused to sink into bitter melodrama, preferring to project her fantasies into the lives of the young dancer and her passionate lover. That couple would be the salve that smoothed over her own unpleasant memories of the paltry world of cheap hotels, taverns, jails, and the disdain suffered therein: Monasterio, through his betrayal of his friend and his promiscuity with women who ate up his shrinking, ill-begotten funds; the great Vergara Gray, crushed by his love for an arrogant woman who lacked the generosity to even offer him the air necessary to remain alive, and suffering; and herself, always second to everyone, always snubbed by Monasterio except when a bout of his own melancholy brought him to her bed looking more for maternal tenderness than sex.

Not even to mention all the others who swarmed around Las

Tabernas Street, grim and lonely, trying to get someone to buy them one more glass of wine so they could fall into their cold sheets and beg for death to take them quietly before they opened their eyes onto another day of anguish. This was the world of the "nighthawks," Elena Sanhueza, the art teacher, had told her.

SHE LET THE telephone ring more than seven times, wanting to complete one perfect cut: a rectangle without regrettable curves or careless smudges on the vellum. Once she'd finished, she picked it up.

"Monasterio's hotel?"

"Yes, sir."

"I would like to speak to Alberto Parra Chacón."

"He doesn't live here."

"Can you please look through your guest registry? It's very urgent."

"I'm looking at it right now. The most frequent visitor we have is a Mr. Enrique Gutiérrez."

"Well, that's not him. I need to talk to Alberto Parra Chacón. About medium height, skinny, nervous."

"Almost everyone who comes in here is nervous, either because someone might see them or because they won't be able to perform."

"I understand. But you must have a list of your guests."

"Of course we do, sir."

"Do you ask them for identification?"

"What a question! It's a city regulation, after all."

"And you don't have a Parra there?"

"*Parra*, like Violeta Parra? No, sir, I'm sorry, we don't."

"In case he shows up, can you give him a message?"

"With pleasure, sir."

"Tell him, please: Order canceled. Come back."

"I'll write that down."

"Don't make a mistake, please. It's very important."

"A matter of life or death?"

"Exactly."

"Rest assured. I'll write it down: Order canceled. Come back."

"Very kind of you, ma'am. Thank you very much."

"And from whom is the message?"

"What?"

"I mean, who are you?"

There was silence at the other end of the line. Elsa held the receiver between her shoulder and her ear, and with her free hands she spread some glue on the back of the clipping and pressed it down onto the black vellum.

"Tell Parra Chacón that the message is from a friend."

"Will he understand?"

"He'll understand."

"Understood, sir."

"Thank you, ma'am."

A friend, the woman repeated to herself and smiled after hanging up.

She picked up the piece of paper on which she had written the message, crumpled it up in her fist, and threw it in the garbage can. "What am I doing, getting myself mixed up with these creeps?" she said to herself, touching the spot on her throat where Alberto Parra Chacón had pressed his knife against her skin.

WHEN VICTORIA TOLD her mother that she was going to disappear for a while, the woman increased the speed of her needle across the sweater she was decorating with cross-stitching and understood this to mean that the girl would go live with the young man with disheveled hair in some run-down rooming house.

She may have wanted to say: *I know I have nothing to offer you but this tenacious and sterile sorrow. How well I understand you, for at times I look at my own hands and want to press them around my own throat until I squeeze out all the air.*

She could have said: *That's wonderful, you have your guy and your dance. You dance what you are, as the critic said. Be yourself. Perfect. I won't take it as abandonment.*

But the mother said nothing to the daughter.

Victoria navigated through the silence, knowing that her bag was packed and ready upstairs, that within a few hours she would place it on her shoulder and wrap herself in her father's overcoat. She had the honesty to tell her mother that hers would be a long absence, so long that years might pass before they would see each other again.

Her mother stopped her needlework and looked at her knees as if they belonged to a distant landscape. She had sunk into a deathly silence. Victoria's leaving could mean only one thing: secrecy, the Resistance. And therefore, death. With any luck, a car from the morgue would one day come get her to identify her daughter's disfigured corpse. She told her as much. She said, "They're going to kill you, my love."

"You got stuck in a time warp, Mama. We are now living in a democracy. Nobody can kill me because nobody is shooting anybody. There's no Resistance. There's no terrorism, no armed struggle. There's not even a political struggle. It's not like in Papa's day."

"You're going into hiding and they're going to kill you. Your picture will appear in the newspapers and many people will come with me to mourn you. After that I'll be alone."

She picked up her knitting and with one edge that ended in an ocher-colored ball of yarn, she wiped the sides of her nostrils.

"You should be happy, Mama. I'm going to be alive and happy somewhere else. Not dead, but dancing!"

"Where?"

"Let's say Brazil."

"Don't leave before I finish this sweater."

"I have to leave tomorrow, and you've still got a lot to do."

"You'll come back and get it when it's finished."

"Of course."

"I liked eating vegetable soup with you. I'm going to miss you."

"Because of the soup?"

"I also liked eating chicken soup with you."

"You never told me, Mama."

"Tomorrow I'll make an apple strudel and serve it with the tea."

"That will be perfect, Mama."

"I figure the sweater will be ready in . . . What month are we in?"

"July."

"We've still got two months of winter."

"To tell you the truth, I really don't think I'll be coming back that soon. Maybe next year."

"I'll be dead before then."

"Why do you talk about death so much, Mama? It's like you stick an ice cube right on my bones. I'll come back on a very cold day with lots of rain, and I'll put on the sweater and I'll say, *Thank you, Mama, it turned out beautiful.*"

Young Ángel Santiago called Charly de la Mirándola and made him an irresistible offer. As soon as Milton ran his race on the big day, Ángel wanted Charly to load him onto a horse trailer and send the stable foreman to wait for Ángel with the motor running at the Vivaceta Avenue exit of the racetrack. Ángel would buy the horse—*at the coup rate*, he considered saying as a joke, but didn't—for a very tempting price that could go as high as three hundred thousand pesos. The good-natured trainer reminded him that the value of the animal would depend on whether he lost or won the race; of course, Ángel said, not to worry. The money could be collected tomorrow on Las Tabernas Street, where Ángel would go to show his gratitude to all the angels who had contributed to helping Victoria get out of the situation in which Lazarus had also once found himself.

With the same coin he managed to call Victoria Ponce. She began by telling him about all her mother's bad omens, but he reassured her by saying that nothing and nobody could prevent the success of this operation. She should go, warmly dressed—*very* warmly dressed—and with her feet wrapped in at least two pairs of wool socks, to the Swiss ranch house, where they would meet to begin their honeymoon. There she would be waited on like a queen by a good friend from his childhood he'd hung out with "flank to flank" on horseback or exploring the woods on foot. She agreed now that she didn't care a bit about her mother's prophecies and that she imagined her life after tomorrow like that of a wild animal running across endless plains. Any remaining symptoms of her illness had disappeared, except for a little bit of fluid remaining in her nostrils, which she took care of with Nova tissues.

VERGARA GRAY DID a final check in the dance studio. Although everything seemed ready—*tutto a posto,* as he used to say to his Teresa Capriatti—a last review of every detail might still reveal a weak link that could mess up the entire mechanism.

What awaited him if he succeeded? A new avalanche of tears for Madame Capriatti, which he would be careful not to shed when he made out the money orders, so as not to smudge the ink.

He would inform her by telephone that the money she would receive on a monthly basis was from the proceeds of "import/export activities I conduct outside of Chile." How honorable and promising of redemption this would sound to his Dulcinea that he, Vergara Gray, had joined the pleiad of great Chilean exporters who, thanks to the free-market treaties signed by the United States, the European Union, and the Chilean socialist government, had taken that small country's economy firmly on the road to global expansion.

But in addition to this vale of tears, he would have the comfort of the girl's presence. If he could just accompany her for a few months, be a witness to her international success, the sorrows of his own life would be considerably mitigated.

Ángel Santiago had painted for himself a picture of his own version of paradise, which differed somewhat from that of Vergara
Gray—an eminently urban animal. In Ángel's paradise, Vergara Gray
would be some kind of overseer of a dozen or so acres that Santiago would buy to grow vegetables and fruit and raise livestock. Ángel
would watch over his land from atop his chestnut horse, assisted by a
vicious dog with large teeth.

Don Nico, so it seemed, would have nothing to do other than
write his memoirs, make *pisco sauers*, and do daily exercises to lower
his cholesterol. To complement the boy's plan, the older man began
to formulate his own.

After taking the book cover on and off *Where I'm Calling From*
by Raymond Carver so many times, he had ended up reading the
story about the death of Chekhov one afternoon before he took a
nap, and, when he awoke, he began to reread with pen in hand to
underline certain passages. Perhaps his partner's plan wasn't so bad,
as long as his small ranch was near a town with a public library. Nor
would he care if the library carried the latest sensations, for he was
such a novice reader that he could start with *Don Quixote de la Mancha*
and continue chronologically until he got to *Madame Bovary*, and by
that time he would be almost dead; thus he could avoid discussing
with the resident cows and sheep any of the volumes that swelled
the ranks of the bestseller lists.

It was ten minutes to midnight when Ángel Santiago arrived
and looked over Gray's shoulder at the notes and sketches they had
made that final day.

"Everything in order, maestro?"

"Everything in order, disciple."

"Anything missing for tomorrow?"

"For us to get a good night's sleep so our heads are clear."

"You checked all the details?"

"Everything's here: car, license plate, pick up Victoria, winter clothes, taxi to the south, east-west highway, Swiss ranch house, muleteer, Schendler jackets, credentials, tool kit, insulated gloves, three waterproof bags, extension ladder, three large backpacks, a dozen or so smaller plastic bags, cash, mineral water, lighter, cigarettes, ashtray, portable radio, and a full tank of gas."

Ángel happily nodded in response to every item on the list, but he stopped in surprise when Vergara Gray came to the end.

"What is it, kiddo?"

"You forgot something, Professor."

The older man looked at him as if the younger man wanted to tell him a joke, but Ángel undid the buttons on his vest, took out the hefty revolver he had stolen from Santoro, and placed it on top of the sketches on the desk.

"This," he said.

T HE RAIN WASN'T torrential, but it was persistent enough to make the few pedestrians out early bend their backs under the slippery scourge. With their eyes glued to the pavement, some covered their heads with newspapers they had bought at the corner and hadn't yet had a chance to read.

The guard wanted to know what they were going to do with that extension ladder. Vergara Gray explained the truth in all its glorious detail: they needed to get to a place that was practically inaccessible, for there were clear indications that the stuck pulley was right under the roof.

They hung the familiar OUT OF ORDER sign, disconnected the automatic relay, and went up only to the next-to-last floor, a slight variation from the plan they had been reviewing for days.

"It would be a pity to have such a ladder and not extend it a few extra yards," Vergara Gray pointed out.

The real motive for the change, however, was something else. In the event of a serious problem, Canteros's goons would knock down the elevator door on the same floor as the office and Ángel Santiago would be riddled with bullets before he had time to put his finger on the *down* button. Being one floor down would give the boy a chance to make a run for it. And even though Gray didn't explain this as he was removing the bolts from the ceiling, it was clear his instructions were not to be argued with.

"We didn't talk about this, kid, but if you hear shots or any other strange noises, don't even think of climbing up there to see what's going on."

"You forget I'm armed, maestro."

"Not even as a last resort."

"I'm not going to leave you at the mercy of those thugs. I'm going to want to find out what's going on and help you."

"I will be happy to satisfy your curiosity ahead of time. If you make it into the room where the safe is, you will see me stretched out at full length, blood pouring out of my mouth. Once you've turned white at the sight of such a spectacle, the gangster's friends will, without blinking an eye, give you the same dose of lead. Only with a supreme effort will you manage to drag yourself to me and reach out your hand, which I will press warmly in brotherly love. But I will not manage to utter the words, *Adiós compañero*, because they will have shot out my tongue. Take these bolts, kid."

The boy did as he was told and placed them in his jacket pocket. "I'll do as you say, maestro. But it sounds like you've been reading too many gloomy books."

"Not really. But I did read that Chekhov story you told me about."

"You did?"

"It was interesting."

"But the story isn't by Chekhov. Chekhov is a character in the story. The author is named Carver, Raymond Carver."

"How do you manage to remember so many details?"

"Remember what a good memory I have, Vergara Gray. I still know all the answers to the questions on the exam Victoria took."

"Do you remember breakfast?"

"Naturally."

The young man leaned the ladder against the left wall of the elevator, climbed up it, and helped the maestro lift up the ceiling so they could lean the ladder against the wall less noisily than the time before but still noisily enough so that someone who might be keeping an eye or an ear on them would hear.

"Hold on a minute," Don Nico whispered, placing his finger on his lips.

Ángel Santiago nodded and rubbed his forehead hard, as if trying to find something inside. After a prudent amount of time, he spoke in a whisper. "You want me to recite your breakfast to you, partner?"

"Okay, but very quietly."

"Two *marraquetas*, two *colizas*, three *hallullas*, three *flautas*, four *tostadas*, three onion rolls, and three slices of kuchen with raisins and candied fruits."

Vergara Gray's face turned as red as the alcoholics who play Santa Claus in the department stores around Christmas and puffed out his cheeks, trying to hold back his laughter. He let out an asthmatic whistle. "You're going to give me a heart attack, you devil!"

"Nobody's ever died from laughing, maestro."

"Now what are you laughing about?"

"Your appetite. Added together, that makes twenty rolls."

Santiago grabbed on to the cable and climbed it quickly to help Don Nico finish extending the ladder. From that height they both realized at the same time that the dimensions of the elevator car made it impossible to extend the remaining section of the ladder. Within seconds, without giving time for doubts to arise, the expert opened the door to the elevator, pulled the bottom of the ladder out onto the floor, and, placing it at a slight diagonal, arranged it so that Ángel could extend it to the height needed.

He closed the door and indicated to the boy that he should come down and smoke a cigarette. "Now that the unexpected has been overcome, the moment to act has arrived."

They lit the cigarettes and, facing each other as they sat on the floor, their backs against the wall, their knees almost grazing each other, they smoked in silence. Vergara Gray took a deep drag and let it out little by little, leaving a thin trail of rising smoke.

"Chekhov," he then said.

"Maestro?"

"As I started telling you: Chekhov and his wife are staying in a hotel on the French coast. That night he feels terrible, the woman calls a doctor, who comes, and when he sees that there is no cure for Chekhov, that he is already dying, he calls the reception desk and asks them to send up a bottle of their best champagne and three glasses. Is that how it goes or have I got it wrong?"

"It's exactly as you are telling it, Professor."

"Then the waiter arrives, the doctor opens the champagne, the cork pops out any old place, the three drink, and in a little while Chekhov dies."

"The great Chekhov, Don Nico!"

"Okay. The next day the waiter returns to the room with a jar with three yellow flowers, not having any idea that Chekhov had died."

"Perfect so far."

"He wants to give the vase to Chekhov's wife, but she is distraught, of course, because Chekhov is dead."

"Exactly. Then comes the cork."

"Right. The waiter is standing there, holding the vase in both hands, calm and collected. I can imagine him very elegant and maybe snooty, when suddenly, poof, he discovers the cork on the floor. And suddenly he is desperate to pick up that cork that throws off the entire order of that room. Right?"

"That is exactly what Carver wrote."

"Then the widow asks him to go to the best funeral home in the city and tell the owner to make the arrangements because Chekhov has died. That he should walk proudly with his head held high as if Chekhov himself were waiting for the three yellow flowers. But while the widow is giving him his instructions, the young man holding the vase in his two hands keeps thinking about how to pick up the champagne cork at his feet. Isn't that the story?"

Ángel spit a speck of tobacco off the tip of his tongue and placed a hand on Vergara Gray's knee. "That's right. That's more or less how the story goes."

The famous safecracker leaned his head against the metal plates and lifted his eyes to the deep darkness of the tunnel that continued up to the roof. From his leather briefcase he brought out a flashlight and shone it on a section of the false wall Lira the Dwarf had made when he was a mechanic for Schendler Elevators.

"In other words," he continued, smoking, "Chekhov is dead and the boy's only problem is how to pick the cork up from the floor."

"I would say that is only one of the themes of the story. Why are you so lost in thought, Don Nico?"

The man massaged his cheekbones with his fingers, as if wanting to relieve some tension, then stubbed out the cigarette in the ashtray. "This is why. Just like I brought the ashtray, the boy wanted to pick up the cork."

"Well reasoned, Professor."

"That is, if that young man and I were on a transatlantic ship that was sinking, let's say the *Titanic*, and the windows in the cabin were dirty, that young man and I would clean them."

"According to what you are telling me and what I can see for myself, I would say you're right."

"In other words, the big stuff and the little stuff happen at the same time. But since we are always living in the little stuff, we don't realize what part of the big stuff is actually the little stuff we're doing."

"That is a great philosophical question that you can discuss endlessly with Victoria Ponce at my hacienda."

"You don't understand me?"

"A little, Professor. But I haven't forgotten why we came here."

"You're right."

"The other day you yourself were saying that we had to stay focused."

"What a memory you have. Better than an elephant."

"Or a stray dog, Vergara Gray!"

"How do you do it? I have to look at my identification card every day just to remember my name. On the same subject, how many languages do you speak?"

"Spanish."

"That's one. Is that all?"

"That would be all, for now. I know a little English."

"Say something."

"*One dolar, mister, please. And you?*"

" '*Put a tongue in every wound of Caesar that should move the stones of Rome to rise and mutiny.*' "

"That sounds beautiful, maestro. What's it from?"

"Shakespeare."

"Professor, I'm really impressed. I never imagined that you could quote Shakespeare, and in English."

"I've been in prison several times, with honorable people, and with Englishmen."

THEY BOTH STOOD up. Vergara Gray grabbed the handle of his tool kit, and Ángel picked up one of the yellow waterproof bags to stuff into the space created by the Dwarf in order to muffle the noise made by the professor as he punched through the false wall.

Every once in a while they stopped their demolition work to listen for anyone who might interrupt them. They soon realized that in the modern soundscape of Santiago, construction noise was constant and implacable. Even so, they kept it to a minimum until they could feel they only had to push lightly on the metal sheet for it to give way. The only question was whether it would fall into the office or tumble down the elevator shaft into the basement. In the first case, it would remain under their control; in the second, the results were less predictable. The guard might wonder at the sounds of a shower of falling metal shards.

The moment had now arrived for the maestro to perform his very particular brand of surgical procedure. He squeezed through the narrow opening and, once on the other side, gestured to Ángel to pass him his arsenal. In a very low voice, he whispered, "This is where we go our separate ways, partner. You go two floors down and wait for me with the patience of a saint."

"Excuse me, maestro, but I would like very much to see the great Vergara Gray in action. Something I could tell my children about."

"The first thing we've got to be sure of is that this future child of yours isn't born an orphan. Go on down, but whatever happens, don't for any reason remove the ladder. The cable panics me, and I'm terrified at the thought of breaking my neck hurtling through the air."

The expert took one step forward as if he were a sculptor about to face a block of marble, and the young man whistled to him: he held out the two other yellow bags with a broad smile.

"Have a good harvest, maestro."

His partner had already entered into his trance and didn't respond. He took the bags without even turning around to look, then made his way to the immense gray safe and stroked it reverently. Ángel took a few steps down the ladder, hung playfully from the elevator cable, then lowered himself onto the platform. In the maestro's bag there was a pack of cigarettes and the book *Where I'm Calling From*, wrapped in the famous graph paper. With a sip of mineral water and a lit cigarette, he opened the volume to page eleven and began to read, probably for the fifth time, from the story "Boxes": " *'My mother is packed and ready to move.'* "

LIKE A POTTER in front of his clay, a worshipper in front of an icon, a dancer with her dance, an actor reading a script, a bird about to take flight, so the safecracker faced the dial of the metal box. In jail, frequent nightmares about high technology, nourished by television and the press, had made him fear the *great outside*. Awaiting him *out there* would be an electronic inferno where his ancient tools would melt. Time would have streaked past him, and he would be reduced to being a lowly retired crook defeated by two powerful rivals: the treachery of his partner—who broke every code of honor that regulates relationships among criminals—and electronic technology, full of incomprehensible digits and secret passwords controlled by remote computer processors.

The second he saw the safe he realized that, after all, he had one thing in common with that pig Canteros: their chronological age.

Although both had been left behind by progress—computers, cell phones, virtual banks, DVDs, semiconductors—the number one gangster of the republic chose a safe that Vergara Gray could fully understand without the assistance of bionic or cybernetic magicians.

In any case, he thought, rubbing his hands together, this was a gesture of generational camaraderie he felt obliged to generously compensate by breaking open this pirate's chest in the most elegant way possible.

He had no apprehensions and felt no hurry as he removed all the tools from his kit and laid them neatly on the rug; the mere fact of having managed to enter this room without any alarm going off proved that Canteros had preferred to place all the bells and whistles at the door to the office.

Nobody could have had the divine insight that the thief would appear via the elevator and thus avoid all the traps that were surely sprinkled along the other route. To achieve such a feat, one needed the blessing of someone as small as the Great Dwarf Lira, who could combine the skills of a mason with the pragmatism of his size. How fortunate he must have felt when chance placed this gift at his feet, and how much sorrow he must have suffered when he was sent to prison and lost all hope of retrieving it.

And what a homage to him, to Nicolás Vergara Gray, that the lad had so dexterously procured the secret—he smiled—of painting this Sistine Chapel!

There's a common saying in Chile for welcoming guests: *The house is small, but the heart is big.* As Vergara Gray manipulated screwdrivers, a Swedish wrench, picks, pliers, wires of different sizes and thicknesses, a stethoscope, a chisel, wire cutters, files, bits, and a drill, becoming more jubilant by the minute at having found such a conventional lock, he composed in his mind the text of a postcard he would send to Canteros: *The safe is big, but your heart is small.*

After he'd worked for forty minutes, the last bolt gave way, and, even though the vast rewards of his labors were now within reach, he paused before opening the steel door and encountering the joy or disappointment of the century. He decided to smoke a cigarette. Just as he was about to light the match, the Andes-brand matchbox reminded him that the marvelous cordillera of the Andes was waiting to welcome him in a few hours. He stuck the unlit match between his teeth and returned the cigarette to his shirt pocket. Wanting to check the intuition that had stopped him from lighting up and had deprived him of a few comforting puffs, he looked carefully around the room until he saw the metal plaque with the outline of a flame: a smoke alarm!

If only that same golden intuition would serve him so well outside the world of crime! If only such extrasensory perceptions would give him the words and the gestures that would win Teresa Capriatti back! He would give all the gold *of others* in the world—he smiled—to live with her!

Then, with perfectly natural movements, without dramatizing even to himself the culmination of all their efforts, he opened the safe. After glancing quickly through several compartments, he tore a corner off one package, then another, then the edge of one in the back, until he was sure all of those wrapped in green paper contained U.S. dollars, and those in blue paper held Chilean money. A little box with inlaid mother-of-pearl was home to some jewels, probably acquired during those patriotic days of yore when the ladies who supported Pinochet had donated their bracelets, rings, earrings, and necklaces to the armed forces to contribute to the refinancing of the nation after the military coup.

Without further delay, he loaded the multicolored loot into the yellow dry bags until he saw that even one more bundle would make it impossible for him to swing the load over his shoulder. He closed it by pulling the twine threaded through metal rings, finished filling a second in three or four more minutes, then carried them to the hole in the wall next to the elevator shaft. Below, as if he hadn't budged for the entire hour, young Ángel Santiago asked him wordlessly what he should do next.

As Vergara Gray prepared to pass him the bags through the hole, the boy climbed the ladder—he thought, remembering Victoria's exam—as fast as a tiger with retractable claws.

The maestro's wordless instructions were brief and unequivocal: *Take each one down and come back for the next one.*

The operation was completed three times with success. Fearing that Don Nico would have difficulty transitioning from the office to the ladder, Ángel climbed up a fourth time to help him carry out this awkward maneuver; once he had made sure the older man was safely on the top rung, Ángel climbed quickly down to the platform so as not to place too much weight on a ladder that could buckle.

Once they were both on the platform, the older man stretched out his arms like a pelican displays his wings when returning triumphantly with his beak full of delicious sardines, and asked his accomplice for an enormous hug.

For a long time they stood there, cheek to burning cheek.

THEY PROCEEDED TO pack a dozen plastic bags full of money into Monasterio's car. They were in a hurry because they had to rendezvous with the guide several hours before the sun set: not even the muleteers who trafficked in drugs dared to make that initial ascent in the dark. By two in the afternoon, Vergara Gray and Victoria were already driving south down the highway carrying the three yellow waterproof bags they would later load into their backpacks for their trip over the Andes. Ángel Santiago, for his part, had taken the plastic bags full of Chilean money to be distributed as dessert for the lunch he had charged Elsa with organizing at Monasterio's bar. He figured it was better to meet them all in one place rather than risk discovery during the very last stage of the coup. After "dessert" he would take a taxi with Charly de la Mirándola to the Hippodrome of Chile and pick up a truck pulling the trailer where an impatient chestnut horse would be waiting for him. That horse would be his mount as he made his way through the intricate trails that led up the mountains.

After reminding each other to remain vigilant, Vergara Gray deposited the young man at the subway station closest to Monasterio's bar. As they shook hands through the car window, Ángel made the maestro promise that he would not wait for him at the Swiss ranch house if he failed to show up at the appointed time. It was very possible that the horse trailer would be slow, and if they left with their guide before him, he would be able to find their trail a few hours later, as he had walked tightropes through those mountains from the time he was a small boy.

All the little plastic bags fit into one big one that now bounced with him happily along Las Tabernas Street. On each one was written the name of the *destinataire*. From the size of the package one could infer the value assigned to the contribution of each of their accomplices. Elsa and Nemesio Santelices were getting packages worthy of top billing, though there was nothing miserly about what was earmarked for Charly de la Mirándola or the unemployed Professor Sanhueza.

But the cherry on top was a bulky bluish package that clearly would not have fit into just any plastic bag. It bore a dedication that would leave everyone perplexed: DWARF. The size of the lettering did not reflect that of the recipient.

As he anticipated the glorious moment of passing out the gifts, Ángel Santiago felt a surge inside him that he immediately identified as joy. The world was a crazy and lovable planet circulating dreamily among thousands of galaxies, and every being who walked by him seemed both grandiose and incommensurable: the shoeshine boy; the peanut seller; the girls who rose early wearing their nighttime miniskirts; the teenagers leaning against the wall at the corner, smoking like grown-up men; the newspaper vendor shouting out the headlines of *El Mercado*; the taxi drivers wiping their windows with rags; the housewives carrying bags overflowing with produce; the children launching paper boats in the water in the gutters; the construction workers with their red hard hats discussing whether Colo-Colo would win that night's soccer game; the group of schoolgirls practicing a dance they had seen on TV; those pigeons and swallows on the edges of the roofs or in the leaves of the trees; the hummingbirds and thrushes drinking from the stone fountain; and all those dogs that suddenly appeared with fight wounds on their scarred ears, rummaging through the garbage cans or trying to mate in the dust kicked up by the cars.

He had one thought into which he seemed to pour the brilliance of the thousand karats of happiness. He had made a wager with himself and had won: the infamy of his years in jail had been pulverized in his memory, and now that he was pure gumption and future, not a drop of resentment ran through his blood. He remembered Fernando, a Spanish convict addicted to horseracing, who—his eyes popping out from behind his glasses—had defined one day in the prison cafeteria the beauty of betting and winning: "The day your horse finally wins, against any and all predictions, against all adverse circumstances, against the probable and the logical, ah! that is the day you feel that you have defeated, for the moment, the force of necessity, when the joyous strength in your heart beats in secret harmony with all things."

The young man burst into the bar, pushing the swinging doors in with his shoulder, and before the group could rise in excitement, he shouted in a heroic voice, "Have the people eaten?"

The "Yes" was loud and kisses were exchanged all around. A few tears fell onto blouses and lapels.

"Everything okay, Angelito?" Elsa asked.

" 'Okay' is a gross understatement. It went *perfectly*."

"And the professor?"

"As he always says, there are four points on a compass. He can be found at one of them."

He made the rounds of the room: the art teacher had been to the hairdresser, who had styled her hair with blue highlights that made her look at least a few weeks younger; and instead of his humble, felt, rain-colored cap, the valet Santelices was wearing a hat that made him look like the owner of a yacht. As for the receptionist, Ángel decided that any adjective he could possibly think of would pale in comparison to how she actually looked: excited, radiant, heavenly, inscrutable, engaged, lucid, promising, savage, euphoric, perfect, mysterious.

Each one received his or her bag, then returned to their real dessert, the standard papaya with Nestlé sweetened condensed milk. There was a hurried consultation between Ángel and Elsa about the blue package for Señor Lira, during which they exchanged suggestions about the best way to get it to him in jail. The woman thought they should open a bank account in his name, but when the boy informed her that Lira still had fifteen years and one day to serve, Elsa was inclined to guard the loot in a couple of mattresses and hire a call girl to visit him, sneaking in small amounts at a time along with cigarettes, alcohol, and, on the days authorized by the more progressive wardens, sex.

After making his rounds of the room, Ángel Santiago was surprised to find that at the bottom of the big bag there still remained the portion destined for Charly de la Mirándola. Taking his leave of the group, he remembered that during the first race, the chestnut horse, Milton, would have run the twelve hundred meters. He had no choice but to leave the package with Elsa and, stretching out both his arms, he said good-bye to everybody with a gesture of embrace and an informal toss of his head.

Once outside, he hurried toward the main street. By way of a final precaution, he didn't want anybody to catch up with him and see the number of the license plate of the taxi he was going to take. The street was partially deserted; everyone was either finishing a long lunch or had gone to take a siesta, and he passed few pedestrians along his way.

When Ángel was just a few steps away from the taxi stop, a thin man wearing a wide-brimmed hat and a beige raincoat stepped out in front of him and pulled a gun out from between the open buttons at his hip. The young man noticed a kind of compulsive decisiveness in the stranger and, opening his arms as if to ask for an explanation, he said, "What's up, skinny?"

Rigoberto Marín, alias Alberto Parra Chacón, involuntarily baptized as Enrique Gutiérrez, decided that an exchange of even one word with the Cherub would afflict him with remorse and make him fail to carry out his job. Without further ado, he fired two shots straight into Ángel's heart.

Certain that his aim was true, Marín returned the gun to his pocket and, kicking aside the gray dog that was sniffing his leg, he watched his victim collapse; without hesitating, he turned toward the subway entrance and descended the stairs.

He didn't know that the weary person he had almost knocked down on the seventh step was the horse trainer, Charly de la Mirándola, who was making his way to Monasterio's bar in the hopes of joining his friends in time for dessert. The horseman noticed a group of onlookers gathering hesitantly around the body of the young victim. When he joined them, he recognized Ángel Santiago, bathed in blood. He forced his way through the crowd, lifted the dying boy's head, and placed it on his knee.

"How're you doing, kid?"

"They killed me, Don Charly."

"Don't worry, the ambulance is on its way."

The young man could see the bubbles of blood pouring out of his chest and felt them gurgling in his mouth. But he managed to ask, "How did Milton do?"

"Came in fourth."

"Did he run well?"

"He was ahead until the final two hundred, then all the good horses passed him in the mud."

"But he's ready for the next one?"

"Definitely, my boy."

The young man's head fell on the trainer's thigh. Ángel Santiago thought he had managed to formulate the question that was bothering him: If the coup had gone so well in every single particular, why the hell did I die?

A T THREE IN the afternoon they hid the car under a pile of straw in one of the barns of the Swiss ranch house. For a few seconds Vergara Gray had driven completely blind through the barn, where the hay and oats let off a nose-tickling dust.

They placed their suitcases and the three yellow bags next to the kitchen table. A fire in the wood-burning stove took the chill out of the air and a chicken was simmering with a generous helping of vegetables in the soup pot. Ángel's friend, their guide, was an energetic man, and after greeting them, he led them to a hitching post where three horses were tied, saddled, and ready to take them through the mountain passes.

"They know the path blindfolded. If we leave now, we'll be in Argentina tomorrow."

Vergara Gray was the one who verbalized a concern that had been growing in both of their minds throughout their ride there.

"We have heard, Mr. . . ."

The guide turned his eyes toward a small stream and with a touch of disdain said, "I haven't asked you your names, and you don't have any reason to know mine."

"Agreed, my friend. We have heard that at this time of year it is impossible to cross the cordillera in this region. Everyone says you have to go farther south."

"You'll find the road south to your left."

"We were just asking, that's all."

"Okay, but please don't insult me. If I tell you that I'm going to get you to the other side, that means I've given you my word of honor."

"Of course."

"I saddled only three animals because Ángel said he was bringing his own."

"A racehorse," Victoria explained.

Again the man turned his eyes to the stream and crushed a pebble into the ground until it disappeared.

"I'm going to leave one of mine saddled up for him. His poor animal is going to stumble into the first ravine. What time did he say he'd get here?"

"Soon."

"He'll have to reheat the soup, 'cause I'm pretty hungry now."

"Let's just go ahead and eat, Don Nico," Victoria said. "Ángelito said he would catch up with us later."

"He knows these passes and gorges as well as I do," said the guide. "When his mother left, he came to live with me. He'd climb that fig tree every day and help me with the planting. The only problem was that he loved horses so much he stole the patron's son's favorite. But you've probably heard the story?"

"We know he was in jail, sir."

"I hate being called sir. If you have to call me something, call me Tito."

"Tito, for Ernesto?"

"Don't complicate things, man. Tito just for Tito."

The three remained silent during most of the meal. They blew on the broth in the heavy metal spoons, held the ends of the cobs of corn spread with butter and salt, and chewed slowly. Even though the host was in a bit of a hurry, looking at the clock face on the little Swiss birdhouse, Victoria and Don Nico savored their meal, chewing as slowly as possible in the hope that Ángel Santiago would appear before they left.

"What are you carrying in your backpacks?"

"Clothes."

"Warm?"

"Sweaters, wool socks, hats with earflaps."

"Good. And what've you got in the bags?"

Victoria and Vergara Gray looked at each other over their spoons. When they turned their eyes back to their bowls and started chewing a piece of squash, the maestro answered succinctly, "Cash."

"A lot?"

"Enough."

The guide began moving his jaw up and down, as if nodding. Victoria winked at Vergara Gray as if to tell him not be so terse, that this was the way people in the countryside opened the way to more serious subjects.

"I don't know what you and Ángel agreed on, but feel free to untie one of those bags and take whatever you think is right."

Their host had broken off a piece of bread and began to play with the little balls of crumbs, stabbing them with his nails to stop them from rolling off the edge of the table. He suddenly left off the game, untied the twine on one bag, sank his arm into it, and pulled out one of the blue packets. He pushed away an earthenware bowl full of tomato and onion salad and placed the package on the table. After pulling back the top and placing a finger inside, he evaluated the thickness of the bundle with the skill of a bank teller, making precise calculations as to how much all those pieces of paper together were worth.

"If you have no problem, my man, I think that with this bundle we are fine as we are," he concluded.

"If that sits well with you, it sits well with me."

"No more talk about it, then; let's get going."

Victoria Ponce sensed the passage of time less by the clock than by the sun, which now seemed to be hurling itself into the west. "Please, let's just wait a little longer."

"We can't, miss. If night catches us on the trail, it's no dice. You don't play games with these mountains."

The first stretch before reaching the foothills was flat, and though it was full of blackberry brambles, rocks, and branches that scratched or stuck into them and their horses, it would seem almost congenial in comparison to the steep slopes their guide's steps would soon take them on.

Sunset coincided with a break in the thick cloud cover, and Victoria had a shock when she saw that along the snowy peak of the mountain ahead of them was a ribbon of a trail no more than a yard wide. Tito noticed the girl's hesitation and with his gloved hand he took the reins of the black horse and led it as he gave her instructions.

"If you get scared, don't pull back on the reins; trying to stop the horse can make him slip. Just let El Salvaje have his way, and don't try to influence him, 'cause you're not a professional, and the horse already knows that. Just understand that the only thing he expects from you are the rumbles of fear, and that deep down he despises you for it. For the animal, you are nothing more than a heavy pack. So don't move. Just imagine that you are on an airplane and your fate has already been decided. You can't ask the pilot to land on some peak of the Cordillera de los Andes."

"It's just that the path gets narrower and narrower."

"That's right. So let me go first. In a few minutes, we won't fit side by side."

"Any other advice?"

"That will be all."

As they gained altitude, Victoria took advantage of every possibility the landscape offered to get a glimpse of Ángel coming toward them. Silence reigned in the group without anybody imposing it. All that could be heard was the tapping of the horses' hooves on the pebbles and rocks, and the dislodged rocks sliding down the hill.

"From here, my friends, there's a stretch of about a half an hour that is very steep. If you get dizzy, lie down on your horse's neck, close your eyes, and let the only voice the animals hear be mine. The only thing I don't want to hear from either of you is you begging me to take you back. You were brave enough to pull off that job, you must also be courageous in your freedom. Are we in agreement, Don . . . ?"

"Call me Tito also," Vergara Gray spit back bravely, trying to control the chattering of his teeth.

"Me, too," Victoria Ponce said.

The climb was accomplished in the very last rays of light. As they advanced, the air became thinner and more transparent, and the ears of the two neophytes were filled with obscure outbursts of sound: wolves, pumas, the pounding wings of birds of prey. The painstaking procession seemed more like a rite of penitence than a triumphal parade of bandits accompanied by warm bundles of bills.

Even the horses seemed grim and stiff from the cold, without any neighing or changes of pace, as if they had been condemned to their trek. The girl thought of the chestnut horse and of the day Ángel's tender companion drank from the pond while they sparred over adolescent philosophy. These beasts of burden, worn down by the torture of these passes on the edge of the abyss, made her incommensurately sad, and she wished she had stashed, along with the dollars and millions of pesos, a few carrots they could munch on along the way, like the coca leaves the Indians chewed on. What sustenance could these animals get from the ice? What heat from the snow that bored into their martyred feet?

And where was her love? Was it possible he had forgotten about the horse trailer, and in the excitement at his triumph had ridden all the way from Santiago, galloping at full speed on the chestnut horse's back?

A little after night began to fall, the caravan reached a flat area covered with shrubs and bushes. Their guide dismounted from his roan and with half a smile went to offer them help. He announced to them that it would be impossible to cross the border tonight, but they had already been through the worst of the trip, and right here, behind some of those bushes, there was a cave so big that they and the horses could camp inside it for the night.

There they could sleep for a while until the first light; then, after two hours on horseback, they would be very close to a village where they would find a hotel and a receptionist who, for a reasonable sum, would not ask them to prove their identities. Right there they could buy suitcases, even modern ones with locks, and clothing more typical of the people in the area until they could lose themselves in the tumultuous ocean of Buenos Aires. If Ángel Santiago did not catch up with them here, the guide would give him all the information he needed to find them later.

Then he asked them to help him clear away some bushes surrounded by rocks and thorns that hid the secret entrance to the cave. All who used it, including the livestock thieves and contraband traffickers, were honor-bound to erase all signs of having been there.

More scratches and cuts appeared on hands and faces, a shrub with thorns like barbed wire made the ballerina's left earlobe bleed, and the semi-liquid mud seeped into Vergara Gray's boots. When they had cleared away a large enough space, the horses entered first and moved all the way to the back with grateful humility; the guide spread out the hay he had carried in his pack in front of their muzzles.

While the animals were chewing on their rations, Tito placed three gaucho blankets on the ground and began to pump up a small kerosene stove where he would heat some water to make instant coffee. Victoria brought her boots close to the flame and after a few seconds she could feel that her heels, which had felt encased in ice, were beginning to thaw; this allowed her to stretch out her limbs and do a series of stretches she usually performed at the bar.

Their guide, who had undoubtedly led other groups furtively across the Andes, suggested they not waste time imagining their future because, according to what he'd seen, running away was a project all in itself.

"Once you run away, you never stop."

Victoria Ponce took off her heavy boots and pushed on one toe at a time to make sure they were all still there. Vergara Gray approached her with a poncho as thick as a woven rug and diligently wrapped it around her.

"Money is money. But the truth is that these winged feet are our only capital, my dear."

"And your head, Don Nico," she responded with a smile.

She leaned her head on the saddle and, as the fog penetrated the cavern, she fell asleep, graced by those light, indistinct hands.

S HE WAS THE first to wake up. A tenuous light was spreading between the shrubs, and the girl intuited that outside the day had already swung open its doors. She ran out of the cave without putting on her boots, anxious to see what the mountains would greet her with today. Once she was outside, neither the cold nor the wind whistling in her ears frightened her away from the spectacle before her.

The small flat area at the mouth of the cave was situated right between the enormous valley that melted into the horizon and the snowy peaks of the mountains. Hanging over those peaks, the sun in all its power betrayed every texture in the landscape, a few goats chewing on leaves, ravines scattered with eucalyptus trees, ebullient walls of water, slopes laden with snow, high peaks like sculptures hewn by an otherworldly goldsmith, flocks of clouds rushing to their own dissolution, and above all that, a sky of such pure blue that Victoria Ponce asked herself if she had ever seen that color before.

Suddenly, like a feathered meteorite that fell from the highest mountain, there landed in a movement of pure harmonic choreography on a rock a few yards away from her a bird whose red crest crowned a red head that floated on a necklace of white plumage.

Once it had found its balance on the rock, the animal stared at Victoria, mirroring her own curiosity, as if they were engaged in a tacit duel to see who looked away first.

Vergara Gray came over to her, placed a hand on her shoulder, and, in order not to disturb the intense communication between the bird and the girl, he whispered, "It's a condor."

She did not take her eyes off her interlocutor, but after taking in a breath of air as pure as on the first day of creation, she replied with a smile, "Scientific name *Vultur gryphus*, of the Cathartidae family. I learned that when I was studying for my exam with Ángel."

"You think he knows that?"

"What?"

"The condor, if he himself knows he is called *Vultur gryphus*."

"I think so, maestro. He looks like a very sophisticated bird. The eyes of a surgeon, and as pedantic as a doctor."

"Doctor of the air."

"Bravo, Don Nico. Very nice metaphor!"

She was about to reward him with a loud kiss on his forehead when, as she turned her head, she saw a tiny figure in the farthest distance, and the gesture of affection remained suspended in midair. Squinting her eyes to sharpen her focus, she thought she could make out the image of a horse and his rider. She felt her heart expand with sudden joy.

"Don Nico, it's Ángel!"

"Where, my dear?"

"There, down there, down by the river."

"I don't see anything."

"A horse and rider. They're coming toward us."

"I can't make out anything."

"Look, Don Nico. It's Ángel, he's coming toward the mountains."

"It's too far away. But it does look like a horse and rider."

"I see it more and more clearly. It's Ángel riding a blue horse."

"No, sweetheart. It is just some rider on a horse carrying a blue blanket."

"It's not a blue blanket, maestro. It's a blue horse."

Their guide came over to them and, stretching himself out with a huge yawn, he said, "Sorry, folks, but it's time to leave."

Victoria Ponce, her face burning, turned to look at their guide; she asked him if down there, on the green carpet that spread into the river, he didn't see his childhood friend Ángel Santiago galloping toward them on a blue horse.

The man stood on the tips of his toes, raised his wool hat, and shook his head. No, to tell the truth, he didn't see anything, but they did have to leave, he was needed for another job.

Then the girl knelt down and, hugging their guide's knees, said, "I beg you, Don Tito. Let's not go yet. Let's wait for Ángel."

The man, surprised, tried to separate the girl's face from his body.

"There's no point. He knows this area as well as the condor. When he gets here, he'll follow our tracks and find us."

"Give me two hours, even just one!"

The two men exchanged a look; shrugging his shoulders, Vergara Gray tacitly supported the girl's request. Then Victoria Ponce climbed onto a rock and placed her hand like a visor above her eyes, gluing them on the plain below.

Tito offered Vergara Gray a cigarette, he accepted, and the two men sat down to smoke under the precarious shade of a barren fig tree.

Antonio Skármeta was born in Antofagasta, Chile. Having graduated from Columbia University in New York City in 1967, he emigrated to West Germany after the 1973 military coup that brought Augusto Pinochet to power. He attained international acclaim for *The Postman*, which inspired the Academy Award–winning film *Il Postino*, starring Massimo Troisi. His fiction has since received dozens of international literary awards, including the Goethe Medal in Germany, the Boccaccio International Prize in Italy, and the Prix Médicis in France. From 2000 to 2003 he was the Chilean ambassador to Germany and he has hosted his own television show dedicated to literature and the arts. He lives in Santiago, Chile.

Katherine Silver's most recent translations include the works of Pedro Lemebel, Jorge Franco, and Horacio Castellanos Moya. In 2007, she received fellowships from PEN and the National Endowment for the Arts. Her collection of modern and contemporary Chilean fiction, *Chile: A Traveler's Literary Companion*, was published by Whereabouts Press in 2003.